Five by Five

CLAIRE WILSON

MICHAEL JOSEPH

MICHAEL JOSEPH

UK | USA | Canada | Ireland | Australia
India | New Zealand | South Africa

Michael Joseph is part of the Penguin Random House group of companies
whose addresses can be found at global.penguinrandomhouse.com.

Penguin
Random House
UK

First published 2024
001

Copyright © Claire Wilson, 2024

The moral right of the author has been asserted

Set in 13.5/16pt Garamond MT Std
Typeset by Jouve (UK), Milton Keynes
Printed and bound in Great Britain by Clays Ltd, Elcograf S.p.A.

The authorized representative in the EEA is Penguin Random House Ireland,
Morrison Chambers, 32 Nassau Street, Dublin D02 YH68

A CIP catalogue record for this book is available from the British Library

HARDBACK ISBN: 978–0–241–68745–1

www.greenpenguin.co.uk

To Callum. Believe

Scottish Prison Terminology

Five by five	Intelligence report
Bammed up	Wound up by others
Banked	Concealing articles in your rectum/foreskin/vagina
Carted	Restrained and relocated to another area
Cosh	Weapon concealed in a sock
Digger	Segregation Unit
Doe	Money
Dubbed-up	Being locked in your cell
Dunt	A good hit/consumption of an illicit substance
Gub	Swallow
Hampden roar	Score
Huckled	Restrained
Moon	Month
Packing	In possession of illicit articles
Pass man	Trusted prisoners employed as hall cleaners
Patched	Ignored
Patsy	Line of cocaine
Peter/Pad	Cell
Piping	Dodgy
Prop	Cocaine
Rat stunt	Making an unfair move
Recreation	Free association
Scoobs/vallies	Valium tablets

Speg	Spice – synthetic cannabis (legal high)
Spin/spun	Cell search
Square go	A fight without weapons
Snipered	Assaulted from behind
Stiffy	Letters passed between prisoners
Tizzy	Etizolam (fake Valium)
Tool	Weapon

HMP Forth Valley
5 x 5 Intelligence Report

REPORTING PERSON: (Person receiving the information from the source)	Officer Molly Rana	PAY REF NO: u0525
SOURCE NAME: (Person providing the information)	Officer Molly Rana	
PROVENANCE OF INFORMATION:	1. How did you come by this information? Overheard conversation. 2. Where the source is a prisoner, what's their motivation for passing this on to officers? N/A 3. Who else knows this information? Other prisoners in the section. 4. As a result of this information, do you feel at risk? No.	

DATE & TIME OF REPORT:	Sunday, 19 August 2018 @ 15:52 hours				
SUBJECT OF REPORT:	Drugs at visits				
SOURCE EVALUATION	A Always reliable	B Mostly reliable	C Sometimes reliable	D Unreliable	E Untested source
INTELLIGENCE EVALUATION	1 Known to be true without reservation	2 Known personally to the source but not to the officer	3 Not known personally to the source, but corroborated	4 Cannot be judged	5 Suspected to be false

Reporting Person's Evaluation

Source Evaluation	A
Intelligence Evaluation	1

Intelligence:

I overheard prisoner Zac Boward boasting about getting drugs in at his visit. He was popular with his peers when he returned from the visit room earlier.

Intelligence that indicates there is a risk to life, safety or security should be passed verbally to the Manager in charge of the area <u>but the source should not be divulged.</u>

1. Kennedy Allardyce

It starts off like any other Monday, the day I'm almost murdered at work.

The nature of my job at Her Majesty's Prison Forth Valley is that it is strictly confidential. No war wounds cover my body like they do on some of the prison officers – because the prisoners don't know I exist. Shouldn't know I exist.

If they did, an attempt would've been made on my life before now. For I'm the one who stands between the prisoners and them obtaining drugs. Smartphones. Weapons. And sometimes, their freedom.

I'm the one who discovers which corrupt officers are working for them. I'm the one who puts them on closed visits. Reports their crimes to Police Scotland. The one who writes recommendations to the parole board not endorsing their early release. And I'm good at it.

Being an intelligence analyst is more than sanitizing raw intelligence reports, recording them on the prison system and disseminating them on to relevant areas. And that's the way I like it.

Until that Monday.

HMP Forth Valley holds 850 high-security male prisoners. From petty thieves to murderers and rapists. The establishment doesn't discriminate. Convicts who are deemed unsafe to be rehabilitated in the community are ushered through our doors. Which is funny, when staff shortages and budget cuts prevent rehabilitation inside, too – resulting in a revolving door of recidivism.

Three intelligence reports are submitted over the weekend: a recruit disclosing that he knows one of the remand prisoners; a smell of cannabis emanating from the bottom level of Hayworth Hall; and one that's more interesting. An officer's overheard a prisoner boasting about the parcel he's arranged to get at his visit. I want to grade the intel higher, but I can't. I don't know the officer. But still. I can act on it. All I need is corroboration.

Zac Boward. A name I'm familiar with, for he is the main drug dealer in Hayworth level three. I've monitored his calls before. Submitted taskings to monitor his associations. Kept an eye on his personal cash account. But I've never been able to catch him out.

Previous intel has been that he introduces and distributes drugs in exchange for protection. The only reason he hasn't been seriously assaulted so far is his brother's connections. No one likes a sex offender in the mainstream halls.

This is what I've been waiting for. A time, a date and a route of entry. I'd started to think he had someone on the inside helping him. It wouldn't be the first time. But it's through his visit sessions.

There are two ways to corroborate the intelligence – monitor his calls, or check the CCTV for myself. Deciding on the former, I log on to the PIN phone system and cue up his last call. As I slip on my headphones, a familiar tingle of excitement makes itself known in my stomach.

'This call originates from a Scottish prison. It is logged, recorded and may be monitored. If you do not wish to accept this call, please hang up.'

'Do we have to listen to that daft message every bloody time?' says a female voice I recognize immediately as his older sister's.

'Who's this?'

'Tegan. Who'd you think?'

'Aw. I dunno.' A nervous chuckle.

'I hear you're getting bullied in there.'

'Aye, right. Where's Mam?'

'In bed. With him.'

'I need to speak to her. And I only have fifty-five pence credit left, so hurry.'

'Aye, right. I'm not going in there. Tell me and I'll pass it on.'

'There's a visit. Tomorrow.'

'Right.'

A hesitant pause reaches ten seconds.

'I need her . . . To do me proud . . . Again. Think about it, but watch what you're saying.'

'A turn?'

I pause the call, unable to believe my luck. I owe Officer Rana a drink. Boward must be desperate, to talk on the prison phone. Pulling my notebook closer, I resume the call.

'Aye. Watch what you're saying.'

'Put me on the visit.'

'OK.'

'What do you want?'

'Some coke. And a ton of her scoobs,' Zac replies, adding the word 'egg' after every syllable to make it difficult for me to decipher what he's saying. But I've become fluent in egg language over the five years I've worked in the IMU.

'I'll pass it at the end. Mam's off her meds again. She can't be trusted.'

'Whatever. Don't let me down.'

'Have you managed to speak to Scout yet, about your mo—'

The call abruptly ends.

Scout? It's not a name I'm familiar with. I run the nickname through the prison records system. No luck. Someone in the prison will know. I send a quick email to the first line managers. The unit managers. Ask them to forward it to the officers in their areas. The civilian staff in education and social work. Make it sound like I'm desperate to know in the hope someone will take pity and clue me in. But I already know the answer to that one. I won't hold my breath.

I type up my own intel report. Make some calls, conscious of the ticking clock above my head.

It's time to catch them red-handed.

Everything's ready. I've practised the briefing. Printed off handouts of the targets.

The briefing's to be held in my Intelligence Management Unit – an office no bigger than a cupboard that only my manager and I can access. I wipe down the surfaces and hoover the corporate royal-blue carpet before any of my guests arrive. I search the walls, making sure there's no sensitive information pinned up. I remove an old i2 association chart and slip it into the shredder.

I fill the kettle. Clean some grubby mugs. I don't have company often. Wipe the grime off the 65-inch CCTV monitor with a paper towel, the weak August sun splicing through the bars and highlighting the dust. The webs in the corners, themselves thick with dust, I'm too short to reach.

The only office in the establishment that's not permitted a pass man, and for obvious reasons. But that means I have to find the time to clean, which is always low in my priorities. As such, a fruit fly glides around the office. Maybe two. I open the windows as far as they stretch in the hope that it'll disappear, as well as to bring in some fresh air to alleviate the fusty smell. Not for the first time, I consider smuggling in a can of Febreze for these situations. After all, I know which front-of-house officers turn a blind eye. I know exactly when I'd manage to get it in.

Victor Saka, my manager and the establishment's head of operations and security, lets himself into the IMU. Other staff think Victor's the double of Idris Elba, but I don't see it. But then, men aren't exactly my skill set.

'Everything ready?'

I raise an eyebrow.

'Sorry,' he says, raising his hands.

Stevo O'Donald from the National Search Team is next to arrive. I'm glad it's him. He knows that if I have credible intelligence, he isn't wasting his time. It'll result in a capture, making us both look good.

'Thanks for coming on short notice, Stevo.' I bend down to scratch Tyson behind the ears. Good. Tyson's the better dog. Spaniels normally are.

'That's all right,' he says, his voice gruff. 'Where did the five by five come from?'

'You know I can't reveal the source.' I grin. 'But it's corroborated.'

Victor and Stevo strike up a conversation about football while I check my briefing notes. Nobody notices my fingers tremble. But it's not through fear. It's excitement. Nerves.

I'm finally going to catch Boward out after months of close calls.

Another knock on the door. DC Erica Wallace and a plainclothes policewoman I don't recognize make their entrance. Their escort stalks off without a word.

'Sorry we're late,' announces Erica. 'This is PC Alli Graham. I don't think you've met?'

I sit up straighter. Lick my dry lips. The PC is stunning. Her sparkling blue eyes. I've always been a sucker for blue eyes.

Erica wears the same white blouse and blue jeans every time I see her, blonde hair tied back in a bun. Glasses perched on the end of her nose, and her expensive black leather jacket. You'd assume she was a headteacher rather than a cop.

Alli Graham is the opposite. Spiky black hair and tanned skin. She reminds me of an ex. I always did have a thing for bad girls.

'Pleased to meet you. Shall we start?' I hand out briefing sheets. The clock ticks louder. Closer.

'I've developed intelligence regarding nominal Zac Boward. He's suspected to be receiving a quantity of drugs at his visits and selling them on for his own protection.'

'Protection?' frowns Alli. Her piercing blue eyes penetrate my heart. I dig a nail into my palm to help me concentrate.

'Yes,' I chuckle. 'He's a bit of a victim in here. Can't fight sleep. And the rest of them won't batter someone if they can provide drugs. It keeps him safe,' I add.

'Is he linked?' Stevo asks.

'Prison Intel at Gartcosh has disseminated unconfirmed intelligence that his younger brother is working as a specialist car thief for the Shire Boys organized crime group.'

'So that's a yes then,' Erica jokes.

Ignoring her, I continue. 'His older sister, Tegan Boward, is due to visit him, along with their mother, Mary. Intelligence suggests Tegan will be in possession of cocaine and Valium.'

Stevo scrutinizes his handout, committing their faces to memory. 'No problem.'

'Standard operation,' Victor says, taking over. 'If Tyson

indicates on her, she'll be taken to the search room, where yourselves will be waiting.'

'Excellent. We'll get a result,' says Erica with a nod and a smile.

We take our places just before eleven. Stevo, in the corridor with Tyson, hidden from view. Erica and Alli concealed in the search room. Victor and I remain in the IMU, glued to the CCTV monitor.

One camera focuses on the front desk. Another's trained on the corridor where Stevo and Tyson wait.

Maria Collins, security officer, is on one knee, stroking the dog and chatting to Stevo and the police.

My knees shake. My mouth is dry as the first visitor registers for the visit. The front-desk officers are aware something's happening, but not what. Intelligence must be kept secret. If it falls into the wrong hands, it can be dangerous.

Not everyone can be trusted. Not even the officers. A lesson I've learned the hard way over the years.

'That's her,' I say, tapping the monitor. I sit back and exhale. Tegan Boward looks unperturbed as she signs in at the front desk. She doesn't fidget. Doesn't sweat.

She swaggers around in denim hot pants that don't match the autumn weather we've been having this summer. Her fake-blonde hair is longer than her shorts. Make-up expertly applied, complete with trout lips. Her mum waddles behind, scratching her greasy hair and removing her navy jacket. But I'm not interested in her. Her daughter gets all my attention.

'She's either been doing this for a while, or she's clean.'

My fingernails dig into my knees. Edge closer to the screen. I'm five minutes away from catching them. Months of work leading to this moment.

'Relax,' Victor chuckles. 'If she's dirty, we'll catch her.'

'It almost seems too good to be true.'

'Hmm. Whatever happens, this might lead to an increase in violence in the hall.'

I stay quiet. I'd rather see a spike in violence than drugs in the hall.

The Boward women take off their jewellery and empty their pockets into blue plastic trays which are then slid through the X-ray machine. Neither mother nor daughter sets off the walk-through metal detector as they make their way to the waiting room. Tegan Boward strolls along like she doesn't have a care in the world. Maybe she doesn't.

'I bet my mortgage the drugs are in her bra.'

'Five minutes and we'll find out. Relax.'

The visits officer allows them through the turnstile and directs them into the waiting room where other visitors are already gathered.

Victor presses his radio and speaks.

'Tango Juliet 007 to Steve O'Donald. Message, over.'

'Send your message, 007.'

'Stand by for the first group.'

'Roger, received.'

The police disappear into the search room as Maria takes up her position at the electronic door.

My fingers rub at my left eye, fighting an urge to tug at my lashes. A nasty habit I've had since childhood.

Maria unlocks the door and motions for the small group of visitors to follow her through. Tegan enters the corridor. She spots the dog; jolts back like she's been shot.

Maria motions for her to continue forward. The cameras pick up the hesitation on her face – as if she's trying to decide whether to continue or to run away.

Her guilt is clear. The intelligence is right. *I'm* right.

She takes a step forward. Stevo murmurs something to the dog.

'I'm scared of dogs,' she says, I'm later told.

Another step. Tyson bounds over and sniffs.

My heart flutters. 'Sit down,' I whisper. 'Sit down.'

If the dog doesn't indicate, we won't have the justification to search her.

As if the dog hears me, he sits. A big shit-eating grin on his face. Maria marches over, careful not to put hands on the visitor, and directs her towards the search room.

'Yes!' I shout, arms in the air like I've just scored the winning goal in a cup final.

I watch as Boward shakes her head. Shrugs. 'I'm innocent,' she pleads.

Maria and Stevo usher her into the search room. When they emerge, Stevo looks up at the cameras with his thumbs up.

'Positive indication from Tyson. Hopefully, anything she has is in a place where the police can retrieve it,' Victor says.

I grimace.

That's the thing with females. They've double the number of hiding places as a man. And most aren't afraid to use them.

The rest of the visitors are screened along with Mary Boward before she's escorted upstairs to the visit room, where she and her son are placed on closed visits. A sheet of glass will prevent anything being passed that might've been missed by Tyson.

The police keep us waiting a full fifteen nailbiting minutes.

'Can you radio down for an update?'

'Let them do their job, Kennedy.'

I squint at the screen.

'Is she in handcuffs?' I ask, caressing my lashes with my thumb.

We both jump when a message comes over the radio.

'Tango Juliet 187 to Head of Operations, over.'

'Send your message, Maria.'

'That's one arrested from the visits, over.'

'Received. Great work, Maria. Out.'

'Yes,' I roar, and my smug smile hurts my cheeks.

'Good work, Kennedy. Shall we find out what's been recovered?'

I nod.

'Put on your name badge. We better go and brief the Governor.'

I roll my eyes. My one act of defiance against the man in charge. But not even interacting with him will dampen my mood, even though he'll give it a good go.

The police take Tegan Boward into custody, along with the 10 grams of cocaine and 120 Valium tablets they recovered from the cup of her bra. As soon as the Governor is briefed, I nip out to the nearby supermarket to get something for lunch, leaving Victor to brief the National Intelligence Bureau at HQ. A communication will go out, banning Tegan Boward from visiting any prison in Scotland.

I stare between the sushi and the plain ham sandwich. It's the cost that settles it. The boring sandwich is fifty pence cheaper. My hands are outstretched, ready to snatch the packet when she speaks.

'Are you that Kennedy Allardyce?'

The woman in the grey jogging bottoms and navy jacket doesn't immediately look familiar. Her brass-yellow hair is tied back in a pony-tail, black, greasy roots showing. She looks at my name badge, the one the Governor's so insistent we always wear, and scowls.

I don't recognize her face, but I should've recognized her voice.

'Think you're big, eh? You're nothing.'

'I'm sorry, can I help you with something?' My hand automatically goes to the prison ID that hangs around my neck, but it's too late. She knows who I am.

'My Zac's a good boy. It's folk like you that can't see past his false conviction. He's trying to better himself, win his appeal, but you can't see that, can you?'

My heart bangs that hard I feel it in my throat. My vision is blurry. This woman knows who I am. What the fuck? I look around, try to attract the attention of the security guard, but he's busy scrolling on his phone.

My face blazes against her scrutiny. Her loud voice attracts the attention of the nearby shoppers. I expect someone to jump in, back me up, but it doesn't happen. I'm not in my safe place.

'Do you know what they call you? Behind your back?' She takes a step closer. The smell of stale vodka seeps from her pores.

I don't move.

'The prisoners can call me whatever they want.' I rub at my eyes.

The woman grins, showing eroded blackened stumps.

'I'm not talking about the prisoners, hon.'

My stomach lurches.

Even though I know I'm disliked because of the job I do, it's not nice to have it voiced. Especially by someone like her.

When she forms her hand into a fist and swings it at me, I still expect someone to intervene. Her fist connects with my jaw and my vision trembles. I stumble back as I register the pain. White-hot and burning. There's blood coming from somewhere. Her cubic zirconia ring slices my cheek. Someone shouts something, but I'm too stunned for the words to register.

For the first time in five years, I feel real fear. My blood flows to my limbs, but I can't move. My eyebrows raise, my mouth opens. Then nothing. Except the growing pain.

I should be able to protect myself, but every defensive stance and action I've ever learned in my annual self-defence course exits my brain. And naturally, I'm overdue to attend. Out of competency. Incompetent.

My muscles tense, anticipating the next blow. A tic in my eyelid. And then it gets worse.

The blade of the knife glints under the lights as she clutches it. My insides turn to ice. Fluid. My breathing quickens: short, rapid breaths. Tears? Or sweat?

'Look,' I say, voice high-pitched, licking my lips and holding my arms out, trying to appeal to her better nature, but it's useless. She doesn't respond to the spirit of common decency. My heart reacting to the adrenaline, pummelling my chest, I fight the flight response my body is screaming at me to adhere to.

She shifts towards me quicker than her weight should allow. I stick my arms up, instinctively knowing she'll go for my face. But I'm surprised when all I feel is a punch as she punctures my unguarded abdomen. I jolt as she grabs my shoulder, sticking the knife in further before yanking it out, a proud smile plastered over her fat face.

It's the sight of my own blood coating the knife that makes me fall to the ground, clutching my wet side. She

14

kicks my face and I vomit coffee and bile over her scuffed Adidas Superstars.

'Scout says goodnight,' she says, before hawking back and spitting on my battered face.

My eyelids flutter as she's pulled away from me. I surrender to the alluring darkness.

2. Adrian Maddox

I'm cleaning my gaff when the screw appears. Working off nervous energy. It doesn't take long, considering I'm stuck in a six-by-nine coffin box. A small bed, laughably called a single, a small wardrobe unit for my clothes, and a desk. Some shelving for my shower gels. A small safe for my valuables. And a tiny door, no bigger than one on a plane, that houses my en suite. I have to walk sideways to enter it, so I don't remove the skin off my arms.

I'd put the word out – about Boward. About how he couldn't be trusted. And now the cons are looking at me in a different light. And with Boward moved to the digger . . . One down, one to go.

And then the path to the top will be clear. I'll be rightfully cemented in as the Top Dog.

'Are you finished with the hoover, Maddox?' growls the screw.

I raise an eyebrow, for I don't have the hoover.

The screw sighs theatrically and storms into my gaff, but not dramatically enough to attract the attention of the others.

'What do you want?' I smirk.

'I have a present for you.' The screw holds out a package. 'From your uncle,' the screw adds, but their hand remains clamped.

I cross my hands over my chest and make no move. It's a game we both like to play. Who holds the most power. It's a pity when they think it's them.

'If it was from my uncle, it'd be a bit bigger.'

'It's time to step up, Maddox. Your uncle has a big job for you. Pass it, and he'll let you into his inner circle.'

The screw thrusts the small baggy into my hand. Not even two grams' worth. Not worth the hassle to try and sell on. 'It's not my birthday.'

'No, but it will be if you do what your uncle wants.'

The smile slides from my face. For months I've been begging him to trust me more. Give me bigger responsibilities. My stomach fizzes. This is it.

'We're about to get a new admission. The infamous kind.'

It only takes a second for it to click. 'No way.'

'Way.'

'You've to give him that, him being a big cokehead and all.'

I look at the powder and frown. Why are we doing favours for him?

'What if he doesn't get put up here?'

'Don't worry about that – that's my problem.'

I lick my lips. My fingertips tingle.

'Oh, and Adrian. You don't want to take a dunt. Nor do you want to be caught with it.'

'Why?'

The screw sneers.

'You don't want to know. Just make sure you give it to *him*. Call it a housewarming present.'

I hold the powder above my head. Under the light. It looks like proper cocaine, but I suddenly don't want it anywhere near me.

'The cunt in gaff 37 owes me a favour. Get him to hold it until the time's right. Tell him from me, it'll clear his debt.'

'One more thing. Questions are being asked ... It's been taken care of, but we'll need to watch ourselves.'

'If it's been taken care of, then we have nothing to worry about,' I say, handing the powder back.

'I'll have more stuff tomorrow. Christmas is coming early.' The screw winks. Swaggers out my gaff. The smile spreads over my face. It's time to put part two of my plan into action.

It's time to take over the hall.

3. Kennedy

'Did you remember to lift your packed lunch? I put in all your favourites.'

'Yes, Mum,' I scoff.

'Don't call me that. I'm only trying to make your first day back better.'

No, you just don't want me going to the supermarket.

'I'm sorry, love.'

We've been sitting in our car outside the prison for almost seven minutes. I can't seem to leave.

'I can take you back home. If you want.'

To be fair, I could take more time off, on full pay, but you have to come back at some point, right? Sitting alone in our flat while Ellie's at work, watching mindless TV for another week, no longer appealed.

'No – just. Give me another minute.'

She nods. Stays quiet.

The weather over the last six weeks hasn't been on my side either. Summer to autumn. Fat drops of rain and frost. Not that I'd wanted to go out.

I laid it on thick during my occupational health appointment. How desperate I was to get back to work. Back to normality. It's easy to lie on a phone call. I might not have been successful if the appointment had been face to face.

'Have you remembered your medication. Your Sertraline?'

I look away, unable to maintain eye contact. 'Yes, Ellie.

Stop fussing. Please.' The unopened box of antidepressants remains stuffed down the back of my bed. I can't bring myself to take them, despite Ellie's relief that the doctor prescribed them. 'They're the best,' she'd sighed.

My stitches came out after two weeks and my wound itched like mad. The gash to my cheek was glued. The bruises healed. Ellie spent six weeks treating me like one of her patients. As much as I love her, I need away from her swaddling. It made things awkward between us; boundaries were blurred, just when we'd been getting on better since our break-up.

Victor phoned once a week. I'd come to look forward to our five-minute chats. Not that he divulged much on what I was missing, but my nose had twitched in anticipation of intrigue nonetheless, like a hungry rabbit. I told him about my itching. My dependence on crap daytime telly. How I had to come back before my brain rotted any further.

I made jokes. Let him think I'd recovered. He wasn't surprised when Occupational Health signed me fit.

'I can't believe people are allowed to walk their dogs on the grounds,' she says as an old man walks past the car with his black Lab.

'It's public property. As long as they clean up their shit.'

She lapses into silence as I stare at my hands. 'Look, he's down near the vehicle lock.'

'He'll be getting watched on the CCTV in the control room.'

The attack on me wasn't spontaneous. That's the thought that's consumed me over the last six weeks. An inside job.

'We can sit here as long as you need to,' Ellie says. 'If you're sure you want to go back.'

Someone told her who I was. Where to find me. A conclusion that's tormenting me. I need to know who it was. I need to come back – it's the only way I'll find out.

The CCTV footage won't keep for ever. I need to know who spoke to Mary Boward before the bitch attacked me. The longer I stay off, the less likely I'll be able to access the footage from the privacy of the IMU. But that isn't my only reason for wanting to return.

'I have to go back. Do you know how much work will have piled up over the last six weeks?'

'We both know that's not why you're going back. You want to find out about him. This Scout.'

'It could be a she . . .'

'Statistically unlikely. And anyway, you said females are the minority in there. That you're the only decent-looking one.'

'What if this person tries again? What if I'm still at risk, but they use someone more . . . effective? I need to know, Ellie.'

She looks away so I don't see the expression on her face. She's been biting her tongue for weeks. Wanting to beg me to quit. Which is ironic, considering I never wanted to work here in the first place. She would hate me to point *that* out to her.

'No one will think badly of you, you know. If you need another few days.'

'I don't care what people think,' I say with weak conviction.

My thoughts return to the job. No one's tackling my to-do list. And I don't like to think about those fuckers getting away with anything. The core nominals, making money over the weaknesses of others.

I'm plagued with thoughts of vital intelligence that's

been missed due to my absence. Snatched conversations in egg language that'll only mean something to me.

The prisoners who'll be out their tits because I'm not there to stop the drugs from entering the prison. Passed through visits. Concealed in property. Thrown over the fence. Or the route of entry that's becoming more prevalent – smuggled in by corrupt staff.

Someone will have filled Boward's shoes. Or there'll have been a power struggle in the hall. A takeover. And because I'm six weeks out of the loop, I'm starting on the back foot. Again.

It's like a big game. Sometimes they win. They get their stuff in. And sometimes I win. And they don't. But recently it feels like they're winning more than I am. No matter how hard I work.

The drug trade inside is enticingly lucrative. Prison prices are three times higher than those out in the community. Even a nice colourful shower gel will sell for £50 a bottle. But when you're up against a senior management team that likes to turn the occasional political blind eye – that puts the human rights of prisoners before all else – it's difficult for me to do the best job I can. Soft-touch Scotland. Especially when there's no incentive for the cons to behave.

'We can't punish families,' they'll cry, before complaining there's too much drug misuse the next day. Or, when I want to organize a lockdown search of an area, the Governor will squirm, knowing any finds will result in an increase in violence and cell damage in the School of Crime he presides over. More bad publicity. Especially in the long run-up to Christmas. Hooch hunts. If we find too many drugs, have too much violence, the Governor doesn't get a bonus.

One thing I haven't missed: the politics.

Another reason I want to come back – the one I'll only admit to myself – I miss the structure. The routine. The pride I take in doing a good job. Even if I'm the only one who's interested in making the place safer for everyone.

And Scout. The bruises have healed, but the thought that the attack could have been an inside job makes me want to cry. What could I have done to be hated so much someone tried to kill me over it?

It's the thought that's kept me up at night, but also the one that's given me the courage to fight back. If someone has set me up, I want to know who.

Ellie's been great. But she has a full-time job and a new girlfriend. If I don't have my job, I have nothing.

The warmth of the car comforts me. I glimpse towards the building, as grey as the sky above it. A plastic bag has been captured by the barbed wire that covers the twenty-foot-high perimeter fence. I watch as it blows in the breeze. Trapped.

'It's got to be an officer,' I lament, and am rewarded with another eye roll.

'It could be a coincidence, babe.'

'That I ask for help from the whole staff group to iden-tify someone and get attacked hours later? She said "Scout", Ellie. That's the name I emailed, like, four hundred people about.'

'Couldn't it just be a well-connected con?'

I shake my head. 'Trust your gut. That's what was drummed into me at my training. It's an officer.'

She sighs. There's no arguing with me when I'm in this mood. I know I'm right, and that's all that matters.

My limbs are heavy. I lack the energy to get out of the car.

Not even the threat of the imminent downpour is enough to get me moving. I could get her to start the engine. Go home. Instead of languishing here in purgatory.

That's what I wanted, after all. The green light to return. So why am I so hesitant to leave the car?

I want her to turn on the engine. Drive away. But when she doesn't, waiting on my cue, I click my belt.

'Right. I'm ready.'

'Phone me if you need me. I'm not doing anything today. Phone me anyway, let me know how you're getting on.'

We both ignore the tone of relief in her voice.

She goes to kiss me, a platonic kiss on the cheek, and I flinch. Almost bang my head off the passenger window.

'Not here, for fuck's sake.'

'Calm down, Kennedy. No one's looking.'

With a deep breath, I grab my yellow umbrella – to protect me not just from the inclement weather but the threat of any harm.

My legs jiggle, but I continue to put one foot in front of the other.

I'll pay for that later, but I have bigger worries than Ellie's hurt feelings. I look around, my head swivelling, eyes out for anyone who might jump out at me. Making sure the dog walker is nowhere near.

The automatic doors whoosh open as I approach the main entrance. I concentrate on the sign in front of me: 'Welcome to HMP Forth Valley', like I've arrived at a caravan park for my holidays. That's how the prison's portrayed in the media – a holiday camp. And if you knew what I knew – you'd agree.

The new governor's a different breed. All about rehabilitation rather than punishment. But what he fails to realize is that 90 per cent of the cons aren't interested in rehabilitation. Most are desperate to get out to return to the crimes that brought them here in the first place.

Sometimes, it's hard not to think that I'm the daftie for making an honest living. But I could never be like them. Earning money illegally and always having to look over my shoulder.

Keeping my eyes straight ahead, I proceed to the front desk, already removing my outer jacket. A solitary candle flickers in the mouth of a premature pumpkin, poorly carved fake webs and plastic spiders are pinned to the counter. Someone must have been bored to put up the decorations this early.

Fresh coffee and the unmistakable odour of a recently cooked slice of bacon makes my stomach gurgle. I've been too nervous to eat.

I remind myself to breathe as I grab a plastic tray and place my jacket and bag inside.

'Morning,' greets Tina, an operations officer who's never had any aspirations of promotion. Her nickname's Marilyn, because she's just as dramatic and likes the attention of other women's men. The only thing she's good for is gossip. She's a magnet for it. The whole place is. If someone farted at the front desk, they'll have shat themselves by the time Tina has made the rounds. Staff at the far side of the prison must've heard I'd been murdered rather than stabbed.

'Morning,' I say as I slide my tray of personal items on to the conveyor belt to be scrutinized under the X-ray machine. I don't recognize the male officer manning the machine. A product of the high turnover of staff. The job isn't for everyone. I can attest to that.

'I haven't seen you for ages,' says Tina. 'Where've you been hiding?' She huddles around her coffee mug for warmth.

I gaze directly into her eyes. Is she trying to be funny or just being herself? Hard to tell with Tina.

'I've been off. Sick.'

I clench my teeth so hard I almost turn them into dust. She must've heard what happened.

'Nice to see you back,' she chirps.

The body scanner doesn't beep when I walk through, confirming I have nothing on me I shouldn't have.

The security procedures for entering any prison are the same as at an airport – but without the alcohol and the excitement of going on holiday to look forward to.

'Is there any truth in the rumours that we're getting women prisoners here?'

I grab my personal items out of the tray. Women?

'I've been off the last six weeks. If a decision like that's been made, I'll be the last to hear about it.'

My face is hot and flushed as I hurry away from them.

'That's her,' Tina whispers to the new guy, before I've made it two metres. He giggles. I speed through the security door, away from their sniggering.

The smell of sour mops, a mixture of bleach and vomit, makes my already sensitive stomach churn. I breathe through my mouth as my heart thuds. Maybe I *have* come back too soon?

I sit in the professional visitor waiting area before my legs give way. Concentrate on my breathing like I've been taught at counselling. In for seven. Out for five. Repeat until my heart cooperates.

The Governor's face smirks at me from a poster on the wall. The plant in the pot below it is in dire need of rescue, the leaves turning brown and wilted.

The controlled door clicks open and Bruce Gordon, Prison Officers Association union rep, walks through.

'Kennedy?' He hurries over and kisses me on the cheek. 'Nice to see you back.'

I swallow down the lump in my throat. 'Thank you.'

'How are you feeling?' He tilts his head in the universal gesture of sympathy.

'Better. Taking it a day at a time. You know . . .' I dip my head, not wanting him to see the shine of my eyes.

'Have you heard my news?'

'No.' I glance up.

'I'm retiring at the end of the week. You'll come to my night out, right?'

I close my eyes. My ally. He can't leave. All the words I've ever learned vanish.

'I thought you were in with the bricks?'

'Yeah . . . Well . . . The job's fucked, and . . .' He pulls his wallet out of his pocket. Opens it to reveal a picture.

'Oh my God. When's she due?'

'Christmas Day.' He laughs. 'Me? A granda.'

'Congratulations. I'm delighted for you.'

'Thanks, hen. I'm going to spend the next two months doing up her spare room and taking her to all her appointments, with her man still deployed overseas.'

'Will he be back in time for the birth?'

'Aye. But it's the best present I could have asked for. Life's too short for this shite, mate.'

'Don't I know that!'

'Did you look into that vacancy with the police I sent you? You'd be more . . . anonymous there. They pay better, too.'

'Yes,' I lie. The grass isn't always greener, but I don't want to sound ungrateful. Plus, I refuse to leave. Not until I've unmasked Scout. It's on the tip of my tongue, to ask Bruce his thoughts, confide in him, but he's been

27

in the union too long. He knows how to hide people's dark secrets.

'Look, I need to go, but I'll catch up with you later.'

'OK.'

I wonder why Ellie never mentioned it. Her father and Bruce are as close as brothers. It's how I got this job.

'And remember,' he says as he waits for the control-room officers to unlock the security door opposite, 'you need to speak to anyone, you know where I am.'

'Thanks.'

'It doesn't matter if I'm in a meeting or whatever. You get someone to radio me, and I'll be right along.'

'I appreciate it.'

His mouth opens and closes, like he's on the cusp of saying something else, when the door's unlocked. He disappears through with a backward wave of his fingers, and I'm on my own again.

I count to ten and try again. Pick up my bag. I fob the door to the key-vend room. A wall of radio chargers blinks at me as I trudge over to the vending machine that holds my set of keys.

The smell of sour mop intensifies. I draw my keys, attach them securely to my key chain and put them in my secure belt pouch. I don't need a personal alarm. I have no intention of leaving the safety of the IMU.

My mind drifts. How many emails will I have? How many incident reports? Intelligence reports? It'll take me the rest of the week just to catch up. If only Victor had allowed me remote access, I could've worked from home. But I should've known better. Silly of me to think the Prison Service would've made an exception for me. Even if by doing so it would've helped them out.

The keys are chilly as I take them from my pouch. I

identify the correct one and slip it into the lock. It resists against me. I try again.

I push at the door. It creaks open while my keys trail from the lock.

'Morning,' says a stranger sitting at my desk. 'You must be Kennedy?'

His pink shirt clashes with his ginger hair. His freckles.

'Who the fuck are you?'

His mouth opens in shock. Thick glasses slip down his nose. Clearly no one told him I like to swear when they told him my name and permitted him to sit at my desk.

I remove the keys from the door, secure them and let myself in. Once I'm inside the IMU, I lock it.

'This door should never be left unlocked. This is a restricted area.'

'Well, actually,' he begins, pushing his glasses up his nose, running a nervous hand through his rust-coloured hair, 'there's a policy about lone workers and—'

'Who *are* you?'

'I'm Jacob. Jacob Bradley. Your new assistant. Why don't you sit down? I'll make you a coffee. Or tea?'

But I can't answer. His bright pink shirt is at risk of giving me a migraine. I note his rainbow lanyard and wonder how he gets away with that.

Jacob explains how he started two weeks ago. A job no one told me was advertised. A flare of anger boils inside me. Is this for real? With the time constraints involved, the post must've been advertised before I'd gone off sick.

Hurt trades places with anger. Can't help but feel I've been replaced. All the times I've moaned about my work-load; I never expected Victor to do anything about it.

'I've been reading policies and such, trying to acclimatize

myself to the conditions,' he explains, handing me a cup of coffee which I don't accept.

I stand. My jacket draped over my arm. My bag on my shoulder.

'I guess you'll want your desk back?' He smiles as if he's made a joke. But there's nothing funny about the situation. I have flashbacks to my own volatile start in the IMU, but it's not enough to pacify my anger.

'Yes,' I say. 'I'll have a ton of work to catch up on.'

'I spent time at headquarters. To learn the job. HQ have been dealing with the intelligence reports in your . . . in your absence.' He coughs. 'I, um, I'll just log off, and you can . . .' He claps his hands together twice.

'We do things a little differently here. From HQ,' I say as I push past him and sit.

My desk is cleaner than I expect. A small pile of intelligence reports is stacked neatly next to unread copies of *NEDitorial*.

'It's only anything that's been submitted since Friday that needs to be dealt with.' He points towards the paperwork in between my keyboard and telephone.

I pick up the pile and transfer it to the other side. Petulant, but he needs to know I'm the one in charge.

I turn my attention back to my main monitor, grit my teeth. There's nowhere in the office for him to work. What was Victor thinking? He sits down at the round table where Victor and I have our morning briefings.

I log on: 1,835 unread emails.

My skin crawls as Jacob taps his nails against the table. Slurps his tea. Tedious. If we're forced to work together, we'll need to establish some ground rules.

'Has someone given you a tour?'

'No. Are you offering?'

'I can't; I'm non-operational. A civvie, just like you. I'm not authorized to escort people.'

He continues tapping his nails and slurping his tea. I grab my telephone and dial a number, knuckles white against the black receiver.

'Morning, it's Kennedy in the IMU. I'm wondering if someone's available to give my new admin a tour. Yeah, just the three halls, gymnasium, health centre, activity buildings, et cetera. It shouldn't take long – less if you don't blether . . . Cheers.' I put the phone down and turn to Jacob. 'Someone from Security is going to give you a tour. They'll introduce you to some of the officers too.'

They'll love him. I suppress a smirk.

'That'll give you a chance to catch up without me pestering you,' Jacob adds.

Maria Collins arrives a minute later. She ignores me, but I don't expect anything less. My first staff corruption investigation was into her best pal, and she hasn't broken breath to me since.

Once they leave, I lock the door. Switch on the CCTV. Change the date. The time. Cross my fingers. But it's pointless. The footage has been scrubbed.

Any clues as to who Mary Boward spoke to before leaving the prison that day are no longer accessible. My hand smarts when I punch the hard drive.

Thwarted, I pinch two of Jacob's Jaffa Cakes and try not to berate myself for staying off so long.

I look between the pile of reports, the emails in my inbox and copies of *NEDitorial* – the mysterious underground magazine that publishes weekly under a shroud of secrecy. I pick up the top copy and begin to read. Sometimes, the content of the magazine appears to be one step in front of Police Scotland's investigations. At other times, the complete opposite. But sometimes it provides me with intelligence. Associations. Enemies. Potential new admissions that can bank an iPhone.

We've made the front page.

Governor in scandal-hit prison bans the word 'prisoner'. Staff based at HMP Forth Valley have been banned from referring to cons in their care as prisoners. Staff have been ordered to address them by their surname, prefixed by 'Mr', to protect their human rights, says an insider . . .

I throw it down, no longer interested in reading it.

The unit smells clean. The small fridge purrs beside me, and the microwave and kettle perched on top are cleaner than I've seen them since they came out of their box.

The bin is empty, the carpets are clean and the air isn't stale.

My thoughts return to the new guy. Can there be room for a second person? Probably. But sharing an office will be a struggle.

'I need to explain the importance of intelligence to you,' I announce when Jacob returns. It thrills me to see him subdued.

'Some people believe intelligence is sexy. It's not. It's dangerous. If you're recording intelligence on the system and it's wrong, it can have a severe impact on the decisions made at a strategic level.'

I pause to take a breath, pleased to see by the worried look on Jacob's face that my words have made an impact.

'I'm eager to learn,' he explains. 'I'm a little overwhelmed by the place . . .'

'You need to get over that. Quick. You need your wits about you in this place, and I'm not just referring to the prisoners.'

'I thought we aren't allowed to call them "pri—"'

I glare at him. Willing him to finish his sentence. 'What's said in this room stays in this room. Do you understand that? Trust is important.'

He chews on his thumbnail. 'I'm looking forward to learning from your experience.'

'It'll take at least six months for you to be confident. That doesn't mean you'll get away with making mistakes,' I warn, hoping I might scare him into leaving. His face pales, accentuating his freckles.

A short time later, keys jangling in the lock mean only one thing: Victor. The only other person who can access the IMU.

I stop typing. Turn down the radio.

There's a line with Victor. You have to determine what mood he's in before you cross it. He's been in the job almost as long as I've been alive. He's seen everything. A walking encyclopaedia of the Prison Service. And although not everyone likes him, he's respected.

A tall, broad man with dark hair shaved so close to his scalp that from a distance he appears bald. We get each other. We trust each other. And in this environment, trust is everything.

It angers me when I overhear people mock his stutter. The only time the stutter doesn't make an appearance is in a time of crisis.

I should've picked up on that.

'Morning,' he announces as he locks the door behind him.

I look over to Jacob to see if he's noticed.

'Morning.'

Victor strolls over to me. 'Welcome back.'

'Thanks. I'm so pleased to be here,' I add dryly.

Normally, Victor understands my sarcasm. Yet his mouth remains set in a firm line.

He puts a piece of paper down in front of me. I scan it before reading more closely.

'Fuck,' I say.

He nods once. 'Fuck.'

4. Kennedy

If this were a normal incident, the command room would be bustling.

Chief commander. Deputy. Communications officer. Atlas operator, keeping a log of every movement. Every decision. Sometimes there'd be a representative from Police Scotland or the Scottish Fire Brigade. Paramedics. The duty manager on the line from headquarters, demanding an update every three minutes.

But this incident is top secret. Only a few people know that we've agreed to accept Fred 'The Villain' Filan from HMP Barlinnie. Filan, one of the most dangerous prisoners in the country. Who has the financial backing and a criminal organization behind him to carry out his bidding.

The intelligence could be wrong. It wouldn't be the first time. But I'd rather act and look stupid than risk Filan escaping from custody on the transfer over.

Fred Filan's trial's been all over the papers for weeks. I'd been hooked, searching social media for updates while I was off. The police have been after him for years. Suspected him to be involved in more disappearances and deaths than they'd the evidence to charge him with.

As a youth, he'd risen up the organized crime echelons fast – he was the leader of the Forth Valley Soldiers, taking over in his late teens, following the disappearance of former leader, Ronnie Lawson.

The Soldiers' arch-enemy, Chet Sangster, leader of rival

gang the Shire Boys, had initially been convicted of his murder. Yet Sangster was later released on appeal, intensifying the hatred between the two camps.

And then Sangster disappeared.

Filan's behaviour while on remand in HMP Barlinnie had been deteriorating fast and, as the only establishment not to have any of his known mortal enemies in it, we'd been obligated to accept him. It'd be a bloodbath should members of the two rival gangs meet.

I place a sweaty palm on the dusty windowsill, my nose pressed up against the cold bars that line the window. Has something gone wrong? It's taking too long.

'I know you must have questions. About Jacob.'

I change position, tap the aeriel of my radio against my chin as I wait for the communication that should've been received five minutes ago.

'I don't,' I lie.

'I need you to accept him, Kennedy. Be nice to him. For me.'

'Is he a relative of a friend or something?'

Victor chuckles. 'Play nice, OK? Train him up. Let him in.'

Filan had been convicted last week and given three consecutive life sentences. He wouldn't be getting out anytime soon. The reason the intelligence had to be taken seriously. Despite its E4 grading: untested source. Cannot be judged. Filan had the financial backing and the connections to make an escape possible.

'Can't the police give us any clue of the source?'

'Would we tell them the source if it was the other way around?'

He grunts, and I turn my attention back to the window, my breath fogging up the glass.

In the distance, I hear the distinctive whump of helicopter blades. My eyes flick up to the clouds. A second later, blue flashing lights illuminate the main road. I press myself closer to the window.

The radio crackles to life. 'Tango Juliet 101 to Victor Saka, head of operations, message, over.' I grip the radio tighter.

Showtime.

'This is Tango Juliet 007. Send your message, over.'

'Open the gates, sir.'

'Roger.'

Victor grabs the nearest phone and dials the number for the control room as I watch the helicopter approach. The flashing lights reflect around the darkened room.

'Open the vehicle lock,' he says, without identifying himself. 'Let the escort vehicles in immediately.'

The black helicopter circles the prison as two police motorcycles screech down the drive, followed by the escort van. An armoured car drives so close behind the van it would've been impossible to sandwich so much as a piece of paper between the two vehicles.

Once the procession is through the gate and into the vehicle lock out of my line of sight, I turn my attention to the CCTV monitor on the wall.

The prison's on lockdown for the vehicles to get from the front of the establishment to the reception block without being hindered. As soon as the vehicles are in the sterile area, the control-room officers lock the gates.

My fingers tremble. Excitement or relief?

Fred 'The Villain' Filan has arrived without incident.

Three officers dressed in riot gear exit the vehicle with Filan emerging behind them in plasticuffs. They'll only be removed when he's safely locked up in a fresh cell.

The police officers hold a guard of honour, ready to jump in and huckle the prisoner if he kicks off. But Filan's small stature doesn't match his reputation. Hard to believe he's the most violent prisoner in Scotland. His chest's puffed out as he exits the van. He doesn't look around but instead allows the officers to guide him to the reception block in the cuffs.

Victor adjusts his tie, clips the radio to his belt and makes sure his name badge is showing. Time to brief the Governor.

Our secret's out the bag. Any member of staff with access to a front-facing window will've watched the cavalcade charging down the drive, adding a bit of excitement to an otherwise dull Monday afternoon.

We march towards the Governor's office and knock before entering.

'Victor,' he announces without looking up from his spreadsheet. 'Everything's gone well, I take it?'

'Yes, Governor. The prisoner's—'

The Governor clears his throat.

'Sorry. Mr Filan has landed in reception and is being processed.'

'The intelligence that he was going to escape was rubbish, was it?'

'That's hard to say, Governor. Would you rather we took the risk?'

Governor Sebastian Canopy picks up his mug. Takes a long drink. 'When is the analyst back at work?'

'I'm right here.' I pout, but he doesn't look my way.

'We need to gather as much intelligence as possible. I want his associations charted. His rivals. It goes without saying, staff safety is paramount. I don't want any of my officers ending up with a missing finger.'

'I believe it was a nose he chewed off, Governor. Not a finger.'

His comments wash over me. I'd been employed at HMP Forth Valley longer than he's been employed by the Prison Service. An accelerated promotion – fulfilling a role that should be earned, not handed out like sweets to bored children.

'Kennedy will be all over it. But in order to keep everyone safe, the staff will have to submit five by fives to the IMU. Managers will have to listen to, and act on, Kennedy's recommendations.'

But the Governor isn't listening.

'Make sure Mr Filan's located in the Segregation Unit for a period of seventy-two hours. No longer than that. I'll expect a full profile and association chart by Wednesday lunchtime. Then we can decide which hall he's going to.'

The Governor turns to face his computer, indicating that the conversation's over.

I nod and escape from his office, pleased with myself that I didn't punch the sanctimonious prick on the jaw.

'He should be in the digger for longer than three days after the stunt he pulled at Barlinnie,' mutters Victor as we storm back to the IMU.

I nod. How can we maintain effective relationships with the staff group when prisoners don't get punished for their internal crimes as well as the ones that saw them admitted here?

'Make sure you embellish your profile on Filan a little. Make it hard for the Governor to put him to a hall.'

'I can't do that, Victor. I have to go where the intelligence takes me.'

'You're right—' he begins, but his apology is cut off by the radio.

'ALL STATIONS, ALL STATIONS, CODE BLUE IN HAYWORTH LEVEL THREE. I REPEAT, CODE BLUE IN HAYWORTH LEVEL THREE.'

We look at each other. And run.

Code blue. Someone isn't breathing.

5. Kennedy

'As first days back go . . .' Victor says as we make our way from the sterile area down the metal coffin corridor into the beast of the prison. Gobbets of spit and bird shit line the route. Gone are the fancy welcoming signs. The fake flowers. The fresh paint. Replaced with sheets of metal with rules sporadically bolted to the metal. No running. Single file. No spitting.

'Feels like I've never been off.'

I zip my black Scottish Prison Service fleece. It's not the open slats at the top of the metal fence that make me shiver. It's this. I feel it too. That all hope, beyond this point, is gone. The false veneer that covers the sterile area doesn't extend on the other side.

'You're OK though? You're still taking the antidepressants?'

'Yes,' I answer, too quick.

'Good. Bird by bird, remember.'

Victor's favourite saying, based on a book he read. 'Bird by bird,' I repeat.

I have to ask. 'Who all knew about the operation? With the Bowards?'

We walk on in silence. I'm scared of the answer I'll get, but I have to ask.

'Operation?'

'With the Bowards. Before I went off.'

'I had to tell the Governor, Kennedy. You know that.'

41

'I'm not saying anything, I'm just asking. Do you think he might have told anyone else?'

Victor sighs. 'I don't know. He might have mentioned it to the other senior managers.'

I clench my teeth His non-answer tells me what I need to know. The whole establishment probably knew.

'Where is Boward?'

Victor rubs his nose. He must've known I'd ask.

'Look, why don't we talk about it later? This isn't the place.'

I stop walking. 'No. Let's talk about it now.'

It takes Victor three more steps before he detects I'm no longer beside him.

'Kennedy . . .'

'Oh my God. He's still here. Isn't he?' The blood drains from my head. Leaves me feeling dizzy.

'It's a complex situation. We'll discuss it later.'

'Discuss it later? You promised me I'd be safe, Victor. Nice to know I'm valued.'

We reach the point of the corridor where it branches off on to the halls: Hayworth, Morton, and the Seg unit in the middle. The third hall, Larkfield, is on the outer grounds. A small unit prisoners can transfer to if they meet the criteria for progression. Home leaves. An external work placement or college course. Prepare them for release.

I pause at the hall we're about to enter. Victor reads my mind.

'He's in the Seg unit. You won't see him.'

'It's not him I'm worried about,' I spit.

Zac Boward's still here. And you can't ban a prisoner's next of kin. It's against their human rights. Even if they commit crimes near the grounds of the establishment.

Like attempted murder pled down to assault to severe injury and permanent disfigurement. She could come up anytime. I could walk into her, anytime. They ban the sister, but not her? Make it make sense.

'You know she got bail, right? On account of her mental health?'

'I was briefed.'

'It's a fucking joke. Bad enough she pled not guilty. What about *my* mental health? What if I see her, huh? What then?'

'You could see her at the cinema. The doctor's. The supermar—'

He flinches, and I know he instantly regrets his words.

'Come on,' he adds. 'We're needed in the hall. We'll discuss it later. I promise.'

I try to keep up. Try to keep my eyes dry.

I wasn't expecting a pat on the fucking back for coming back to work, but I was expecting to get treated better than this. Bruce was right. The job *is* fucked.

I follow Victor up the concrete steps. He swipes the access point with his fob and the door clicks open. Fresh autumn air turns to body odour and boredom. Eau de Bawbag.

The whiff of sour sweat intensifies as we climb the stairs to the top wing. At least in a hospital bad smells are masked by bleach. Prison smells of boiled food, dirty mops and body sweat. Fresh paint if a VIP's expected.

The hall's unnaturally quiet. No shouting from the windows. No banging on doors. Eerie. Unnatural. I shiver, but not because I'm cold.

The stained walls are painted a calming pink, which is supposed to help reduce the violence. The centre console, where the prison officers normally work from, is deserted. The wing splits into east and west sections, separated from each other and the console by bright red grille gates, each section holding approximately sixty prisoners.

The activity is all on the west side. Someone's put up a curtain outside cell 37. I saunter up the section, feeling brave in Victor's presence, and wave.

'Kennedy! Nice to see you back,' says CID officer Derek Glasgow.

'Thanks. Better circumstances would've been nice. The job's still fucked.'

'One off the numbers though?' he jokes.

Victor's death stare behind us raises the hairs on my neck.

'Any idea what's happened, Derek? Suicide?'

A CSI technician takes photographs inside the cell. The repetitive click of their equipment punctuates the silence. The camera is flashing with such an intensity there should be a risk warning for epileptics.

Derek shakes his head. 'Nah. Gonna have to wait for the post-mortem. I can guess, though.'

'We'd rather wait for the facts,' Victor says.

I chew on my bottom lip. 'Can I look?' I ask, surprising myself.

'As long as you don't enter the cell or touch anything. It's still officially a crime scene.'

I take a deep breath. I've never seen a dead body. I clasp and unclasp my hands as I take a step forward. Pop my head into the cell without crossing the threshold.

Maybe this could've been avoided if I'd been at work, I can't help but think.

The body lies face down on the bed. No obvious blood spillage. No ligature. No syringe or other obvious drug paraphernalia.

His blanket's fused with his mottled torso. I take a step back. I've seen enough.

'Did he leave a note?' I ask over my shoulder. Victor shakes his head.

'Not that we've been able to find.'

I make a mental note to listen to his last phone call. There might be clues there. Listening to phone calls is boring half the time. But listening to a call knowing it's the last one someone has ever made is tough.

I look at the deceased. Kalvin Jones. I'm not familiar with his name. The prisoner means nothing to me. But somewhere, his mum's getting a life-changing knock on the door. Will she care? Or will she see it as an opportunity to make money? Some do.

The residential officers go round all cell doors on both sections, making sure the other prisoners are as OK as they can be, given the circumstances. The last thing we need is another death. But that's the thing with suicides. They're contagious. And that's what it looks like we're dealing with here.

My arms pucker under my fleece. It isn't being close to the corpse that bothers me, it's the unnatural silence. Like they've all died.

The hall door clicks open. Two men enter with a trolley. A body bag. I hurry to the grille gate as they set foot into the cell. I don't want to see this part. Victor remains where he is, head bowed. Even the CID are solemn.

I'm closest to the centre console when the phone rings. The shrill ring makes my head pound. When it becomes apparent no one's going to answer, I pick up the receiver.

'Good morning, Hayworth Hall.'

I glance up at the clock on the wall, amazed that I'm right. It is still morning.

45

'Sorry to bother you, but I can't remember if I have a visit with my son this evening.'

I tug at a lash while the woman talks.

'Give me a minute, I'll find the visit sheet.'

I search the desk for the clipboard detailing the day's movements. Court appearances. Education. Work parties. Visits.

'Can you give me your son's name and date of birth, please?'

'Sure. His name's Kalvin Jones and his birthday's the . . .'

I don't hear the rest of the information as it takes all my resolve not to drop the phone.

'Give me one minute, please,' I say, pressing the hold button before she has the chance to reply.

I place the handset gently on top of the desk. Look around for someone to help.

'Derek,' I shout, motioning him over.

'What's the matter? I need to witness them removing the body.'

I point at the phone.

'Don't tell me the wife's tracked me down?'

I shake my head. 'It's his mum,' I whisper. As if she might hear me. 'The deceased's mum.'

'What does she want?'

'To know the time of their visit. Look,' I say, pointing at the visit sheet, 'she's listed to attend at 7 p.m.'

'Then tell her that.'

'I can't,' I squawk. 'Her son's lying dead not five feet away. I can't tell her to come up.'

'Kennedy, you have to. She has to believe everything's OK until Uniform can tell her.'

I shake my head, unable to speak.

Derek sighs. Picks up the receiver. 'Hi there, your

visit's at seven, OK?' A pause. 'Sure, I'll let him know. Thank you.'

I tug at an eyelash. 'Thank you.'

'That's one you owe me, Allardyce.'

'She'll be told before she has to leave for the visit, right?'

He shrugs. 'Should be.'

I open my mouth, but nothing comes out.

'Come on. Let's get you away from the phone in case it rings again. Do you want me to get you a cuppa?'

'No, thanks.'

Ten minutes later, the trolley rolls out of the cell and back towards the exit. Officers hang their heads. All conversation ceases. All that can be heard is the squeak every three seconds from one of the wheels.

As soon as the body's removed, the cell's locked over with a security seal. It'll remain that way until it's no longer deemed a crime scene. Then the pass man will be paid a higher wage to clean it out ready for its next occupant.

A female officer emerges from the staffroom behind the centre console, holding a tissue to her swollen eyes. We briefly make eye contact and my heart contracts. I've never been attracted to an officer before. Her hair, her cheekbones. Who is she? Following her out is Tim Reilly, the unit manager of Hayworth Hall.

'How are you?' he asks, gently nudging my shoulder.

The female keeps her head down and leaves the hall.

'Not bad. How are you?'

He shrugs. 'You see it all, pal.'

'How's your wife keeping?'

'Good days, bad days.' Another shrug.

I change the subject. 'Who found him? The body?'

47

'Officer Rana. I've let her go get some fresh air – compose herself – before the police take her statement.'

'Rana?'

'She's new.'

It occurs to me moments later where I've seen the name before – the intel report. About Boward. And now I have a name to the face.

'Have you tasked the officers to ask the prisoners—'

He doesn't let me finish. 'Yes. Every prisoner's being asked what they know, Kennedy.'

I smile at him. 'I knew I could trust you,' I say. Loud enough for Victor to hear.

As managers go, Tim Reilly is one of my favourites. I'm glad he's on duty. Glad it happened in his hall.

'Make sure officers put in intelligence reports,' I instruct. 'Doesn't matter how minor . . .'

He salutes and walks away.

'Anything?' Victor asks.

'Not yet. Either the other prisoners don't know anything, or no one's talking.'

'Did you expect anything less?'

Number-one rule in prison if you want to survive is don't talk to officers: don't be a grass.

'Do you think this is the work of Filan?'

I frown. 'He's only been here two minutes.'

'He has a lot of reach, remember. I'm under no illusion he'll have come here banked. The digger pass man is located here. He could've couriered drugs up to the hall on Filan's behalf?'

I'm not convinced. The death seems like a suicide to me. And Filan's been here less than two hours. That's not enough time to make new connections.

'It'll be interesting to see which officers are brave enough to admit they know him, if any,' Victor continues. 'Keep me posted, yeah?'

'Will do. I need to get back to the IMU so I can start my checks.'

We hear the breathing before he speaks. His breathing louder than his footsteps.

'Mr Saka?'

Victor and I look up. 'Yeah?'

He's grown a beard since I last saw him. It makes him look younger, despite the grey around his chin. Still the same thick glasses. If the Prison Service had a height restriction, he would never have got in.

'You know how this has happened, right? Because of that monster in the digger.'

My lips part, but Victor launches in first.

'Let's not jump to conclusions. And it's the separation and reintegration unit, not the digger, may I remind you.'

'Bit of a coincidence,' he scoffs. 'I hope you're planning to ship him right back where he came from. This is the start of it, mark my words. My mate worked with him on remand in Barlinnie. He's a fucking animal. He chewed an officer's ear off there.'

The officer slumps off without another word, rubbing subconsciously at his own lobe.

'Who put fifty pence in him?' I joke.

'You know the Bloodhound, if he hasn't got something to moan about, he might spontaneously combust.'

The Bloodhound aka Darren North. The officer the prisoners hate because he refuses to be conditioned. Incorruptible. And likes the word 'no'. Thrives on making the prisoners' time as difficult as possible. Preferring to wind them up and leave his colleagues to diffuse the situation. He liked to submit reports to me that were only occasionally intelligence. Most of the time they were rants about his colleagues or prisoners calling him names.

My spine prickles, and I look up. Three officers huddle around the centre console. They turn their heads as I make eye contact. Distrust comes off them in waves. I shiver.

I'm not welcome here.

6. Kennedy

By mid-afternoon, cell 37 on Hayworth level three re-opens. The police have taken all the photographs and evidence deemed necessary to begin their investigation.

Jacob's been tasked with shredding documents we no longer need to keep for audit purposes. Intel reports. Incident overviews. Use-of-force paperwork. The constant whine of the shredder grates on my nerves. Almost as if Victor's done it deliberately to avoid having the conversation that he promised earlier. Explaining the decision-making behind Boward still being here and not in the Barlinnie digger. But at least it means I don't have to make small talk with Jacob.

The Estates team will rearrange the IMU first thing in the morning to make space for him. The unit is no longer my safe space.

Another three hours before Ellie picks me up. My eyes are gritty with a fatigue that makes itself known in my bones as I start a to-do list. Research the deceased. An i2 association chart and summary profile of Fred Filan so a decision can be made on his future location. I can't decide where to start. Both tasks as urgent as the other.

But first I need a coffee. But I'm stopped from doing so by the sound of keys rattling in the lock. Victor sticks his head through the door.

'Are you busy?'

I point at my paper-strewn desk.

'The Governor's asked if you'll go down to Hayworth

three and pick up the deceased's property. He's meeting the family first thing in the morning and doesn't trust the officers to pack it . . . respectfully.'

My shoulders sag. Couldn't we have cleared out the cell after the body had been removed to save me having to go back up there?

'Are you joking?' I know he isn't. Victor's not the type to bullshit. 'He asked for me personally?' I add, rolling my eyes.

'It needs to be done, Kennedy. And you're the only one *I* trust to do it.'

'Fine.'

'Do you want me to come with you?' Victor asks.

'No,' I lie.

'I could help you?' Jacob offers.

Ignoring Jacob, who's cocooned in a moat of paperwork, I grab my fleece and stride from the unit. The coffee will have to wait, I think as I look at it mournfully. One thing's for sure, I won't get offered one in the hall.

Four black rucksacks are lined up on the centre console. No brand names or logos. Smart. Respectful.

'Do you have a spare pair of gloves?' I pluck at my lashes.

'Nope,' replies Officer Ray McCredie, who continues typing. All-round prisoners' friend and enemy of the IMU. His colleague smirks beside him, slurping from a mug.

Heat explodes on my cheeks.

The Bloodhound exits the staff office situated behind the console and hands me a new box. 'Here. Rather you than me,' he says in his thick Aberdeen accent.

I mumble my thanks and grab the bags. Stride over on unstable legs. I slip on the gloves before I enter. My palms immediately begin to sweat. A layer of dust coats the 19-inch TV. The counter. I close the cell door to avoid spectators and breathe the smell of rotting fruit out my mouth.

The old bedsheet that's been used as a curtain has been pulled from the wall and dumped on the ground. The window pushed open the two inches it allows to try to get rid of the stench.

I start with the toiletries. A used toothbrush. A glasses case with black spectacles inside. A half-used tube of toothpaste. If the deceased possessed any shower gel, then someone's already stolen it.

I place the contents in the first rucksack, ensuring the toothpaste lid is tightened, and zip the bag. Everything in the cell now belongs to the mother.

Jeans. Tops. Jumpers. Underwear. Some clean. Most dirty. The release of dust makes me sneeze and I get a lungful of detergent and body odour.

Before I start the final bag, I press my hands into the small of my back. Crack my neck. I could sit, but I don't want to. He died on the mattress, after all.

There's a handful of DVDs. One book. Intelligence suggests drugs are passed around the section inside films and CDs, so I inspect every case. It'd be embarrassing for the property to be handed over to the mother, only for her to find drugs.

Sweat forms along my hairline. I swat it with my fore-arm. I grab the book and stand by the window. The cold air that whistles in is welcoming, but my top still sticks to my back. My underarms.

'Tre. You there, bro?'

I pause. Listen to the conversation being shouted between cell windows. Tre Sinclair. The tallest prisoner we've ever had the misfortune to house. Six foot five and an aspiring MMA fighter. His afro adds another couple of inches to his height. I've been trying to get him moved for months. But the senior managers failed to act on my recommendations.

'Aye, mate.'

'You p-egg-acking?'

My interest is piqued. Someone's inadvertently providing me with intelligence – Tre Sinclair, another known hall dealer, currently in possession of contraband? I make a mental note to task Security to search his cell.

I strain to hear. When Sinclair doesn't answer, I return to my task. Sinclair isn't stupid enough to have a conversation at the windows. He knows anyone could be listening.

I place the rucksacks by the cell door before I give the cell another spin. Pick up the book that has 'Property of HMP Forth Valley' stamped on the spine.

A piece of paper falls out and flutters to the floor.

A stiffy. If prisoners want to write to each other, it has to be treated like any other mail. If it isn't in an envelope with a stamp on it, then I have authority to read it. And, of course, why would they pay for a stamp when they can pass them to each other for free?

> K, you better not fuck this up for Scout, or I'll rip fuck
> out of your face. Don't go running to the screws again.
> You know who.

The paper flutters to the ground and, this time, I have to sit down on the cold mattress.

Violent shakes shudder my body. My vision blurs. I hyperventilate. That name again. *Scout.* I didn't imagine it. I didn't make it up. And now I've found his name in a dead man's cell.

Am I next?

It takes a few minutes to regulate my breathing. When I do, I pick up the note. Stuff it into my pocket before I pick up the rucksacks. The urgency to get back to the IMU overwhelms me.

The muscles in my arms sing as I dash out of the hall, without giving the officers the satisfaction of asking for help. The straps dig into my skin as I make my way to Victor's office, having to stop every few minutes to change hands.

But it's nowhere near as sore as the headache that swells and pounds in my head.

7. Kennedy

I slap the stiffy down on Victor's table. 'Tell me I'm crazy,' I begin.

He picks up the note and scrutinizes it, his frown deepening the closer he gets to the end.

'I don't know what to say. Maybe you should go home until we can figure this out. Find out if the police have had more luck identifying him.'

'I'm safer here, Victor. I'd rather stay at work.' Where there're cameras, I want to add.

'Very well.'

'First I'm attacked. Then his name's found in a dead man's room. This is beyond anything we've dealt with before, Victor. I don't know what to do.'

I brush crumbs off the round table. I should feel relieved. That I'm not going crazy. But the piece of paper is proof, and all I feel is fear.

He steeples his fingers. 'We have to keep an open mind. Let's not make two and two add up to five. But. At the same time. Be careful. Until we know what we're dealing with.'

My stomach roils. My mouth waters.

'Do you feel up to observing an interview? Might take your mind off things.'

'An interview?' I frown.

'Integrity interview. Potential corrupt officer.' A grimace. 'Ray McCredie.'

He fills me in and the fatigue abandons my body.

I check the time. Ellie will be here soon to pick me up. My knee jiggles under the table.

Victor's office is meticulously tidy, to the point of OCD. No dust on the window ledge. No cobwebs between the bars on his windows.

The only sound is the breeze from the open window swirling the blinds and my shoe bouncing off the floor.

'Are you ready for this?' He looks up, peering over the rims of his glasses.

'Of course.'

'Then why is your leg dancing?'

'Nerves, I guess.'

'You've done nothing wrong. He has. Allegedly. If he was doing the job he's employed to, then we'd be getting on with other work right now.'

I nod, seeing the sense of Victor's words. But some parts of the job never get easier.

The phone rings and I jump. I let out a breath as he answers. I'm not the one on trial here.

'Victor Saka.'

I pinch a chocolate from the bowl in the centre of the table.

'You're entitled to bring a union rep with you, Ray. But the meeting's due to start in two minutes. I do need to speak to you today.'

My head springs up. Victor meets my gaze. Rolls his eyes. I shake my head.

'Can you bring your first line manager?'

I frown at the phone, trying to concentrate, but my superpower lies in my memory and not my hearing.

'OK. See you in five.'

'Someone's arse has collapsed,' he says as he hangs up.

'Is he coming?'

'Aye, he's coming. If I have to go down the hall and drag him up . . .' He takes a sip of his water before he continues. 'He's refusing to come unless he has a union rep with him. Bruce is away to some conference at the college.'

'Fantastic delaying tactic.'

'Exactly. But we'll see him this afternoon, you can guarantee it.'

'I bet you he uses the death in custody to get out of it.'

'The odds are too poor,' he jokes.

When there's a light tap on the door, I deploy my poker face.

'Come in,' Victor shouts. The door opens slowly as Ray McCredie pops his head into the room. He sees me and jolts. Now he knows it's serious.

Could McCredie be Scout? Unlikely. He's never come across as anything other than a weak guy with a penchant for other men's women. The guy would shag a barbershop floor if it was hairy enough.

With his oblong head and dyed blond hair, brushed forward to mask his receding hairline, I'll never understand how he gets all the women. He must have hidden talents.

Following Ray into the office is the worst manager in the history of the Prison Service. How he managed to get his pips is the cause of long-running jokes. The favourite being that he found them in a lucky bag.

First line manager Clive Clifford was promoted at a time when all you needed was nine years' service under your belt. It didn't matter if you were a racist, homophobic, sectarian, sexist piece of shit – seeing as he's all four.

'Afternoon, fellas. How are we?'

Ray shrugs, attempting to give the impression that he doesn't give a flying fuck. But the tremor in his digits betrays him.

'Can I get you a drink?' Victor continues. Classic interview skills.

'Nah,' he answers, abrupt. Rubs his legs.

I look at Clive. Wait for an answer.

'I'm fine, thanks.'

'Can you close the door, Kennedy?'

Victor wants Ray's nerves shredded. Prolongs the silence. I get up slowly, placing my notebook and pen on the chair before I trudge over, depress the handle and close the door properly.

Victor doesn't start until I'm seated. My stomach churns. Excitement and nerves.

'Right, we'll get straight to it, shall we?'

'Please,' Ray croaks. His confidence and swagger, gone.

'How do you like working on the threes?'

Ray frowns, thrown by the line of questioning. Clive politely coughs into his hand. I lick my dry lips.

'It's all right.' Ray rubs at his nose. Flicks his hair with a finger. 'It's good, yeah.'

'How do you get on with the prisoners?'

He shrugs. 'I like to think I get on with everyone. There's a couple too anti-authority to converse with. You know what it's like. And some will say we've the worst up there,' he rambles.

Clive nudges Ray's knee under the table. If Victor notices, he doesn't mention it. But I'm clocking everything.

'Is there anyone you're particularly close with?'

Ray's waxed brows meet again. He takes a second to form his answer.

'Not really?' He shakes his head to emphasize his point. 'Has someone said something? If someone's accusing me of something, I deserve to know so I can challenge them.'

His conviction would be more believable if he weren't

vibrating with fear. It's clear by his reaction that he's guilty of something.

'Why do you think that? You had a run-in with someone?'

Ray sits on his hands. Beads of sweat form on his upper lip, nestling into his cupid's bow, until his tongue darts out. Like a frog with a fly.

'You know how it is. Sometimes you have a disagreement with some folk, they take it the wrong way. Snowflakes. Go greeting to managers instead of settling it out. Like men. It's a different generation these days. Weren't we just saying that on the way up, Clive?'

Clive grunts. Keeps his beady eyes trained on the table.

'Who have you had a run-in with?'

Ray can't seem to make eye contact and focuses his attention on the open window.

'No one.' Another shrug. He shrugs that much he's at risk of losing the epaulettes on his shoulders.

'Shall I tell you what I've heard?' Victor begins.

'Sure.'

'I hear you've grown quite close to Caleb Dyer.'

'Rampage?' He chuckles, but it's a nervous one. 'Rampage is all right. If you know how to manage him. Not many do.'

Caleb 'Rampage' Dyer. Unpredictable. Violent.

'And how do you manage him, Officer McCredie? If you don't mind me asking.'

'It's easy, really. It's about respect. I show him respect if he shows me respect. That's how I treat all the prisoners.'

'Would you ever cross the line of duty to reward this so-called respect?'

'I don't know what you mean.'

'Have you carried out a task at the request of Caleb Dyer?'

'No. Not me.' He sits closer, both hands on his legs.

'Are you scared of him?'

McCredie chuckles. 'As if.'

'Does Mr Dyer say "Jump," and Officer McCredie, with eight years' experience as a residential officer, say "How high, Mr Dyer?"'

The smile slides off Ray's face. It takes all my composure not to grin. I hate the officer and everything he stands for. His loudness. His desperation to be friends with those in his charge. To be seen as a good guy.

'I'm not scared of prisoners, and I absolutely refute any fucking allegation that I am,' he says, slamming his hands on the table.

'I'm not swearing, or raising my voice towards you, Officer McCredie, and I expect the same courtesy from you.'

Clive digs Ray in the ribs.

'I've done nothing wrong.' Ray McCredie levitates off the chair. Like he can't decide whether to stay or go. Victor takes the moment to change tack.

'How did you get on with Kalvin Jones?' My ears prick up.

'The same as any prisoner,' he says, and shrugs.

'He was admitted to the establishment last month. He's been assaulted on four separate occasions. Am I refreshing your memory?'

Ray clears his throat. 'There's a lot of violence on my wing. Unresolved external issues, mostly. Impossible for us to prevent it until after the fact. They see it as grassing – letting us know if they've issues with each other on the outside. We seem to breed violence up there.'

Ray adopts a smug grin, thinking he's in the clear.

'Mr Jones had an outstanding charge for rape.'

The smile dissolves from Ray's face a second time. I

pretend to write something down on my notepad, the atmosphere tense. Awkward.

'Do you have a problem with those who commit sexual offences?'

'No,' he answers immediately. 'I'd be in the wrong job if that was the case. And can I just say, I think your timing's awful. You are aware what happened this morning, right? How Molly and I found a dead body? I could've ripped the arse out of it and taken the rest of the shift off. Instead, I stay on, to be faced with this bullsh—'

'I put it to you, Officer McCredie,' Victor resumes, ignoring his outburst, 'that you informed Caleb Dyer about Kalvin Jones's alleged sexual offence and, in turn, Caleb Dyer assaulted Mr Jones.'

'I refute that allegation.'

'If you can turn your attention to the monitor.'

All three heads turn to the left, where the monitor hangs on the wall.

'Can I ask you to look at the footage and then answer the questions I ask afterwards?'

Ray audibly gulps. The puce colour leaches from his face. Does he know what he's about to watch, or is he conditioned to fuck?

The footage plays. Ray sits at the console, tapping away at the computer. The lanky frame of Caleb 'Rampage' Dyer appears. He's holding a mop. Several seconds pass before Ray McCredie motions him over. Dyer approaches the officer. Their foreheads almost touching they're that close.

Victor pauses the footage. 'Can you tell me, Officer McCredie, what you're discussing with Mr Dyer?'

All eyes are on McCredie as he scratches his head. His stubble. His ear. His nose.

'I can't remember,' he mumbles.

'Lunch choices? Visit applications?'

'I'm his personal officer. I'm probably talking to him about his sentence management. He's doing a long time, you know. Some might say his sentence was harsh.'

'He caused over twenty grands' worth of damage in the secure unit he was housed in. He seriously assaulted a fellow inmate.'

'Aye, but he was young. Led astray in that secure unit. I'm sure we all done daft shi—' Another nudge from Clive. Harder this time. 'Stuff when we were his age. They reckon he took the blame, anyway. He shouldn't be here,' Ray sniffs.

'I've never permanently disfigured someone. Have you, Kennedy?'

'Not that I can recall, sir.'

'How about you, Clive?'

Clifford has the good grace to blush. Victor accepts his silence and moves on.

He presses play. McCredie and Dyer are deep in conversation.

Rampage Dyer takes a step back, recoiling from the officer. He shakes his head before asking a question. Ray McCredie holds up four fingers.

'What's the significance of the four fingers?'

McCredie's face turns crimson.

'I take it you can't remember?'

'A lot happens in a week. You'll remember that from when you used to work in the halls.'

Feeling brave, Ray turns to me and smirks. Now it's my turn for my face to go red. Nothing stays secret in the prison. Everything's remembered, even from five years ago.

When I started as a prison officer and didn't even last a day.

The footage replays. Rampage's body language tells a story. His chest's puffed out and it's clear he's shouting. Rampage begins to gesticulate with both arms, pointing in the direction of the east side of the hall. Victor enlarges the footage and McCredie's smug grin is there for all to see.

'I'm going to fast-forward this part.'

More figures appear on the screen, moving around at speed. Prisoners return from their work parties. Pass men head behind the hotplate and dish out the lunch.

Pass men. So called because they're given a pass to move around unsupervised. But there are several meanings for pass men.

Being a pass man is a position of trust and respect. It doesn't take a genius to work out who'd given the job to Rampage Dyer. They're supposed to keep the hall clean, serve the food and clean the dishes. But in reality, the pass men are used to distribute drugs around the hall. Whether they want to or not. It's a fine line between having strong characters but not violent bullies. Like Rampage.

Two officers, including McCredie, observe the portion sizes and make sure there's no subversive behaviour going on. Victor plays the footage. Rampage comes out from behind the hotplate and speaks to one of the other prisoners. They look around.

The footage pauses. 'Can you tell me the name of this prisoner?' Victor points to the prisoner in dark glasses who's picking up a sachet of salt and a slice of bread.

Officer McCredie takes his time. Squints. 'It's hard to say. The footage isn't clear.'

'It's Kalvin Jones,' adds Clive.

Ray turns around at such speed, a look of shock on his face like the manager's scudded him across the back of the head.

'Correct.' Officer McCredie licks his lips. 'I can't make him out there. Your eyesight must be better than mine.'

Clive shrugs. The manager's worked long enough with Victor to know this is going somewhere dodgy, and he's out to save himself.

The footage resumes. Rampage marches over to Kalvin Jones and hits him on the side of the head. Jones is floored immediately. Rampage gives him a beating while McCredie watches.

'Why didn't you intervene?' Victor asks.

'I instructed him to stop. He refused to comply with my instruction. I put him on report for it.'

'Why didn't you pull him off?'

'I had no back-up. He seemed violent. I done a risk assessment and deemed it unsafe to intervene.'

And right enough, as soon as more officers appear, McCredie pulls him off, restraining him on the ground.

'It doesn't appear to me like you felt unsafe.'

McCredie sits straighter. A hint of a smirk on his face. 'That's my call, isn't it? I didn't feel safe, so I waited until my colleagues turned up for the support.' He sits back in his seat, triumphant, and crosses his arms over his chest. For him, the case is closed.

'I don't think we're going to get much further here today,' he adds, wanting it to be over.

'You're right. I can't prove anything. But know this, McCredie – my eye is firmly on you. One more thing goes wrong when you're on duty and I'll have you up on a code of conduct before you can blink. You're free to go. For now.'

My heart constricts. Could McCredie be involved in Kalvin's death? Along with Rampage? Could either of them have written the stiffy? Could I be at risk from McCredie? He scowls at me, and I look away. If I am at risk from him, I don't want to antagonize him.

'I'm not leaving until you tell me who's tried to stick me in,' says the cocky prick.

'Source protection is paramount. We cannot disclose sources. Someone with your level of service should know better than to ask.'

'Maybe we should get back to the hall . . .' Clive's suggestion falls on deaf ears.

'I was surprised to hear Mr Dyer suffered no consequences from the assault we just watched,' says Victor.

'I'm not a gaffer. The gaffers make the decisions.'

'Hmm. Interesting his misconduct report was thrown out in the orderly room hearing due to the wrong charge being given. That wouldn't have been deliberate on your part, would it? "Chase the sex offender out the hall and I'll make sure you get away with it," ' Victor adds.

My teeth pierce the inside of my cheek. I taste blood. Despite there being CCTV of the assault, Dyer has been found not guilty due to a technicality with the paperwork. The prison rules are a joke.

'Is that what someone is saying about me? That I falsify records?'

Victor plants a smile on his face. 'You're entitled to apply for your Subject Access Request. It'll provide you with a list of all the intel the SPS holds on you. And Ray, I strongly urge you to apply for yours.'

He scoffs. 'My SAR? What's the point, when all the important bits will be redacted?' He crosses his arms over his chest again like he's won.

'Yes, but it will show you just how many entries there are . . .'

Ray's face reddens. He really is a weed. We know he does favours for prisoners, tips them off before they're searched, but nothing to suggest he traffics contraband. Not enough for suspension, but the case is building.

'Over the last two months, every act of violence within Hayworth level three has happened when you've been on duty. Nothing seems to happen when you're on double turn or rest day. Weird coincidence, eh?'

Victor switches off the monitor as Ray scarpers from the room. Clive hangs back.

'Can I help you with something, Clive?'

'Can we speak privately?' he replies, glancing at me.

'Anything you want to say to me can be said in front of Kennedy.'

Clive rubs at his nose. 'He's a good officer, Victor. He's good with the lads. Keeps them in control. I don't think there's any cause for concern here.'

'Really?' Victor says, a wide grin on his face.

'Yeah, well, I thought you might appreciate my opinion,' he says, not grasping the extent of Victor's sarcasm.

'Thanks, Clive.'

He rubs his nose a second time before he trudges from the office. As soon as he's gone, Victor turns to me and shakes his head.

'Some people, eh?'

'I thought you had him there.'

'That was never my intent. I just wanted to spook him.'

'Object achieved.'

'Imagine we actually have officers that use prisoners to get folk they don't want moved off their hall. It sickens me.'

'I know. But we'll get him.'

'He's on the list.' Victor grimaces.

'He's never come off it.'

'I want you to keep an eye on him, going forward. Anything comes in – I want you to tell me immediately.'

'Don't I always?'

'I know.'

I lick my lips. 'Do you think . . . I mean. Could he be this Scout?'

'As I said earlier,' he says after a beat, 'we have to keep an open mind. Follow the intel and see where it takes us.' His sympathetic glance makes me want to cry.

By the time I return to the IMU, I'm drained. I look around at the work I haven't been able to get through due to the events of the day. The threatening letter I recovered from Kalvin Jones's cell is taped to the whiteboard – not that I need the constant reminder.

I pack my things into my small bag and switch off the monitor. My eyelids are heavy as I make my way down to the exit.

At first, I think she's a visitor and then she turns and I recognize the SPS logo on her black uniform-issue fleece.

Her hair's long and sleek, tied back out of her face. She has the most golden eyes I've ever seen. Modest make-up. As I step closer, the small piercing in her nose glints under the fluorescent light.

It's the officer from the hall. A feeling I haven't felt in so long runs through me. Like someone's switched me on. Molly Rana. The officer that inadvertently led to me being attacked by submitting the intel about Boward. But I won't hold that against her. She was only doing her job.

I smile, my heart fluttering. She smiles back. I open my mouth to say something, anything, but at the same time she turns her back to me and I continue walking on jelly legs until I'm outside.

Ellie flashes the car lights, and I run towards safety, comfort and the promise of an early night.

I might not have uncovered Scout, but I have uncovered the stiffy – a clue that might identify them. Before they come for me again. And for now, that's enough.

8. Kennedy

'Yes, you have to go,' Victor says as he answers the phone.

'How did you know that's what I'm phoning about?'

'I want you there, Kennedy. Don't be late.' He has the audacity to hang up on me.

I've attended debriefs before. Boring hours I'll never get back. Slyly appointing blame. Homing in on trivial details. But that isn't why I don't want to go. It means I'll be stuck in a room with the Governor. In the eight months he's worked here, he hasn't yet remembered my name. And this is someone I meet with regularly.

'Morning,' Jacob singsongs as he enters the office. The idea of attending the debrief instantly sounds more appealing.

'Morning,' I mumble, turning my attention to my computer.

'I can't believe how different the office looks,' he says as he removes his jacket. It isn't that different; our new desks face each other. New filing cabinets have been installed and shelves have been hung. It already feels claustrophobic.

I ignore him as he rambles on about the layout, how his fingers are numb from the hours of shredding. 'Sorry I couldn't help you out.'

'I don't need help,' I answer coldly.

'Sorry.' His face twists into a scowl. 'I didn't mean to imply you need my help.'

He's wearing a bright lime colour today. A dangling

dreamcatcher hangs from his right ear. All that's missing is a feather boa.

Remembering Victor's warning, I soften my tone. 'Elton John called. He wants his white specs back.'

Jacob laughs. 'They suit me better,' he says, snapping his fingers.

I log into the PIN system. Search up the last calls made by Kalvin Jones. It's something I'll get asked at the debrief and I don't want to give the Governor the satisfaction of me not being able to answer his questions.

Meanwhile, yesterday's stiffy taunts me from where I hung it on the board.

Jones's final call lasts less than three minutes. I stick my headphones on and play the recording. Pen and notebook ready to write down any intel. If he did indeed take his own life, there will be some indication in the call. There always is.

'Mam?'

'That you, Kalvin?'

'Aye.'

She takes a draw on her cigarette.

'What are you after now?'

'Can't I phone you without being after something?'

'Of course, but that'll mean hell's frozen over.'

'How?'

'Never mind.'

The silence between them reaches almost thirty seconds.

'Why do I feel like you're psyching yourself up to ask me something you know I'll say no to?'

Kalvin lets out a deep sigh that ends in a sob.

'I hate it in here. I want to come home.'

'It's your own fault you're in there. Didn't I warn you? Stay away from the lads, I said. Bad news. And what happens? I'm proved right.'

I pause the call to take a sip of water to dislodge the lump in my throat.

'I'm sorry. I should've listened. But I haven't touched anything for three days now. I spit down I haven't. Are you proud of me?'

'I don't know if I can be proud of you again. You forget I'm out here. I'm the one getting dirty looks on the street. I've had to apply for a new council flat. I don't feel safe here any more since that dogshite was pushed through the letterbox.'

'I've asked to be moved to another hall. The protection one. I might settle in there better.'

'Are you in trouble?'

The third silence feels the longest.

'No. It's just. I don't want to get dragged into anything. I can't sleep either. If I could just sleep . . .'

'Keep the peace. There's worse folk in there than you. Don't be causing no trouble.'

An audible sob.

'And don't cry. I can hear you crying. Do you want to get picked on? A repeat of school? Man up, for fuck's sake.'

'Sorry,' he sniffs.

'Is there anything else? My programme's about to start.'

'I'll phone back tomorrow?'

'Don't we have a visit?'

'Yes. And – I need to tell you something.'

'What?'

'Not on this. I'll speak to you at the visit.'

Her annoyance is clear through her irritated sigh.

'Save your money then, Kalvin.'

'Bye, Mum. I love you.'

But she ends the call.

Will she ever watch her programme again, knowing she chose it over the last words of her son?

Was that the mind of a suicidal person? I chew on my bottom lip. I can't help but feel disappointed. There was no mention of Scout. Nothing that brings me any closer to identifying them.

The call takes seconds to download. It'll form part of the evidence for the Fatal Accident Inquiry. The police investigation.

Jacob makes me a coffee to take to the debrief. My plan to work on Fred Filan and his association chart delayed again. I send a quick email to the analysts at Barlinnie. Maybe they've already done the work and could share it with me.

I march to the boardroom, keeping my head down to avoid small talk I don't have the patience for. I push open the door and step inside. The room's been painted during my time off. The walls are now corporate blue and there's a clean matching carpet. The large table takes up most of the room, with fake plants dotted in the four corners. The blinds are closed, and I choose not to open them, preferring the dark.

A sixty-inch TV hangs on the wall. It's supposed to be used for presentations and CCTV footage, but the senior managers pretend to have meetings during sporting events.

Empty water glasses are grouped in the middle of the table but are not accompanied by water jugs. I pick a coaster and put my coffee mug on it.

'You're back then?'

I flinch. The hairs on the back of my neck rise and sway as if there's a draught. I don't want to look up but, at the same time, I don't want to show any fear. Loathing.

He switches on the light and I squint against its brightness.

'And give you the satisfaction of me not coming back? Never.'

I force myself to look up. Brace myself for his perpetual smugness.

'Not everyone is cut out for this job. But you already know that.'

'Yeah, not all of us can be lining our pockets.' I hold my hands under the table so he can't see he's getting to me. My eye twitches.

Crawford Docherty – the unit manager of Morton Hall – has always been a dick. Nice to me when I first started (another womanizer who'd shag a stab wound if he thought it'd be tight enough), but when I investigated his friend, Lila Deil, who moved on before I had her sacked, our mutual dislike, and distrust, grew.

'If you want to accuse me of something, sweetheart, you better make sure you have proof.'

And that's the thing. Gut instinct isn't proof. But I'd put everything I own on him being dirty. Corrupt. I've so far failed to prove it. But every dog has its day. And he's a fucking dog.

We ignore each other until the other staff arrive. And only then, when the room is full, does it occur to me. Is one of them Scout? Am I breathing the same air as the person who wanted me harmed?

The door opens and the Governor strolls in. He looks at me, and I stare back until he looks away. Out of all the governors I've worked under, he's the weakest. A belief I'm not alone in holding. Many of the officers parody him. From his plummy, nasal voice to his incessant blinking.

'Thanks for making the effort to come to the debrief,' he announces, pushing his glasses up his nose. The attention of the officers is focused elsewhere. The lack of respect speaks volumes.

'We're directed to have these hot debriefs to ascertain if there's anything that could have been done, or done differently, should we ever find ourselves in this . . . um . . . circumstance in the future.'

The Governor pauses, looking around the room for someone to continue. Victor sits to my left, doodling on a piece of paper. It might look like he isn't listening, but Victor never misses a thing.

The Governor's face flushes as the realization strikes him – he hasn't learned anybody's name. He can't invite anybody to speak. He attempts to read the name badges of the frontline staff and fails. He turns to Jacob, who's been drafted in late to take the official minutes.

'For the benefit of Jacob, if you can announce who you are as we go around the table and let everyone know what your duty was on . . . on yesterday.'

It's like an awkward first date. No one offers to speak up. No one looks directly at the Governor.

'Victor. Can we start with you?'

Victor looks up. 'Sure, Governor. Victor Saka, head of operations.'

Introducing myself at meetings always makes me feel awkward. This time's no different. I squirm in my seat, waiting for my turn.

'Kennedy Allardyce, intelligence analyst.' I keep my eyes on the boardroom table. They all know who I am.

'Tim Reilly, Hayworth Hall unit manager.'

'Clive Clifford, Hayworth Hall. First line manager, on duty when the body was discovered.'

'Ray McCredie, residential officer, Hayworth level three. I found the body, along with Officer Rana, who gives her apologies. I also put the code-blue message over the radio.'

Disappointing. The debrief would've been more interesting if Molly Rana had attended.

'Mira Bhatia, clinical nurse. First responder to the code blue.'

Beside me, Jacob furiously scribbles in his notebook, trying not to miss anything. On the other side, Victor continues his doodle. A dog on a skateboard.

'Thank you all for coming,' repeats the Governor. 'I know we're all busy—'

'Do we know how he died yet?' McCredie asks.

'No. The post-mortem will be carried out soon, depending on priorities in the community.'

The atmosphere in the stuffy boardroom is tangible. No one wants to be here, especially the Governor.

'It's obvious, isn't it?' McCredie scoffs. 'Fred Filan transfers here the day someone dies. It doesn't take a rocket scientist, does it?'

Clive Clifford places a warning hand on his arm, mutters something under his moustache, giving me flashbacks to the interview with McCredie yesterday.

'Let's not jump to conclusions,' I jeer.

'Filan's been in the Seg unit since he arrived,' states Tim. 'How can he be responsible?'

I smile over at him, thankful for support where I can get it.

'Aye, but still,' McCredie continues, 'you're not telling me he hasn't got his fingers in all the pies with his history. And what are the IMU doing about that?' He crosses his arms over his body.

I dig my nails into my hands to release the anger. Bite

my tongue so I don't say what I want to. But it doesn't work. I can only stay silent for so long.

'We can't do anything if we don't receive intel telling us what's going on and who we should be looking at,' I say, my voice bored. Eyeballs, not crystal balls.

'Maybe if the Intel staff came down to the hall more often, they'd have a better understanding of what's going on,' McCredie huffs.

'We need to know what's going on, who to look at before we can let you know what's going on,' Victor says.

'Bit of a chicken-and-egg scenario,' Clifford jokes, attempting to lighten the mood. Everyone ignores him.

'Aye, I know that,' McCredie agrees, backtracking to save face. 'But you put five by fives in and hear nothing back.'

I open my mouth to bite. When was the last time he submitted anything? It's not my job to pat them on the back and tell him what a great job they're doing. But Victor gets in there first.

'We can't always tell people what's going on.' He glares at McCredie. 'And I think we're getting a little off track here.' He raises his eyebrows at the Governor for back-up.

'Quite.'

My fingers reach for my lashes. But it doesn't calm me. I'm riled up and ready to verbally attack.

'Who was the deceased?' I ask. 'How long had he been in the section? Was he a known drug user? Who did he associate with? Was he in debt? Did he ask for protection the day before he died?' I deliberately make eye contact with McCredie, who quickly looks away, his face colouring. Prick.

'Well?' I say, prompting him to acknowledge me, deliberately making him wriggle. Enjoying it.

McCredie shrugs and is sharply nudged by Clifford. 'I'll look into it when I get back to the hall,' he mumbles.

I give him a satisfied smile. If he wants to try and look smart, I'm here for it. Sometimes, the officers forget we're supposed to be on the same side.

'Can you run us through the events of yesterday?' asks the Governor.

McCredie clears his throat. 'A normal morning. Nothing sinister. The section seemed settled.' He coughs again. 'Good atmosphere. Relaxed.'

The Governor shuffles paper.

'Why wasn't he on the protection?' I ask.

'No space for him,' Clifford answers.

I ask myself for the hundredth time: why do we accept prisoners we can't accommodate? Then I look at the Governor and understand. The other governors – the ones who've worked their way up from the bottom – are taking the piss.

Our Governor's an anomaly. No experience of prisons or how they need to be run. Dangerous, when you're the overall decision-maker. Normally, a deputy governor makes the decisions, only telling the governor in charge what they need to know, but the dep had gone off sick just a few months after the Governor took up post. Another coincidence.

'Who was the last person to see him alive?' asks the Governor. This time, McCredie stops himself from shrugging at the last minute.

'I'm not too sure, Governor. I'll check the rosters and report back.'

'Isn't that something we should know? Haven't the police asked?' the Governor demands.

Silence fills the room.

'They've asked for the CCTV footage leading up to

him being locked up the night before and the body being found the next morning,' I say, staring at the door.

'Right.'

Everyone looks at Clifford, who is busy biting his thumbnail. 'I'm just back from leave, Governor,' he says, spitting the chewed-off bit of nail on to the floor. 'I'm not up to speed with who's on the wing. I think an intel briefing from the IMU would help me and my officers. Work together and that. Share info.'

'I think we need to reconvene this meeting once we have all the relevant facts,' Victor suggests. 'We're getting nowhere.'

'Don't we have to have the debrief within twenty-four hours?'

'It's seventy-two hours, Governor,' Victor whispers, loud enough for everyone to hear.

'Oh yes. Very good. If the Intel team could accommodate an information sharing with the officers, please. It seems there's a problem with communication here.'

Victor grabs my arm to stop me from biting. 'Of course, Governor,' Victor says, looking over at Tim Reilly. 'Shall we pencil in a meeting?'

'Sure. I'll check the diaries and get back to you.'

The Governor nods, desperate to be away from the front-line workers, preferring the comfort of his ivory tower.

'Shall we say in forty-eight hours?' He looks around at the faces staring back at him. He opens his mouth to confirm the date and time when a chorus of buzzing fills the room.

We look at the personal alarms attached to our belts, except for Jacob and the Governor, who never bothered to lift one.

'What's going on?' demands the Governor.

'There's something happening on the exercise yard of Hayworth Hall,' says Clifford, pressing his radio earpiece further into his ear to get the relevant information from the radio communications.

Without a further word, Victor and I troop out of the boardroom towards the IMU to get the incident up on the CCTV.

'Come,' Victor says. 'It'll be quicker to cut through the sterile area.'

We take a different exit and hurry down the corridor. Shoes squeaking against the laminate floor. We take the stairs rather than wait for the lift. Victor radios ahead to make sure the door's unlocked.

We barge through, careful to make sure it's relocked behind us. 'This way,' pants Victor.

The small incline is steeper than I remember. But the roars and screams from the direction of the exercise yard are enough to make us hurry.

'There,' I say, pointing redundantly.

Two colours battling on the exercise yard. White shirts versus the red tops of the prisoners. Training from long ago flexes my muscle memory. But when Victor senses what I'm about to do, he reaches out and holds me back.

'They have weapons.'

Crude razors melted to the ends of toothbrushes glint in the morning sun as they're pulled back by meaty arms.

I press myself up against the chain fence. Hopeless.

'It's not your fight, Kennedy. Look, there's more staff.'

There's no fear as twenty officers run into the exercise yard, batons drawn. Orders barked. 'Drop your weapon! Drop your fucking weapon!'

'Come on, ya mad bastards!' roars a gobshite brandishing a cosh.

Ignoring the instructions of staff, three prisoners continue kicking the shit out of someone lying in the foetal position.

Some prisoners hold their hands up as soon as the officers arrive. They're escorted from the yard one by one.

'This has the potential to become a serious incident. Should we set up the command room?'

'Nah. Look which manager's dealing with it,' Victor says, motioning with his head.

I squint my eyes. Big Gus McInnes saunters into the yard with no fears over his personal safety. His presence is enough for half the remaining cons to drop their weapons. Ex-MMA, ex-military, he's one of the few white shirts the prisoners respect. His wild red hair and beard clash with the colour of the prisoners' tops.

My shoulders loosen. Four prisoners are left in the yard. They don't know how to proceed and look to their ringleader for command.

Tre Sinclair.

It's time to get out my 'I told you so' T-shirt. The one that, after five years in the job, I'm sick of wearing. Because them acting on my previous recommendation to transfer Tre Sinclair would've prevented this.

He'll get moved now though. That's a guarantee.

Tre Sinclair motions his head towards the hall and his troops stand to attention. One by one, they walk towards the officers, arms raised.

The prisoners are wearing blue nitrile gloves. Any weapons they've handled will not carry their fingerprints.

Three prisoners remain on the ground. Dead, unconscious, or simply catching their breath? The nurses are on standby, waiting for the all-clear to attend to their clients.

The officers are cautious, batons raised. Any one of the

prisoners could still be in possession of a manufactured weapon. It's the first question that'll need to be asked. How the hell have they managed to smuggle them out of the hall? Each one should've been subject to a rub-down search on exiting the hall.

But for now the priority is ending the incident without anyone getting hurt. But the body language of Sinclair and his troops is obvious. They want to hurt. They want to see blood.

Big Gus McInnes puffs out his chest. It's like any game of chess: you must take out the right pawn to win. He holds out his baton with one hand and the other hand is up in warning.

'Drop your weapon, Sinclair.'

I count the seconds. One. Two. Three.

Gus jabs Sinclair on the arm with the baton, causing Sinclair to fold like a fragile bed sheet. As soon as Sinclair's on the ground, his troops freeze and the white shirts pile on top of them. Controlling limbs, minimizing the risk of injury. And just like that, it's over.

More officers pile into the yard and take control of the remaining prisoners. One by one, they're dragged to the digger, where they'll stay until alternative accommodation can be found for them in separate establishments.

Blood coats the blades of artificial grass. I close my eyes, but I can still see it. The blood. My scar twinges. My eye twitches.

'Show's over,' Victor says as Sinclair, the last person to be relocated, is compliant enough to be huckled to the digger. Tears of pain, anger or frustration roll down his face.

'Is it just me, or is the violence escalating?' I say.

'It's not just you.'

9. Adrian

It's just like I imagined it. The cell bars are like icy fingers as I press against my window, watching the carnage on the exercise yard below. As soon as the last fighters are carted to the digger, I'm unable to keep the grin off my face.

First Boward. And now Sinclair. The path to the top is clear.

I waited for something to go wrong, for Tre's bottle to crash, but it didn't. He never seemed the type, to be fair.

My plan started the night before, when I called the Bloodhound a prick. You just had to look at him the wrong way and he placed you on a misconduct report. No strikes. No warnings. There had to be a valid reason for me not attending my allocated time in the fresh air. Being involved in the fight wasn't part of my plan. You can't leave your cell if you're on misconduct report. Removed from circulation until you appear in the orderly room for punishment.

None of the other screws would react to being called names, but the Bloodhound was different. That's why it had to be him.

Tre wanted me out there, backing him up. But I couldn't let that happen. And now he's in the digger, the gullible fool. It's my time to take over the hall. A king in the queen's hotel.

Tre Sinclair might be bold, but he isn't smart. All it took was for me to say things in his ear. Make it out like he'd have to act first. Save face. Any situation can be manipulated if you're smart enough. And I have smarts in spades.

I'm waiting on my orderly-room appearance when heavy footsteps stop outside my door. The key clanks as it's inserted in the door. Ray McCredie's face appears. One of the better screws.

'Maddox. Come here,' he says. 'I have a job for you.'

'I'm on Rule 95 until my orderly room.'

'I think the gaffers have more important things to worry about than your adjudication.'

I follow him out into the wing.

'You'll have heard what happened?'

'No,' I lie, playing dumb.

'We're short on pass men since they're all in the digger. You're on trial. Don't let me down. I've stuck my neck out for you.'

I didn't expect this to happen so soon. Out of the cons on your wing, you're deemed the most trusted. A position that's yours to fuck up. Unlocked all day, two helpings of recreation and two portions of every meal. And access to the PIN phone to make calls whenever you want.

Most times, the screws leave you to get on with it. If you do what they demand of you and don't give them too much hassle. Make it seem like they're the ones in charge.

Pass men become invisible to the screws. They'd have conversations about people, forgetting there're prisoners around. Who's shagging around on their wife? Whose gambling's in a bad way? Who can't shake the bottle? Or the powder.

All information is power. And being a pass man, you're loaded with it.

Kai Spencer, an armed robber, two years into a five-year stretch, polishes the centre console as I approach.

'Hear you need my help,' I shout across the wing.

'Adrian Maddox on the pass? Nice one.' Spence beams

as he watches me stride towards him. There's nothing worse than being on the pass with a complete bam.

As suspected, the screw leaves us to get on with it.

'The first thing you need to learn is the most important.' He motions for me to follow him.

We go into the pantry, over to the sinks. On the wall above the sink is a list of every regular screw, what they drink and how they drink it. Even down to which cup is theirs.

'Are you for real?'

'If a screw wants a brew . . .' He leaves the rest unsaid.

'Lazy bastards.'

'It's nothing for you to worry about yet, bro.'

'What do you mean?'

'They won't trust you. You'll need to earn it. You won't be allowed to make them a drink until they're satisfied you won't spunk in it.'

I can think of one screw I'd like to indulge in a little body fluid revenge, but I'm not about to risk my new job. Replacing Tre Sinclair, in more ways than one, is only the first part of my plan.

The afternoon passes quickly as I follow Spence and Rampage – the other pass man – around the hall, dishing out clean towels and helping to serve the food.

From my vantage point in the servery, I watch the Bloodhound closely when he puts on his fleece to go to the union to complain. He's the one screw I'll never win over. Not that he likes any prisoner. That one's in the wrong job. He just about had a heart attack when he saw me helping on the pass.

'When was he in the orderly room?' he'd demanded.

'Pipe down, eh? We needed the help, or would you rather get your hands dirty behind the hotplate?' argued

McCredie. 'Nope. Didn't think so.' The two other screws backed him, leaving the Bloodhound outnumbered.

'I need to make a call,' I say when an hour passes. I dash over to the PIN phone on the other end of the hall so the screws can't listen in to my conversation. I put in my personal code and dial the number. It goes straight to voicemail. There's no point in leaving a message, cos he doesn't listen to them.

My knee jiggles as I type in another number.

'Hello.'

'It's me. Adrian. I need to speak to him. I've . . . fucked up. I trusted the wrong con, and, well . . .'

The click of a lighter. An exhale. 'He knows,' says Uncle Shay.

Fuck.

'Is he angry, Shay?'

'What do you think?'

'I can make it up to him. I'll sell what I have. Make him money.'

'You know the job you were supposed to do. Someone will be in touch. Don't speak over these phones.'

He ends the call and I hurl the receiver at the wall.

'What are you doing?' Spence says. 'You break that phone you're off the pass.'

'Bad news,' is all I can bring myself to say. Fucking bad news.

We're having a cup of tea mid-afternoon when McCredie approaches. 'I need you to do something, but you aren't going to like it. I don't want to hear you moan; just know you'll be rewarded for it.'

Spence's face turns white. He knows what's coming. I don't.

'What is it?'

'He wants us to clean out gaff 37. Don't you?'

'Aye. We need it back in circulation as soon as.'

'Come on then,' I say. 'The quicker we get started, the quicker we're finished.'

Spence stays where he is.

'What's the matter with you?'

'I don't want to go in there.'

'Don't be a chicken head. Come on.'

I like Spence, but sometimes I feel like he's not cut out for life inside. It isn't for everybody. Only the strongest survive.

We grab bin bags and sprays from the cleaning store. The screw leaves the gaff unlocked for us. But Spence freezes at the door. I push him inside.

'He's dead, bro. Gone. He isn't going to attack you.' I march inside. 'Fucking stinks in here, eh?'

'Doesn't it bother you? At all?' Spence asks.

'What? That he's dead and I'm still alive?'

'You know what I mean.'

'No. I don't.' I glare until he looks away. 'He was a wee worst cunt. In for a naughty one. The wee scumbag shouldn't have been so greedy. And if he was still alive, I'd burst him, the mess he's left me in.'

I supervise as Spence cleans the gaff. Every item the guy owned has already been removed. There's nothing left for stealing, unless I'm in the market for dust. Dirty bastard. When Spence's fingers shake, it angers me.

'Give your head a wobble, eh? Pull yourself together.'

'Do you think we'll get questioned?'

'Why? We weren't involved.' I sneer, pushing past him as I exit the gaff. If I stay with him a minute longer, I'll knock the pussy out. He doesn't try to follow me as I stride back to my own gaff.

We're locked up after dinner so the screws can have their break.

I scrub my hands in my tiny en suite and, only when I'm done, I put my ear to the door. The hall's quiet because it's *Hollyoaks* time – a programme prisoners only watch when they're dubbed up. A programme like that is the closest thing some of us get to an attractive lassie. And after all, *EastEnders* clashes with rec.

I pull my bed board away from the wall and, using the thick plastic knife I've borrowed from the servery, I pluck away at the loose skirting board.

It's time my uncle starts seeing me as a serious contender for his firm. I can be useful to him. He just has to believe it. But my bad decision-making has earned me a black mark against my name.

It took some practice, banking the drugs Uncle Bar set me up with – especially when my sentence kept getting deferred. But when the judge had enough and remanded me, I was ready.

'This is your chance to prove yourself to me, wee man,' Uncle Bar had warned when he'd heard I was facing a stretch. 'We'll split the profits 70/30 in my favour. Don't let me down.'

I'd managed three Kinder eggs. All containing various tenner bags of drugs. By the time I was finally sentenced, put on the escort van and brought here, I was surprised when no one commented on the smell of shit. It'd leaked from me like I'd had a dodgy kebab. It'd taken all my resolve not to puke everywhere when I'd finally, and gratefully, removed them from my arse.

But there was a problem. Tre Sinclair was top dog. If he caught me selling gear on his wing, the crazy bastard would've taken my face off.

I had to get rid of him. Without being a fly grass.

But first I'd befriended him. Got him onside. And then told him I'd heard his co-accused, located down on the ones, turned Queen's evidence on him, and was going to attack him at court. Naturally, Tre wanted to get him first.

And now both are in the digger, awaiting immediate transfer to different prisons. I'd solved that problem, and I'll solve the problem with Uncle Bar too. I just need to think.

As a pass man, I can't risk my status by getting caught with anything. Can't afford to bring attention to myself. Especially as the Bloodhound isn't my biggest fan. That fat bastard will be looking for any excuse to sack me off the pass.

I put my hand in the hole where I've hidden my discarded Kinder eggs and grin. It's time to take over.

There's a new top dog in HMP Forth Valley. And his name is Adrian Maddox.

No one's going to get in my way.

It's the beginning of the end of the first period of recreation when everything changes.

'One on!' roars McCredie, to no one in particular.

The Bloodhound races out from the office opposite the entrance, his jaw dropping at the sight of the new admission.

I take a few steps closer, hanging around the console to observe.

'What's he doing here?' he asks.

McCredie shrugs. 'I was asked to bring him here.'

He's right in front of me. Chicken Filan.

'After everything that's gone on in here the last few days. That'll be right.'

McCredie shrugs and heads towards the staff office behind the console.

'See you later, Weedy McCredie,' says the new admission.

The smile drops from his face and he scurries past me. Meanwhile, the Bloodhound's on the phone. I can't make out the conversation, but his face turns crimson.

'Turns out you are where you're supposed to be. No one bothered to tell us.' He waddles down the section, leaving the new admission with no option but to follow him.

Fred Filan. Uncle Bar's mortal enemy. The one I'm supposed to sort. A flare of fear flashes through me. Legs weak, I grasp the console for purchase.

Composing myself, taking a few deep breaths, I follow them down the section. Pull it together, I tell myself. If anyone sniffs out my temporary weakness, I'm fucked.

'In here,' says the Bloodhound after he unlocks the door. Cell 37. At least it's clean. But it needs a paint.

Filan dumps his plastic bag on the mattress before he closes the window. The air's still permeated with a bad smell, like bleach mixed with shit.

He reads the graffiti on the walls as he unpacks, variations of the same message. *Anti-Screw Crew 110%. You can turn the locks, but you can't stop the clocks.* A couple of crudely drawn swastikas. *KJ wiz here.* The Bloodhound scrutinizes him closely.

'I'll get the pass man to bring you some bedding and towels.'

I dive away from the gaff so I don't get put on report. I don't want to give the old bastard the satisfaction.

'Maddox. Get some bedding and towels and take them to 37.'

I flee to the kit store, where I have the solitude to breathe.

'Here you go,' I say. He turns around. Glares at me, but there's no recognition there. He doesn't know who I am. I can work this to my advantage.

'Put it on the bed.'

'You're Fred, right?'

'Who the fuck's asking?'

'I'm Adrian. I run this hall.'

He doesn't appear to fear me as much as I'm wary of him. I dislike him immediately.

'Is that right?'

'Yeah. Stick with me and I'll make sure you're all right though,' I smirk.

He ignores me. It gives me strength. I'm taller than him. I have similar chib marks on my body from gang fighting. I've never murdered anybody, but I have it in me to do so.

'Someone died in here the other day. The screws say he was murdered. That's the kind of thing that goes on in a hall like this. If you don't watch your back.' My tone isn't threatening, but threat is implied.

'Piss off now, son.'

I chuckle. It's easy to forget how emotional your first night in custody is. Once that door locks. Trying to keep it together and failing. Even someone as high up the criminal chain as Fred Filan will feel it soon enough.

Maybe he'll do me a favour and hang himself.

The servery is empty when I go to make myself toast. With shaking fingers, I grab what I need. The more I try to control the shakes, the worse they seem to get.

10. Kennedy

Like most Saturdays, it was teatime before I knew it. I'd spent the day in bed, willing the clock to stop speeding towards the time I'd have to start getting ready.

Dark blue jeans, boots and a Guns n' Roses top. There's no need to get properly dressed up. I'm not staying out for long.

'You don't have to go, Kennedy. No one's forcing you.'

I roll my eyes. Ellie has her new fancy woman coming over. Anything's more appealing than suffering that. And if I say anything, it'll end up in another argument.

I copy the TikTok video, but my make-up still looks a mess. 'It's just for an hour,' I say, reapplying eyeliner.

We'd got the mortgage together when we were still in love. She should've seen the warning signs when I let the estate agent believe we were best friends. It isn't as if it was a lie. Now the one I'd take a bullet for is the person holding the gun.

'You look beautiful. You really suit that colour.'

I soften. Always a sucker for a compliment. 'Thank you. It's the one you got me for Christmas last year.'

We were best friends and lovers. But the pressure she put on me to have a child proved to be our downfall. After all, how could I know how to be a mother when I had no point of reference? All I'd learned from the woman who birthed me was disappointment. Selfishness. Ignorance. I'd rather not inflict that on my own. Plus. The whole me-still-being-in-the-comfort-of-the-closet thing.

The two of us were too stubborn to move out of our dream flat so we called a truce and continued living together. I moved my stuff into the second bedroom. The one she had her heart set on being the nursery.

It's been almost a year, and we're in a good place where we pretend to be happy for each other. We're still friends. But deep inside, the candle still flickers time to time. I didn't end it because I didn't love her. I ended it because she deserved someone who'd take her out into the light. Give her what she deserved.

'Don't mention the "C" word. It's too soon.' We laugh as I wipe the cotton bud around my lids.

'Would anyone notice if you didn't go?' she tries again.

'I'm just going for an hour,' I say as I apply blusher to my cheeks. 'Just to show face.'

'Do you want me to come with you?'

'No.'

'You might've actually hesitated for a fake second. I've known Bruce longer than you have anyway.'

'Yeah, but I've actually worked with the guy. You only know him through your dad. It's different.'

'It's not, though. I was a bridesmaid at his wedding.'

'You were five. Your dad was his best man.'

'If Dad wasn't abroad, he'd be allowed to go,' she says, scowling.

'Ells, this is a work thing. Your dad used to be his governor.' I soften my tone, so I don't pay for it later. 'It's just an hour. I don't need my hand held.'

It's burned me up all day, the thought of attending Bruce's leaving night. A small part of me wants Ellie to come, but the reason why she can't is the reason why we split up in the first place. She can't ever know how much I'm hated at the place she forced me to stay.

'Do you want me to make a fake emergency call in an hour? Help you get away?'

'Nah. I'm a big girl. I can make my own excuses.' The truth is, I'm hoping no one notices me leave. Or arrive.

'I wish you'd let me come. We're only friends anyway. Nothing more.'

I squint in the mirror to make sure I haven't smudged my eye make-up. 'Have a good time with Kym,' I say as I make my way to the front door. I don't give her the opportunity to reply.

Dread pulls at the bottom of my stomach as the taxi driver beeps his horn. Just one drink, I tell myself as I stagger over to the waiting taxi. I've had a few already. For courage. And I'd never been able to master the art of walking in heels.

'Where we off to, love?'

Ellie can't ever know how disliked I am. Not with her dad being who he is. Who he was.

'The Gatehouse Inn.'

All thoughts of Ellie are replaced by Scout. I've come out early enough so that it's daylight. And I plan to be in a taxi home before it gets too dark. I can't help but think: will Scout be in the pub? Will I be safe?

'By the prison?'

I nod.

It'll be fine. It'll be fine. It'll be fine. I swallow saliva.

The driver, sensing my unease, doesn't speak until we arrive at the pub. I don't want to think about Ellie. I don't want to think about Scout. She doesn't understand what it's like. For me. In this environment. Being something I'm not. This is for Bruce.

'That'll be six pounds, love.'

Officers stand joking outside the pub. Smoking. Unfriendly

faces. I pretend to search for change in the bottom of my purse until they go back inside, such is my fear of walking by them when they've been drinking. When they can say anything they want and blame it on the drink.

I grab my bag until my knuckles hurt. Breathe in. And out. I'm out in public, I remind myself. No one will try anything in a busy pub. I'll get home before it gets too dark. Maybe Ellie could come for me?

'Are you OK?'

'Yes,' I breathe. 'Just give me a minute.'

I pay the taxi driver and totter outside the pub, catching my breath and psyching myself up to go in. With another deep breath, I open the door and walk in, holding my head high.

I proceed straight to the bar. The laughter behind me intensifies. Paranoia? Conversations blend into one noise. I hold on to the bar. Practise my breathing until my vision clears.

'Can I have a bottle of Bud, please?' The barman nods and grabs one from the fridge. I watch as he pops the cap off and places it on the counter.

'Is that everything?'

I hand over a note and wait on my change. Only then do I grab the bottle and take a swig, hoping it'll calm my nerves.

'You came,' Bruce says, placing a hand on my shoulder.

'Jesus, Bruce, you scared me.'

Prison staff have taken over half the bar. I peek at them all. Is *Scout* here? My heart flurries. The lager tastes like battery acid in my throat. I don't want to be here. This was a mistake.

'Sorry, love,' he slurs.

'Can I buy you a drink?' I offer after I give him a kiss on the cheek. His breath smells of stale alcohol.

'I have plenty on the table. I'm glad you made it.'

'I wouldn't come out for most,' I confess.

'I know, hen. And I'm touched. Now, you come and sit with me. I'll look after you.'

I smile at him. I've bought a drink. I'll drink it. I've shown my face. I don't have to stay any longer than I'm comfortable with. Objective achieved.

Bruce took me under his wing when I first started. When I wasn't sure if a career in the Prison Service was for me. I'd wanted to join after growing up watching *Prisoner Cell Block H* and *Bad Girls*. I was accepted as soon as I turned twenty-one and completed the six-week training a few months later.

I didn't last one shift. My first morning, I attended an alarm. A lad had been attacked. Left for dead. I'd written my letter of resignation by lunchtime. The job isn't like it is on TV. I'd been issued several rape threats and serious violence only two hours into the shift.

I'd spoken to Bruce for advice. As Ellie's dad's best friend, I'd met him a few times out of work. He managed to get me into a non-operational role in the Intelligence Management Unit. A secret role where I could have as much, or as little, prisoner contact as I'd like. He'd saved me.

Ellie could only think of her dad's reputation. She'd forced me to stay in a place where I was unhappy so her dad wouldn't look bad. I should've been stronger at the time. So, when she pressured me for a baby, there was only one choice I could make. And it broke the two of us. It's not her fault. It was how she was raised.

I follow Bruce to the table. Plaster a smile on my face and pretend I'm happy to be here. I sit with my back to the wall. I see everything. The officers and, more importantly, the exit.

Some of the officers greet me whereas others don't acknowledge me. I'm fine with that.

My skin prickles. Jimmy 'McWhackle' McCall glares at me from the opposite table. If I'd known he was coming, I would've stayed at home. McCall got his nickname from his time in the 1980s when dragging prisoners into cells and slapping them around was not only accepted but expected. McCall couldn't move into the twenty-first century and still deemed it acceptable in 2015. He was the second officer I got sacked.

My hands shake under the table. Bruce remains by my side, like a guard dog. But I'm off as soon as I finish my drink. It's not just Forth Valley staff here. There are officers from the other prisons. The college. Other union reps.

Years of working in the IMU have thickened my skin. But I've never associated with officers where alcohol is involved. I brace myself for a veiled insult. Some of the officers have been out drinking for hours. I fight the urge to check my phone. To pull the mascara from my lashes.

'Watch, there's the jail polis,' slurs a voice to my right. I glance up sharply but can't distinguish who's spoken. I tremble. Sweat collects at my armpits. Trickles down my sides. My heart pumps adrenaline around my body. I look towards the doors. To flight.

'Who's going to the bar?' shouts one of the officers I recognize. Intelligence suggests he has a huge cocaine problem. But the Prison Officers Association won't let us drug test to prove it. He rubs at his nose at thirty-second intervals. Sniffs.

'It's your turn, ya fanny,' shouts another.

Being surrounded by so many people under the influence makes me uncomfortable. It always has, on account of my handsy father. The rum that spoiled him for a fight.

97

I'm fidgety. I struggle with the smell of alcohol. A precursor of danger. A warning. I breathe through my mouth to stop me smelling stale beer and eggy farts. Bruce returns and stands next to me, like a shield, and instantly I feel safer. He won't see any harm come to me. No one will say anything in front of him.

My neck prickles again; the hair on the back of my neck stands on end. I look up. But it isn't an angry officer staring back at me. Instead, there's a man I don't recognize in a tweed flat cap gawking at me over the rim of his pint glass. I stare back until he looks away first. I hate this bar. It brings out the weirdos.

When I feel him stare again, I don't give him the satisfaction of my attention.

'Do you want a drink, doll?' a bald officer says, staring at me intently.

'No, thanks,' I say, shaking my full bottle at him.

'Are you sure?'

I smile my fake smile again. Point to the bottle. 'I'm fine.'

'Are you Bruce's daughter? You look dead familiar.'

'No, but I have worked at the prison for the last five years,' I deadpan.

'Get that lassie a drink,' he orders no one in particular.

'Are you having a good time?' I ask, trying to keep the conversation light. From experience, explaining exactly where I work in the prison will go one of two ways. I'll get verbal abuse in a half-joking manner, or I'll be completely ignored.

Baldy wanders over to the bar with the kitty and I breathe out.

Bruce ruffles my hair. Cheeks flushed. 'Are you OK?' he says.

'Of course.' My jaw aches with all the false smiling. Not

for the first time, I wish Ellie was here. Every time the door opens, expectant hope engulfs me, and I curse my own stubbornness.

The backshift trickles into the bar. The DJ calls out for karaoke singers. I focus on my own drink. Pick at the label on my bottle.

'You know what people say about that?' says a female voice. I peer up at her from under my fringe. I know what she's going to say before the words leave her lips, but I humour her, nonetheless. Because it's her. With the long brunette hair. The piercing gold eyes. Dark skin. Molly Rana. She's wearing a revealing red floral jumpsuit that clings to her slim frame.

'Go on. Tell me,' I say when my tongue loosens from where it's been stuck to the roof of my mouth.

'It means you're sexually frustrated. Or that's what I saw on TikTok anyway.'

'If you saw it on TikTok then it must be true.' As soon as the words are out, I feel my face heat up, but she chuckles.

'Can I sit?'

'Of course,' I say, moving to make room in the booth.

'You're the girl that works in the IMU, aren't you?'

I nod, deflated.

'Do you like it?'

'It's OK.'

'I'm Molly, by the way.'

'Nice to meet you. Kennedy . . . I mean, I'm Kennedy. Whereabouts do you work?'

'I'm based in Hayworth just now, but I haven't been there long. I used to work with the sex offenders in Barlinnie previously, and yes, it's different, and no, I didn't enjoy it.'

Her eyes are like pools of sunshine and I'm drawn right in.

'I'm sure all the sex offenders would've appreciated your sex tips.'

'Excuse me?'

The joke falls flat. I want the ground to open and swallow me.

'God.' I cringe. 'I swear that's my first,' I say, pointing to my bottle. 'I meant what you said about me ripping off the label. It sounded funny in my head,' I babble. To my relief, she chuckles again. It sounds velvety and comforting, like chocolate spread on pancakes.

'Can we start over, please?' I say. 'Do you know Bruce well?'

'Can I be honest with you?'

'Please.'

Her words tickle my ear. I get a whiff of cigarette smoke from her and, for a second, it disappoints me.

'I don't really know him. I couldn't bear another Saturday night in front of shitty telly. Is that terrible?'

'No. Not at all.'

For don't I know exactly how it feels to be lonely?

My mouth opens, to share my confession, but I change my mind at the last minute, plugging my mouth with the bottle instead.

'Why did you move from Barlinnie? Was it your choice, or did you come to Forth Valley on a promotion?'

I think of everything I want to say before I say it so I don't stumble over my words. She has that effect on me. Could reduce me to a mumbling wreck with one look. One smile. She's stunning, and my heart hasn't beaten properly since she turned up.

'I liked it there, but it messed with my head. It takes a special person to be able to work with the protections their whole career. And then . . . There was a confrontation.

With a sex offender.' She shudders. 'A story for another time, I think,' she adds.

'How long have you been in the service?'

'Five, six years? Plus, Forth Valley's my local, so . . .' she adds with a shrug.

'That makes sense.'

'Can I get you a drink?'

'Great, yeah, if you don't mind.' But I don't want her to leave. To break the hypnosis she has over me. She smiles. A smile that makes my heartbeat fluctuate in a dangerous way.

'Of course I don't mind. You're the only person in here who hasn't stared at my tits.'

I look down at her cleavage before dragging my eyes away as my cheeks heat up. Thank fuck for shitty Saturday-night telly.

'Be right back.'

As soon as she walks away, I shiver. I haven't felt such a sudden attraction to a female since I met Ellie years ago. But I don't shit where I eat.

I flinch when a glass is dropped behind the bar. Five seconds of silence follow before the officers start clapping and jeering towards the bar staff. I clutch at my chest. It's too boisterous for me.

Molly and I are trying to make each other comfortable at a night out neither of us wants to be at. That's all it is, I tell myself as I keep glancing over my shoulder, watching her. I drink down the warm bottle. She looks back at me with a disarming smile, and my insides melt.

Damn.

There's nothing wrong with a crush. Some window shopping until the real thing comes along.

A hint of a smile is on her face when she returns. She stops to talk to Ray McCredie. My hearts squeezes in jealousy.

'It's getting busy in here, eh?' she says as she offers me a fresh bottle and a shot of something bright green.

'Yeah. It's been ages since I was last in a pub . . . I feel a bit overwhelmed.'

'Has that got to do with . . . ? Sorry, it's not my place to ask.' Squirming under my gaze, she takes a deep pull on her own drink.

'Ask what?' I brace myself, knowing what's coming.

'I was stupidly going to ask if it's because of the, um, what happened to you. The stabbing.'

I smile wryly to let her know she isn't making a faux pas. But my insides squirm all the same.

'It's OK. Speaking about it won't break me. It's since before then, to be honest. I went through a bad break-up and I guess I lost my confidence. My ex moved on quicker than I could. I didn't want to see them all over each other in a bar.'

She removes her black leather jacket as she listens, and I see it. The delicate rainbow tattoo on her wrist, like an orange segment.

'Ouch. Sorry to bring that up. That sounds more painful than what you went through with the Bowards.'

'I don't know about that.' I giggle nervously. 'Two different kinds of pain,' I add, surprised at my own honesty. I grab my lager bottle and swallow noisily.

But in a way it was. My injuries healed. My trust hasn't. And yet. Here I am, confessing my life story to a stranger. This is what happens when nerves and warm beer combine.

'Ladies and gentlemen,' announces the DJ. 'Next up to sing is Ray McCredie.'

'We can talk about something else if you like?' she says, sensing my unease.

'Has Bruce paid you to mind me?'

'I'm sorry?'

Another joke falls flat.

The opening notes of 'Unchained Melody' play. Molly and I look at each other and roll our eyes. McCredie has been joined on the small stage by another officer, who knows he's attractive, by the way he swaggers.

'Never mind. I'm not particularly good at making jokes, clearly.' I raise my voice to be heard over the karaoke.

'It's OK. I can be the funny one.' She leans in closer, and I can smell her watermelon perfume. My heart jolts. Molly is doing this thing to my insides. Like all my pulse points heighten, until I can feel them, beating away in sync with each other. Maybe it's the beer. The anxiety of being out of my comfort zone.

'Tell me something about yourself,' I say after a beat. My turn to change the conversation.

'There's not much to know. I'm twenty-seven, passionate about music and football. Arsenal is my team. My talents include avoiding difficult conversations and getting sad over things I saw coming. I'm a high-adrenaline kinda chick. Here for a good time, not a long time,' she winks, and I shiver. Her confidence impresses me.

I open my mouth. Close it. Rack my brains trying to think of something else to ask when all I can think about is how much alike we are.

'Married? Kids?'

'Oh no. I'm far too young for that kind of commitment. In fact, I also went through a bad break-up recently. I started the relationship with bad intentions.' She screws up her face. 'She was married. I fell in love. She chose him. I was just . . . an experiment. To satisfy a curiosity.'

I'm surprised when a tear escapes her eye. I wonder

how long ago the break-up occurred and feel instantly jealous.

'I'm sorry,' she says as she slaps away the tear. 'I did say I get sad over things I saw coming.'

There's something about this girl. I want to know her. I want to be friends. More than friends. The attraction deepens. I'm about to take her in my arms, comfort her, when she brightens up and changes the subject.

'What about yourself?'

'It's never happened for me either.' I knock back the shot. Apple Sourz. 'I haven't met the right . . . person.'

'I understand that. It's harder for me to find someone because I don't want kids,' she adds with a shrug.

I flip my head around. 'You don't want kids? I thought I was the only one.'

'You don't want them either?'

'Oh no. Never have. I like to hold a baby, but I like to hand it back even more.' I lick at my dry lips. 'It's how my last relationship ended, actually. She wanted different things.'

'She?' says Molly, eyebrow raised.

She gives a throaty chuckle and my insides quiver. 'Wow, how about that. Two selfish bitches.'

'Are you two behaving?' Bruce interjects. I move away from her. Disappointment floods me.

'Yes, we're behaving.'

'Then you're doing it wrong,' he says with a wink before he's swallowed back up into the crowd.

'I'll miss him.'

'Yeah. One of the good ones, I hear.'

'One of the last good ones.'

'It's nice to see so many folks coming along for his send-off. Wait a minute. That sounded a bit morbid, didn't it? He's not dead.'

'Just a bit. Although, he might feel like he's dying come the morning after all the whiskies he's knocked back.'

I catch myself looking at her cleavage again. How the red jumpsuit clings to her body. I moisten my lips. Look away. Take another drink to distract myself. I want to kiss her. To hell with everything else. Her conversation's refreshing. Her natural talent for it puts me at ease. I want to stroke her hair. Have her hold me.

The truth is, I fancy her. I don't want to get swept along on an imaginary wave. I've been single so long I might pant at any female attention. Genuine or not. Friendly or not.

'That's a nice watch.'

'Oh. Thanks. Present from the parents for my twenty-first.'

'Wow. How generous. That must have set them back?'

Ellie's dad had a similar Tissot. I'm sure there wasn't much change left out of a grand.

I hide my own beat-up first-generation Fitbit under the table. The one that's not a financial priority for me to upgrade.

McCredie and Co. stop singing and the bar descends into raucous applause. He wasn't that good.

'Are you singing?'

'Oh no. I'm not planning on staying much longer, to be honest.'

'Everything OK with your drink?'

'Yeah, I only came out for the one.'

The rowdy bar steals my attention. Ray McCredie's reappeared, shooting me dirty looks. The sudden urge to flee is overwhelming. He can say what he wants to me, but not in front of her. I can't take the embarrassment.

'I know your game, madam. You want to stop drinking so you don't need to buy me a drink back.' The glint in her eyes confirms she's joking. I'm staring at her lips, wondering what they taste like.

My heart stutters. Somewhere in my subconscious, an alarm is ringing. *Be careful, Kennedy. You're fragile too.*

'I need to go to the ladies and powder my nose,' I say as I pull myself up from the table. I must get away from her. To think. To rest my heart.

'No bother.'

She leans back to let me out. My legs brush past hers, and I hope she doesn't notice them tremble. It's just the alcohol, I tell myself as I make my way to the ladies.

My face is hot, my cleavage sweaty. I check my phone. A message from Ellie containing question marks. I ignore it. Put the phone back in my bag. There's too much going on in my head for Ellie's presence to complicate things further.

I tingle with a pang of something. Meeting Molly has opened something that's been closed for too long. Regret? Longing? Desire? Passion?

The bar's busy enough that no one will notice me leave. Bruce will understand. I made the effort. And the amount he's drunk – he won't be able to remember saying goodbye.

With my mind made up, I check my reflection in the mirror, enjoying the cool solitude. Beads of perspiration dot my hairline. I sprinkle some cold water on my pulse points and practise my breathing. In for seven. Out for five. I'm in control here.

Now I've decided to leave, my hunger returns. Anxiety hasn't allowed me to think about food without feeling sick all day. Not even the smell of Ellie's toast at breakfast tempted me to eat.

Bruce is half out the exit. Trying to have a conversation

on his mobile phone. He says goodbye and puts the phone away.

'Come here, you.'

He opens his arms, and I find myself entering them. He gives me a quick squeeze and plants a whisky-smelling kiss on my forehead. I fight the urge to vomit.

'Having a good time?'

'I am, hen. I'm truly blessed so many have come out. Mind you, some are raging alcoholics that'd go to any night out.'

I smile against his shoulder. A whiff of sweat clings to my nostrils. It's strangely comforting.

'Are *you* having a good time? It doesn't look like you are.'

'Aw, don't be like that, Bruce. You know I'm no good in a crowd. Anyway, I'm not staying out much longer. I'll say my goodbyes here while you're still sober enough to remember.'

'Aye, and you know how prison rumours start, so I suggest you both disappear if you want to get to know each other better.'

His words slam into my heart. 'What do you mean?'

'Molly's out and proud.'

My mouth opens and closes.

'I'm not as daft as I look. I notice things,' he goes on. 'Plus, I play golf with her dad. A good family.'

My vision blurs as my heart races. A pain erupts in my gut. 'I, ugh . . .' But no one is listening in to our conversation, no matter how much the alcohol has raised Bruce's voice.

'Get to know her. Have a good time. She's a great lass.'

'But she's an officer and . . .'

'And what? You shouldn't hold it against her if there's a connection. You deserve to live your life the way you want to live it. Don't get to my age with regrets.'

'I've seen too much . . .'

'Yes,' he interrupts. 'So have I. But what if she's The One? You build these walls, Kennedy. You're just making a prison . . . for yourself.'

'Jeez, that's cheesy. But. Some prisons can keep you safe.'

'What have you got to lose?'

'My feelings. My reputation.' My heart.

'Exactly! Why do you give a fuck what these fuckers think? It's no one's business but your own. Live a little. Have a lot of fun. Throw out the rule book.'

'I . . .'

'You're a lovely wee lassie and you deserve some happiness. You need to stop saying no to people before you give them a chance or you're going to be alone for ever. Is that what you want?'

'Bruce, I . . .'

'Nope. Unless you're about to tell me I'm right, then I don't want to hear it.'

'You're right. I'm such an awkward overthinker, I hurt my own feelings.'

He squeezes me into an even deeper hug. 'Go and give her a chance, love. I saw the way she's looking at you. And mind and invite me to the wedding.'

'I'm surprised you aren't pushing for me to get back with Ellie.'

'Ellie's a great girl. I love her like my own daughter. But she's not the one for you.'

He lets me go and climbs the stairs to the gents before I can say another word. In theory, I agree. His words continue to penetrate the protective part of my brain as I make my way back to Molly.

It's different for Bruce. He's a guy. He doesn't understand what it's like to be me. Female. The scrutiny I'm already under.

'Oh, hey there. I thought you'd gone home without saying goodbye,' says Molly as she appears beside me, holding my jacket. Before I can say anything, she continues, 'I don't mean to sound forward, but do you want to get out of here?'

I accept my jacket. Molly doesn't need to say any more. The atmosphere around us has changed. Two young ops officers glare at each other, ready to strike over a spilled drink.

Behind her, Bruce descends the stairs with his thumbs up but puts them down when Molly looks round.

She puts her head to mine and whispers in my ear. 'I have a bad feeling we might witness something if we stay. I can walk you to the taxi rank if you want to go home instead.' She's smiling. An eyebrow raised.

Her words don't register. I can smell her coconut skin. Her apple-smelling shampoo. Her fruity perfume. She scores brownie points; the fact she doesn't want to stay either.

'Where do you want to go? For something to eat?' It's her smell that does it. Convinces me to go away with her. After all, two lesbians can be friends. And I'd very much like to get to know her better. Be her friend. I'm not ready to say goodnight.

The gossip drums will be banging for the rest of the weekend if we leave together. But I don't have to worry about that any more when a young officer pushes one of his colleagues.

'Here you, ya fucking dick.'

Molly grasps my hand. 'Let's go,' she whispers as she pulls me away. All eyes are on the officers scuffling at the side of the bar. No one sees us leave.

Her hand is soft in mine, and I can't help but stroke it

with my thumb. To my disbelief she strokes back. When we're outside, we burst out laughing. The moment's gone as she lets go of my hand.

'Give me your phone,' she commands.

'Why?'

She takes it from me, her thumbs punching in digits.

'There. Now you have my number.'

What do I need her number for? But the last thing I want is to ruin the moment between us.

She winks. My God. The spark.

She likes me too.

11. Adrian

I can't stop thinking about him. Not when I'm dubbed up for the night. Not when I brush my teeth and not when I lie in bed and try to get to sleep. Filan looks like a nobody to me. All the stories I've heard over the years don't compare.

With the dark circles under his eyes and the streaks of grey in his shaved dark hair, he looks middle-aged. He's smaller than me. I'll take him for a square go – I'll just make sure there's a tool handy. He's a dirty bastard. Just because he's lost his freedom doesn't mean he's lost anything else. In captivity, he'll just become more vicious. Like us all. A caged animal.

I'm unlocked early to help dish out the Sunday fry-up, but I turn my nose up at the congealing grease. Instead, me and the other lads make cheese toasties in the pantry and the smell lingers. Cheap cheese and crumbs. It masks the smell of the stale alcohol coming from the screws' pores. Must have been some night out, the way they're all hanging out their arses.

It's only when I go to spoon sugar into my mug that I notice my hand shaking. The next few days are going to be interesting. Someone's going to have to show Filan the ropes. And that someone will be me. Keep your enemies close and that.

I stir my tea, but it cools untouched in the mug. I slip into my gaff and gub a few vallies to calm me down. Chewing on my bottom lip, I saunter to the PIN phone. As I'd worried, the call goes unanswered. I try Uncle Shay's number and it's answered on the fifth ring.

'It's me. He's here,' I say.

'OK.'

'Get more stuff in. I'll get it done this time.'

'Are you stupid, wee man? You've fucked that route.'

I bite my lip until it bleeds. 'Tell me what to do, then. Get me normal stuff. Heroin. Hash. Scoobs.'

'You know what to do. Get it done the old-fashioned way. No more excuses. The big man wants him off the numbers. And then we'll talk about getting you more gear.'

'It's not that easy. Not after the last stuff. We're being watched.'

I hang up first. Give myself a bit of control. The scoobs begin to dissolve in my system and, despite the call, a calmness descends inside me.

Filan's room remains locked until later, when I'm serving the evening meal with Spence.

'What's with the new celebrity? Isn't he coming out to play, Ray?'

I breathe out of my mouth. The smell of stale alcohol comes off in him waves. Vodka. My mouth waters, but not in a hungry way.

'The higher-ups are too scared to bring him out in case there's trouble.'

Disappointing. But somewhere deep inside, there's also relief. I can't do anything if the screws keep him locked up. But for their protection, or his?

'Do you want me to make him up a plate and take it to his gaff?'

The officer shrugs. He doesn't give a fuck if Filan eats or not. But when it's just the scraps left, he changes his mind. Or his hangover improves. I throw a bit of every-thing on the plate. A few soggy chips and the smallest slice of pizza, the toppings already picked off by the other pass men. I grab two slices of bread, a sachet of salt and some brown sauce. Too bad if he's a ketchup guy – there's none left.

'No trouble,' warns the screw as he unlocks the gaff. Technically, I'm doing his job for him. And if it goes tits up, he'll be the one to get his baws booted.

'Are you hungry?' Standing at the door like a spare prick at a wedding, waiting to be invited in. Filan's lying on his bed, his right arm covering his eyes.

'Leave it on the table,' he barks.

Willing my hands not to shake as I enter his gaff, I do as he says. It's been a while since I've found someone as intimidating as Filan. But 'con' isn't just short for convict. It's short for confidence, too. And to survive in a shithole like this, you need to have it in buckets.

I leave the gaff without speaking, and he's locked back in.

'There won't be any trouble at rec tonight,' I tell Ray once I'm back. 'I swear on my mum's life.' It doesn't matter if he knows she's been dead for three years. He isn't the type of screw to give a flying fuck. That's why we put up with his awkwardness. The desperation he portrays to be our friend. It comes from a place of fear. A bully victim with a bit of power in his white shirt.

'It's not my decision to make. Go and clean the hotplate or I'll give the pass to someone else.'

I raise my eyebrows and he flinches. We both know who's really in charge here.

I sigh and march over to the pantry. I could've dis-obeyed the prick, but he has Bloodhound back-up nearby.

'What's he like then?' Flakes asks, the visit-room pass man.

I shrug. 'He doesn't say much. Doesn't look like a triple killer either.'

'He's a dangerous bastard,' Flakes says. 'My old man says I've to keep away from him.'

'Does he tell you to look both ways before you cross the road too?' The lads laugh. It emboldens me.

'My dad knows him,' Flakes adds. My eyes widen, but I'm fed up hearing it. It's been whispered up and down the section all day. If I had a pound for every time someone said they personally knew Filan, I wouldn't have to punt drugs for a living.

'Put the word out,' I instruct. 'No one touches him until I say they can.'

'As if anyone's that daft,' Flakes mutters. I ignore him, leaving Spence to do the dishes while I make myself another tea.

Spence walks into the pantry and motions for me to follow him to the store cupboard. He's pensive. His complexion pales. 'What's the matter?'

'The guy in gaff 3 is asking where his stuff is.'

I snort. 'You know where it is. In transit.'

'What do you want me to say? I checked; he's paid for them.'

I rub at my nose. 'I'm not really in the mood for more problems, Spence, mate.'

'I know. But we'll have an issue here.'

I've promised more than I should. But I can't back down now. Not when things are going well.

'We don't. I'm getting more gear in soon. But tell him the price just went up.'

If the guy's desperate, he'll pay. I'm the only one that'll be holding, after all.

'I thought we didn't want problems?'

'We? You're not turning chicken on me, are you? I don't associate with chickens.'

'You know what I mean.'

'If he has a problem with the new price, tell him about the weapon I have in my bed box and ask him if he wants to make its acquaintance.'

I walk away, letting Spence know the conversation's over. He's turning out to be a right fucking blouse. My face remains poker straight but, inside, I'm anxious. I have bills to pay too.

Fuck, I think. Fuck.

Sugary tea inside is a drug. I can't drink it if it contains any less than six spoonsful of sugar. It gives you a boost when there's nothing else around. And the hall is as dry as a nun's fanny.

A decision is made to let Filan out for the last ten minutes of rec. They can't lock him up indefinitely. They'd only succeed in embellishing the mystery surrounding him if they make a special case out of him. Put him on a pedestal. Better to rip the plaster off now.

He wanders out into the hall and over to the pool tables, stands back and takes in his surroundings. Every game stops. Ten seconds later, the novelty wears away and we turn back to our games, our conversations, our own troubles.

He swaggers around the perimeter of the section, staring ahead, not looking in any particular direction.

'If anyone wants to come for me, I'm ready,' he announces, flexing his muscles. Almost everyone in the hall averts their eyes. Fucking shitebags.

The screws at the bottom of the hall stand, ready to pounce if the trouble they've been worried about breaks out.

But no one takes Filan up on his offer. He waits for a few minutes and walks back to his gaff before the screws can force him to. He's set out his stall. Smart of him too. I no longer need to put the word out. Filan can take care of himself. You don't get to the top of a criminal organization if you can't.

He stands at his gaff, arms crossed over his chest. A few of the other cons walk up to him, offering gels. Coffee sachets. Other items they're able to share. Fucking pussies. I look around my hall. A couple of the elders have gone back to their gaffs, not wanting to be involved in anything that might happen.

Filan's reputation proceeds him. It's only then I notice rec is only half full. Some wee chickens haven't come out to play at all.

The next day, Monday, is different. Almost like they've assessed he's no longer a risk, based on nothing happening in the space of a few minutes the night before. His gaff's unlocked after the rest of the herd go off to their education classes and their work parties, scrambling for anything they can get that might help them not return to prison life.

That's why I'm better on the pass. I was born into this life. There's no changing me now, no matter how many qualifications I gain while I'm inside. The thug life is the one for me.

We're out cleaning the hall – Spence doing all the work while Rampage and I fuck about with the radio stations. Rampage is the second-tallest prisoner I've ever met. His height and demeanour intimidate everyone, including me. He shaves his hair every week – not because he thinks it makes him look hard, but because he thinks it makes him invisible on the CCTV. He hangs about with me because I can control him with drugs.

Flakes is waiting to be escorted to his pass cleaning job

in the visit room when Filan emerges with his towel and toiletries. I motion to the other guys.

'Close your mouth, Spence,' I whisper. He watches him move across the section like he's some sort of God. The boys should know I'm the only God around here. Spence closes his mouth and returns to mopping the floor.

'Doesn't seem like such a hard man,' Rampage offers. And he should know. Rampage is addicted to violence like other folk are addicted to drink or drugs. A mad bastard. The only reason he's given the pass job's because the screws fear him. It's easier for them to just give into him than try to discipline him.

Good for me, too, because they never put him on report. It's not worth the hassle. If he could be trusted, I'd give him my stash to hold for me. The screws never select him to get spun. But the big cunt would gub everything. And I'm out of pocket enough as it is, gear-wise.

'Better to keep him on side though,' I suggest, looking directly at Rampage.

We wouldn't normally be friends, but I need his muscle and zest for violence as much as he needs the scoobs I can produce. Which is at least every weekend.

We huddle close by as Filan emerges from the shower, having chosen to dry himself behind the privacy of the cubicle.

'All right, mate,' I offer. He nods once in acknowledgement before retreating to his gaff.

I hear the breathing before I turn around, rolling my eyes in the process.

'We're not doing anything, Officer North,' I say in my most sarcastically sweet voice.

'When are you not up to something? You're on the pass, aren't you? Is that floor supposed to be clean?'

117

'We're in the process of cleaning it. You've interrupted us,' Spence says, pushing his dark-framed glasses up his nose.

'Get back on with it then,' he orders, walking towards the centre console. I stick my middle finger up to his retreating back and pull it down when he turns around at the sound of the others giggling.

'Prick. That guy's due a slap,' I warn.

Rampage raises his head. 'Just say the word, brother.'

'Nah. Not you. Someone else.'

Rampage shrugs. He's better at dragging folk into cells and battering them for me. But not a screw. He's too valuable to me to be sent down the digger for a month. Or worse – shipped out to another prison like Tre Sinclair.

'I wonder what they're saying about the dead boy,' Spence says.

'They don't know anything,' I say, annoyed he's brought it up again. Haven't we spent enough of the last week talking about it?

'Don't overthink things.'

'But—' he begins.

'Forget it,' I say, a little sharply. Spence clears his throat.

He's normally a good cunt, or so I thought. Maybe he can't handle the scandal after all. It's not as if he killed him. He just passed him a fucking note.

'If anybody knows anything, they'd have pulled us by now. Forget about it. I have.'

Rampage shakes his bullet head, sick of hearing about it too. I don't want to have to hit Spence, but if he doesn't shut the fuck up then it'll quickly become the only option.

'There's another shipment coming in soon,' I say. There isn't, not yet, but I feel the need to change the tone, atmosphere, conversation.

'I'm pure buzzing,' Rampage says, his face cheesing.

Everyone relaxes at the change in conversation. Even Spence joins in with the laughter.

'Tell me it's not always as boring as this,' Filan says, attracting the others' attention like flies around shite.

I turn around mid-sentence. Blink. 'Come and meet the guys,' I say. Filan swaggers over, making eye contact with each of us.

'Spence, Rampage,' I say, introducing the troops.

'How are we doing, lads?'

Spence mumbles his reply. Rampage stands taller. Puffs out his chest.

'Rampage? What kind of name is that?'

'If you ever cross me, you'll find out.'

We shoot the shit for a while. Tell Filan how the hall works. Rampage is a long-term prisoner – four years so far with a couple of civvie charges still to go to court for after battering a few folks in here, and Spence has just over two years until he can apply for parole.

'You'll have back-door parole, eh?' I say.

He squints at me, and my insides squeeze against my will. 'What do you mean by that?'

I regret speaking, but I can't back down. Not in front of the boys.

'You'll die in here. Leave in a box. Three life sentences. You aren't ever going home.'

To my relief, he chuckles. 'Not me, man. I'll be out of here soon.'

'What? You confident you'll win your appeal?'

But Filan doesn't say anything. He just shrugs his broad shoulders.

'Adrian can supply a bag of brown easier than you can get fresh bedding in this camp,' Spence says.

I glare at him. He needs a slap after all.

'Good to know,' he says, but doesn't look me in the eye.

'Scr-egg-ew,' Rampage says. The screw hovers about in my peripheral vision, breathing heavily. The Bloodhound.

'Who's Darth Vader?' Filan asks. We all laugh.

'That's the Bloodhound. Has a knack of smelling out trouble, drugs and phones. You don't want to get yourself on his radar, Fred. He's a fucking bug,' Spence says.

'That's why we talk in egg language when he's around,' Rampage whispers. 'It drives him crazy. He can't understand what we're saying.'

I can't have Filan knowing all our secrets.

'If you're talking about anything piping on the phone calls, you need to learn the egg language,' Spence offers.

I clench my jaw. It dawns on me. They like the cunt. The enemy.

'I'm sure Fred won't need to use the PIN phones.' I fake-grin. 'I bet you came prepared, eh? Some beat-the-boss phones and some gear up your jacksie?'

'What the fuck is egg language?' Filan asks, ignoring me. He can cast his net as wide as he wants, but he's getting no catch from me.

'You insert the word "egg" into every piping word. They can't make out what you're saying. But the other person needs to understand it too, otherwise you're wasting your time,' Rampage explains.

'You know they listen to our calls, right?' Spence says.

Filan nods. 'It's not my first dalliance with the criminal justice system. A few associates have been in here. Innocent though, they were.'

'Oh aye? Who's that, like?' Rampage asks, and I can feel the power shifting from me. 'Maybe we know them.'

'Big Dom Murray?' Spence guesses.

Filan shrugs. 'One of a few.'

It's clear he doesn't want to continue the conversation. And since it's too close to revealing who I am to him, I need to steer the conversation in a different direction.

'We better get on with the cleaning, lads. I don't want to give the Bloodhound the satisfaction of sacking me off the pass.'

It bothers me more than I'd like – that Filan doesn't seem to know who I am. I'm with the Shire. He should have all our faces imprinted in his brain.

None of the screws seem to care Filan's out his gaff when he's supposed to be dubbed-up. He grabs a mop pole and helps with the cleaning. When we're done, he makes a round of teas in the servery. The bastard's cutting my grass. Trying to take over. I can't allow it.

What's his game? He should have the lads running about after him. I chew on my thumbnail, watching him.

'I know you're new,' says the Bloodhound behind me. I turn around, expecting to be nose to nose with my white-shirt nemesis, but he's turned his attention to Filan.

'You don't have permission to be behind here. I'll let it slide because you're new and the others are taking advantage. But don't come behind here again. That's the rules.'

His hand is in his trouser pocket, clutching his baton. I'd love to take it off him and acquaint it with his head.

'I don't follow rules. That's why I'm in the hokey-pokey in the first place.' Filan glowers at him until he blinks. Looks away to see where the other screws are. Hoping for some back-up. When another screw approaches, the Bloodhound opens his mouth again.

'Come on then,' he says. 'Back to your kennel.'

The others are watching intently, waiting to see who'll

snap first. And I have to admit it, even just to myself, Filan's a cold bastard.

'Look,' Spence says, trying to cool the moment. 'We're just trying to make Fred feel welcome.'

'I don't care. I'll lock you all up and you'll all be looking for new jobs.'

'Come on, lads. It's not worth it,' I say.

'You know,' Filan pipes up, 'one of these days, someone's going to put you on your arse. Pri-egg-ck.'

Rampage chuckles and Spence stares blankly, fearing for his trusted position the most.

'Is that a threat? Are you threatening me?'

Filan shrugs.

'I didn't hear any threat,' Spence says. It's like a knife to my chest.

'Me neither,' say Rampage and Flakes, playing along. I remain quiet.

'You pass men are getting too fucking cocky. Maybe I'll pass my concerns on to intel. Get them to come down and spin you all. Now wouldn't that be interesting? You can join the rest of the idiots on the ghost train.'

Rampage was at an agent's visit or he'd be in the digger, too. Spence had been at education. But only Rampage was disappointed at having missed out on the madness.

A flicker of fear licks at my heart. Before the situation escalates further, Filan swaggers from the pantry and returns to his gaff. The Bloodhound locks us up and I'm grateful for the solitude to compose my thoughts.

I press the emergency buzzer while looking at my bed box. My hiding place.

'What do you want, Maddox?' Thankfully, it's not answered by that dickhead.

'I need to speak to my personal officer. Urgently.'

12. Kennedy

'Good morning.' She smiles. 'Am I allowed in?'

My heart thuds. I desperately want to drag her into the office before she's seen, but I don't want her here when Jacob comes back, which he will be any second.

We went for tapas at the new restaurant in town after leaving the pub. She gave me her number. But it's not clear if she's looking for a friend, or something more. Not that it matters; I'm not looking for more. Not with a white shirt.

The restaurant staff chucked us out at closing time, and we'd walked to a wine bar, where we'd stayed for another hour until that closed too.

It scared me, how much we had in common.

'Thought you were only staying out for one?' Ellie asked when I let myself into the darkened flat in the early hours of Sunday morning.

'Jesus, you gave me a fright.'

She was wrapped in a pink fleece blanket, staring at the joint Netflix account, but with nothing selected to watch.

'I waited up for you. You didn't answer my calls.'

I cleared my throat and asked after Kym.

'I cancelled on her. I was going to meet up with you.'

Reluctant to spoil the night by telling her what really happened, I kissed her on the forehead and wished her goodnight. I stripped off all my clothes and climbed into bed. But I was too excited to sleep. All my thoughts turned to Molly. I hoped that somewhere, she too was alone, excited about me. I allowed myself to have that fantasy. I deserved it.

By the Monday morning, my confidence in my pulling abilities had wavered.

My thoughts had been consumed by her every minute since. What I'd say when I bumped into her. But now she's standing in front of me every word I've ever learned vanishes from my head.

I want to breathe her in, even just for a couple of seconds. 'Um, sure.' I open the door wider to allow her access. 'Do you have intelligence to pass on?'

There's nothing wrong with a little harmless flirting, I think as I close the door behind her. No one gets hurt over a casual flirt.

'So, this is where it all happens, eh? I've never been in here before. The infamous Intelligence Management Unit.'

She stares at the walls, and I jump in front of her before she can see the stiffy on the wall. No one should be allowed in the IMU without Victor's authorization, but the need to be in her company outweighs the rules.

She looks good in her uniform. I've never been attracted to any of the other female officers. A delicious first.

'Most officers haven't,' I reply, maintaining eye contact. 'What can I help you with?'

'My gaffer's sent me over to talk through the suicide.'

'We haven't had confirmation it was a suicide.'

'Oh, you know what I mean,' she adds with a flap of her hand.

Her hair gleams under the light. What does she use to make it so shiny? I want to touch it, to see if it feels real. As if it has a mind of its own, my hand jerks up before I come to my senses.

'I have everything I need in the witness statement you

submitted. I don't need any further information. The police might, but they'll contact you.'

She stares at me like she's waiting on me to say something else. I glance at the clock above her shoulder. Any second now, Jacob's keys will be thrust in the lock and the moment will be gone. But Molly doesn't seem to want to move, and neither do I. Does she feel it? The connection between us? Or am I projecting again?

'I lied about the suicide.'

'I'm sorry?'

'I just wanted to see you.' A cough. 'To make sure you're OK?'

'I'm fine,' I say, chewing on my bottom lip. Nothing's going to happen. Not here. Not at all. Not ever. But it's not good because, if I'm honest with myself, I want her to reach down and kiss me. I watch her lips as she talks. A flick of her pink tongue. I take a step closer.

'Good. Must be my phone then. Cos I never got any calls or messages yesterday.'

My cheeks inflame. 'Um.'

'It's OK. If you don't want contact with me, I'm a big girl. I was just expecting something, is all. A text telling me you got home safe would've opened communication between us,' she smirks.

This time, I can't look her in her eyes. Or I might lose myself in them.

'I thought I better come check you hadn't been in a horrible accident or something. I mean, we had a good time, didn't we?'

'I enjoyed it too.'

'Then why haven't you kissed me?'

My head snaps up. Her eyes are trained on mine. I swallow.

'Is it cos I said I didn't like Harry Potter?'

'What kind of person doesn't like Harry Potter?' I croak.

'I guess I like my books and films to be more . . . female driven. I thought you were the same.' Her grin widens. I take a step back.

'Don't you want to kiss me, Kennedy? That wasn't the signal I was getting from you on the other night.' She takes a step forward and I'm wedged against a filing cabinet. If she makes another move, we'll be touching. The smell of her watermelon perfume's already rendering me light-headed.

I nod, and she nods back, mirroring my body language. Half of me wants this to go further and the other half of me is silently screaming for Jacob's return.

'Do you fancy going out for a drink? I might not be from this area, but it doesn't mean I don't get lonely too. Plus, you owe me for going quiet on me. I couldn't sleep for worrying about you,' she jokes.

I open my mouth and close it again, trying to get my mind clear enough to think of a polite way to knock her back. But a fog's descended.

'Come on, babe. It's just a drink. I'm not asking for marriage. Not yet.' Another flash of her white teeth.

Keys jangle on the other side of the door, and I'm saved from answering. Someone's trying to get in. But who? Jacob or Victor?

'You have to go.' I grab her arm and shove her towards the door.

Molly frowns.

'It's Jacob or Victor,' is all I manage before Jacob appears, clutching some papers and two mugs.

'Hello,' he says, looking between us. 'I don't think we've met.' My face blazes as I look away.

'Molly's an officer in Hayworth. This is Jacob, my glamorous assistant.'

Jacob puts the items down on the filing cabinet to shake Molly's hand.

'Pleased to meet you,' they both say.

I can't breathe. These two parts of me existing at the same time. In the same place. It's too much.

'Excuse me,' I wheeze, pushing past both.

'You didn't answer my question,' Molly shouts.

'Yes,' I answer in a moment of weakness.

I scurry from the office and walk right into Victor.

'I need to talk to you,' he says, but I keep on walking.

'I need the toilet,' I shout over my shoulder, hoping he'll head back to his office rather than the IMU.

My face is cherry red when I walk into the ladies. I sprinkle water on my face, staying there until my armpits have dried.

But despite everything, I smile as I think about the way Molly asked me out. She wants to see me again. She likes me. And as much as I've tried to deny it to myself, I like her too. There's something different about her. Sincere. If anything, we might be able to become good friends. Anything else is a bonus.

'Time for a hot drink – what do you think?' says Jacob as he watches me yawn. I smile and he mirrors my yawn.

I have so much going on in my head, stuff I can't talk to Ellie about, that I'm considering confiding in Jacob. He's picking up the job quicker than I would have given him credit for. Maybe his impartial advice would be helpful.

'IMU, Kennedy speaking,' I answer when the phone rings.

'Hi, Kennedy. It's Erica at Forth Valley CID.'

At the other side of the office, Jacob juggles with the kettle, trying to get my attention.

'Away to fill it up,' he mouths. I nod and return to the call.

'How are you, Erica?'

'Not bad. Look, the reason I'm calling is to inform the prison there's a delay with the post-mortem.'

'How come?'

'To be brutally honest, a murder in the community's taken priority. They're dropping like flies out here.'

'I'm not surprised. It's not a power struggle linked to the different Serious and Organized Crime Groups, is it?'

'Put it this way. No great loss to society.'

'Say no more.'

'Can you let the relevant people know?'

'I'll go and inform the Governor personally.'

Erica chuckles before ending the call. She understands my disdain for the man in charge. She has the same thing at Police Scotland. A fact we'd bonded over when she'd been chosen as prison liaison.

The Governor's suite is brighter than the corridor. Motivational quotes line the blush-pink walls. The blinds surrounding his office are closed, but light filters through the slats.

Margo, the Governor's PA, is absent from her desk. I sigh as I scratch the back of my neck, enjoying the temporary heat from her electric radiator.

I peer through the window of his closed door. The Governor is staring at his desk. But that isn't what's caught my attention. Whispering into his ear, his arm around the Governor's shoulder, is Jacob.

'What the fuck?'

I continue snooping as the Governor stands and Jacob

envelops him in a hug. An intimate hug. Rubbing each other's back.

I march from the office as quick as I can, tripping over a rug in the process, stumbling out the door, hurrying away before they find the source of the noise and realize I've rumbled them.

Jacob and the Governor? The Governor and Jacob?

Rumours of the Governor's sexuality have circulated around the prison since he started. Not that it bothered me.

But I can't help but think – I'm right! This *is* how Jacob got the job. And Victor never let on. This place never changes. Fucking nepotism.

Are they lovers? Has the Governor deliberately put him in the IMU to spy on me? He's been looking for a reason to get rid of me for a while. I don't dance to his beat. And Jacob, pretending to be a friend ... What's been said? What's been reported back? I slate the Governor every time his name's mentioned.

The walk back to the IMU's conducted in a blur. Thoughts muddle in my head. Does Victor know? Is it an open secret among the senior managers?

I dislike Jacob as it is, without having to watch what I say in front of him too. Is he along there now, moaning about my swearing? Is that the type of guy he is? Good for him if he's in love, but don't be using it against people.

A friendly face appears in front of me and it's enough to calm my racing heart.

'I was just looking for you.'

'Oh no.'

'I have a few dates pencilled in for the intel meeting,' Tim says.

'Oh yeah? How's life in Hayworth?'

'Don't ask. Any news on the cause of death?'

'Another couple of days. There's been a delay,' I answer, distracted. 'Can you let the Governor know at wash-up?'

'I'm on my way to a meeting with him now.'

'I think he's in with someone.'

'I can wait.'

It takes all my resolve not to blurt it out. But it isn't my news to tell. And I don't like it when I'm the one being gossiped about.

I head back to the IMU, racking my brains for anything negative I might've said about the Governor in the few days since I have been back at work. I'd have had more respect for Jacob if he'd been honest from the start. At least then I'd have known I could trust him. It's now clear I can't. And working in this type of environment, trust is everything.

13. Adrian

'I have a message for you. From you know who.'

The screw steps into my gaff. I stay where I am on the bed. Bags of drugs rain down on the covers.

My jaw drops. But it's a sign that somebody, somewhere, is looking out for me. This package has got me out the shit. Temporarily.

'Scout intervened on your behalf. It's not fair we're all missing out because you can't be trusted. But Bar says this is your last chance. Fuck this up and you're out. Do you understand?'

'Aye. It wasn't my fault the last time.'

'It never is.'

We glare at each other. Neither of us wanting to be the first one to look away.

'You better be quick. The Bloodhound's been trying to get us to do cell spins all afternoon.' The tip-off isn't for my benefit. The screw will lose out too if this is found.

I can't afford to lose my stash to the Bloodhound. I'd played my last hand to get this in. If I fuck it up, I'm as good as dead.

'Hide it somewhere. I'll take care of that prick.'

But the screw doesn't move. I raise my eyebrows and watch as an item is removed from the heel of their boot.

'What the fuck is that?' I take it from their outstretched hand.

'A tool.'

'How much did Bar pay you to smuggle that in?' I

grimace. The blade of the knife is around five inches long and is sheathed in black ceramic. It won't set off the metal detector. I automatically think about how much I could sell it for, but that's not why it's been smuggled in. 'Let me guess. For Filan?'

Gold eyes glint. A hint of a smile appears. I know it is, so I almost don't notice the silence. But when I look again, I get a nod of acknowledgement.

'Of course. To start with.'

We share a knowing smirk.

'Make sure there's no prints on it.'

'Hide it with the rest. For now.'

The screw goes to pick up the stash. 'Leave me some,' I say. 'I have orders out.'

As soon as I'm alone, I take the towel I stole earlier and rip it up into long strips, tying each strip to another until the line is long enough. I pull the ends to make sure it's tight and won't disintegrate.

The Bic razor blade glints as I remove the fingers from nitrile gloves, stuffing 0.2 grams of coke and pollen into each finger. Once the drugs are secured to the line, I shout out to Spence.

'You ready, Spence bro? Santa's been early.'

'Aye, man. Swing it,' he says, the relief palpable.

I carefully put the line out of the window and pass the drugs to the gaff next to me, swinging the line until Spence grabs it. He'll have his own line and distribute the product down into cells on levels two and one.

As soon as they hear the window lines in operation, the cons start begging me to give them tick.

'I'll give you a shot of my phone credit if you give me a gram,' shouts someone on level two.

I don't answer. Spence's my main guy. He sorts out all

the deals. But it might be useful to make a call using someone else's PIN. I need to speak to Uncle Bar. Find out where I stand with him. Explain things to him properly.

I miscalculate and still have a couple grams left over. Having product in my gaff gives me a different kind of anxiety. But an idea forms by the time the screws unlock for dinner.

I swagger out of my gaff and nod at the others. Spence is behind the hotplate dishing out the food. The person I'm searching for is looking weary at the end of the dinner queue. I stride over.

'All right, Kyle McGregor the hotplate beggar?'

Kyle peers up at me through his greasy fringe.

It's difficult for me not to recoil in horror. For, in fact, Kyle is a stink bomb. It's up to the cons when they shower. If they shower. The screws are powerless to put someone on report for being a tramp. They can only put us on report for refusing an order, and some of the screws can't be arsed filling out the paperwork. Instead, they stay away from him. Like most of us do.

At first, it occurs to me to hide the stash in Kyle's gaff. But I have the same problem with him that I have with Rampage and Flakes. The guy from the other night. Fucking junkies.

'How are you?' I ask, remembering to breathe out of my mouth.

'Are you talking to me?' he stutters.

I try not to stare at the open wound on the corner of his mouth. It's easy to refer yourself to the health centre. I can't understand why the wee guy willingly walks around with a blood-festered crater on his mouth. Fuck being an addict. Luckily, the only thing I'm addicted to is making paper.

'Yeah, I'm talking to you. Just seeing how your day's going.'

Kyle crosses skinny arms over his skinny body. Injection marks have scabbed over. A tremor to his demeanour. Sweaty face. Dark circles under his eyes. Kyle's in withdrawal.

'When's the last time you had a hit?'

Kyle's eyebrows droop so low they cover his eyes.

'What the fuck's that got to do with you?' He'd have more conviction if he didn't look so terrified.

'Because I might be able to help you.'

We take a step towards the servery.

'We might be able to help each other out,' I add.

Kyle chews on his bottom lip. 'I'm not gay.'

'Neither the fuck am I,' I say, fighting the urge to clip him over the head.

'I'm just saying. Folk have promised me shit in here before, but they just wanted me to suck their dicks.'

'Too much information.' I grimace, holding my hand up to shield myself from his words.

'What do you want to eat?'

'Do junkies eat?' Spence says. 'That's news to me.'

'Be nice to my new friend, Spence.' I wink over Kyle's head to show there's a game in play.

'You want extra, my man?' Spence says.

Kyle's face pales. Doesn't know what to say. In fear he's being led to a beating. He licks at his crusty lips, fresh blood beads through the scab and I know I won't eat now. The wee jobby's ruined my appetite.

'Just a plate of chips,' he murmurs, looking everywhere other than at the two men being unusually nice to him.

'Give him double,' I command. Kyle's eyes widen as Spence scoops up more chips and dumps them on his plate.

'There ya go.'

I grab my own plate of food and steer Kyle to an empty table.

'Sit down with me.'

There's no way I'm going to eat with the stench that's coming off Kyle. It's like he's took a dump and hasn't bothered to wipe his arse. The smell of shit soaks the air around him. The tramp must be nose blind.

'Eat,' I urge. 'We'll talk when you're finished.'

Kyle picks up a chip and nibbles the end. 'You know, I'm not hungry. Do you want my chips?'

I strain to hear him over the noise in the hall. Cutlery clanking off plates. Carry on. The heavy murmur of conversations.

'No.' He might've only touched one, but he's tainted the rest. 'You must be able to manage more than half a chip.'

'Look, what do you want? I don't feel too good.'

I drop my plastic fork on to my plastic plate. 'I can make you feel better. You understand what I'm saying?'

Kyle's eyes widen again, finally getting the message. 'What do you need, and how soon can I get paid?'

'Well, see, that's the problem. The favour I need is the kind that'll get you dragged to the digger immediately. Understand?'

Kyle gulps. Then nods. He's at the withdrawal stage now where he won't turn down much to get his precious drugs. He can't.

'How am I going to pay you if you get carted right away?'

'You can give me the stuff first.'

The wee cunt doesn't even care what needs to be done. It's a shame he can't take care of himself better. We could've been friends.

'No offence, mate. But I don't trust junkies. You'll take the hit and be useless to me. And then we'll both have a new problem.'

He scratches his nose, his ear and back to his nose again. He wants the conversation to be over. The hint of a hit is all he can think about.

'I promise I won't take it until I've done what you need. Please. I'll do anything.' He wrenches on the chair as a spasm of pain and craving takes over.

I suppress a smile. 'You promise me?'

Kyle nods. It's going to be easier than I think. At that moment, Officer Cunto walks past.

'I want the Bloodhound done. He has to be out of action for a few days. Can you handle that?'

It's not possible for Kyle's face to get any paler. 'You want me to assault a screw?'

'You do catch on quick, don't you?'

'I'm not much of a fighter,' he whispers, scared to be overheard by the intended target, who's looking over at us and scowling.

It'll raise a red flag, that I've been sitting beside Kyle right before he commits the assault, but they won't be able to prove anything.

'One more thing. You can't tell anybody about this conversation. When they ask what we're talking about, tell them a lie. Tell them you're chasing a pal's act. Trying to pay for protection – I don't give a fuck, just don't mention my name.'

Tears well in his eyes. He's the kind of idiot who likes the screws because they leave him alone. Keep him safe.

Kyle scratches at skin that only itches inside his head. It's going to fuck everything up for him, but the drugs mean more to him. Haven't they always?

'There's more Bobby Brown there if you keep me sweet.' But he can't hear me. The brown is calling.

I retrieve the small tenner bag of brown from my hiding place and disappear it up my sleeve. My gut telling me to be careful. At any time, Security could burst into the hall and spin our gaffs. Any minute now, I could lose. No one tells you being a successful drug dealer is a fucking headache.

Kyle shivers outside his room. Pathetic.

'Have you got it?' His nostrils flare like he's trying to sniff it out. He's learned not to trust anyone, like most in here.

'Yeah, but you're not to take it, mind. Not until you're in the digger.'

I flash the small baggy at him. Tears wet his lashes. He wants to beg.

'You'll get another bag in a month when you come back to the hall. Extra for every week that fuckwit's off his work.'

If they ghost him to another prison, it's not my problem.

He reaches out a tentative hand, but I keep the heroin out of reach. This is getting too suspicious. The Intel mob will check the cameras to see what led Kyle to commit the assault.

'Bank it.'

Kyle continues to shiver like he's glowing.

He lifts an arse cheek and wiggles. Sticks them up his arse with God knows what else to enjoy in the digger.

Kyle stumbles from the table. Looks around. Finds his target. Almost like the screw smells out the impending trouble, he strides over.

'What are you doing in there?' he demands, loud enough to be heard over the clinking of the pool balls and the mumble of conversation from other prisoners.

No one's paying attention to Kyle. No one ever did. He visibly vibrates as he takes a step towards the screw.

'If you don't answer me, you smelly wee pikey bastard, I'll put you on report.'

In one fluid movement, Kyle punches the screw right on the side of the face. The Bloodhound goes down and it's goodnight from him.

The hall goes quiet as everyone digests what's just happened. Kyle jumps on the screw and begins kicking and punching, but the Bloodhound can't feel a thing. His eyes roll to the back of his head.

The prisoners begin whooping and chanting, drawing the attention of other screws. Watch on in frozen fascination as the screws attempt to pull Kyle from the Bloodhound's body. His white shirt drenched in fresh blood.

Kyle screams like a madman as the screws pile on top of him, trying to gain control of his body.

'I'm not a fucking pikey.'

Another screw radios for a nurse. 'Code red. Code red. Hayworth level three,' he squawks.

A screw takes the Bloodhound's pulse. The relief on his face palpable. Shit. The bastard's not dead. Multiple white shirts hurtle into the wing, following the sound of the alarm. At the front is the hall manager. Paedo Clive.

'Show's over, folks,' says Paedo Clive as they begin shepherding the herd back to their gaffs. Rec is over five minutes early, pissing everyone off, despite the fact they've enjoyed decent entertainment. They all wish they'd been the one to put him on his arse. To make him bleed.

'That Kyle's mad,' someone cackles.

'He done more than you,' someone shouts back.

Some cons are refusing to return to their gaffs. Demanding the five minutes they're owed. More officers are requested over the radio. 'Trouble in Hayworth three,' commands a screw. If the screws aren't careful, there'll be worse than a fight. We're on the cusp of a riot.

I caused this, I want to roar. Let everyone know I'm the top dog. I run the hall. This is my camp.

The weaker ones are restrained first. Rampage grabs some pool balls and sticks them down his boxers. More screws arrive. More cons are restrained. 'You'll get an extra five minutes tomorrow,' pleads Clive, the workshy bastard.

The nurses arrive, heads down as they hurry over to the Bloodhound.

Some begin to return to their rooms without the use of force on arrival of the gym personal training instructors. They aren't like the normal screws, even though they are. But they're sound about it. You can have a laugh with them. You don't want to piss off the PTIs or you'd find yourself on the wrong end of a gym ban. And for a lot of us in here, the routine and structure of the gym is the only positive thing we've got going for us.

It's only me and Rampage left. We've lost Flakes in the confusion and Spence was one of the first to return to his gaff. Chicken head.

'Are we doing this?' I shout over to Rampage.

'Back to back, brother.'

'Let's fucking have it.'

Ray McCredie's in my face. 'Reedy weedy McCredie,' I spit. Normally we can tolerate him, but this is an 'us versus them' situation.

'I thought you enjoyed being out on the pass, eh?' he says, trying to get me to see sense. 'I done you a favour and this is how you pay me back? Go back to your room, Maddox.'

But the madness is in me. Went too far. I was supposed

to stay in the shadows while McGregor took out the Bloodhound. I'd never been one to stop and consider the consequences.

'Weeeed. Weeeeeeed.'

'Return to your room and we'll forget all about this.'

I look over his shoulder. The Bloodhound's receiving medical treatment on the ground and five screws are lying on top of Kyle. I hope they like the smell. They can't move him until me and Rampage are secured back in our gaffs.

Five screws pounce on Rampage and, for him, its game over. Yet only Reedy McCredie is trying to talk me down. Don't they think I need five screws too? Do they think I'll take this?

The cons that've been put behind their doors bang and kick them. Whatever they're shouting is lost in a cacophony of beautiful noise.

As soon as the screws go to put hands on me I dart over to the other side of the hall.

'I want to make sure he's OK,' I lie, darting away as soon as anyone comes close.

As soon as the hall's locked up, the prisoners continue kicking their doors, making the noise almost unbearable. I jump up on to the pool table and kick the balls around. It's important I don't hurt anyone. For my plan to work. And I don't want a civvie charge from the police.

The lads will make sure the word goes out that this is all on me. No one will grass. I'll be cemented in as the rightful leader. And where's Filan? Stayed behind his door, the shitebag.

'Come down and I won't put you on report,' Paedo Clive says. I stay where I am, watching the nurse run towards another screw with her first-aid bag. Rampage didn't go quietly.

'Come down before we drag you down,' says another screw menacingly. I jump down and they descend on me, putting me in holds and dragging me to my gaff.

'Make sure he's put on report,' Paedo Clive says.

'But—' I protest. He smiles at me.

'I said *I* wouldn't put you on report. I never said anything about anyone else.'

'You're a fucking prick.'

But he just smiles at me as I'm pushed into the gaff. I stop resisting in the hope they'll leave me alone. If they decide to fuck me up by spinning me, I'm fucked. I've taken it too far. I always do.

The door slams behind me and I rub at my red wrists. The cunts were more forceful than the situation required.

Later, my personal officer presents me with my report. And like a good little boy, I sign it. The nurse checks my wrists and issues me with an ice pack for the swelling.

'I need you to do something for me,' I say as I hand back the signed paperwork.

'If you want me to get rid of this report for you, then forget it. Everyone saw what you did. Haven't I already warned you about being fucking stupid? Drawing attention to yourself?'

'I don't mean the report.' Instead, I nod my head in the direction of the table.

'I need you to put that with the rest.'

The threat of gaff spins isn't gone because they've phoned an ambulance for the Bloodhound. There's still a risk I can get done. Especially when the CCTV's checked.

With a sigh, the screw scoops up the remaining stash.

'Now. Fuck off.'

Restricted: Confidential

HMP Forth Valley
5 x 5 Intelligence Report

REPORTING PERSON: (Person receiving the information from the source)	Clive Clifford	PAY REF NO: u19079
SOURCE NAME: (Person providing the information)	Kai Spencer	
PROVENANCE OF INFORMATION:	1. How did you come by this information? Witnessed it. 2. Where the source is a prisoner, what's their motivation for passing this on to officers? Fear for safety for himself and others. 3. Who else knows this information? Unknown. 4. As a result of this information, do you feel at risk? Yes.	

DATE & TIME OF REPORT:	Tuesday, 9 October 2018 @ 18:52 hours				
SUBJECT OF REPORT:	Weapon				
SOURCE EVALUATION	**A** Always reliable	**B** Mostly reliable	**C** Sometimes reliable	**D** Unreliable	**E** Untested source
INTELLIGENCE EVALUATION	1 Known to be true without reservation	2 Known personally to the source but not to the officer	3 Not known personally to the source, but corroborated	4 Cannot be judged	5 Suspected to be false

Reporting Person's Evaluation

Source Evaluation	C
Intelligence Evaluation	2

Intelligence:

The above prisoner has confided that there's a knife located somewhere in Hayworth level three. He might give good intel in exchange for a move to the top end?

14. Kennedy

I'm watching the CCTV footage from last night when Victor appears.

At first, I don't notice he's holding something in his hand. He takes a seat at the meeting table.

'Come and see this.'

I switch off the monitor and give Victor my full attention.

A clear sharps tube is on the middle of the table among other production bags.

'We got it?' I ask. Jacob remains focused on his own work.

'Yes.' A lockdown search had been organized for first thing. The intel about a knife being present in the hall too significant to wait. Especially with the way the violence was going in Hayworth.

Choosing the sharps tube first, I hold it up into the light.

It isn't like any knife you'd find in the establishment. Not even the cook house has a knife that big. Or sharp.

Scout says goodnight. I shudder at the memory.

In five years' service, I've never recovered such a significant weapon. Does it belong to Scout? In that moment, I know the knife was for me. I'm still at risk, despite the police not being able to corroborate any intelligence.

My fingers tremble as I take a closer look. I can't shake the feeling that I've just saved my own life. A knife inside is meant for someone's ribs. Heart. Throat.

'It was found in the loft space when Maria in Security

was replacing the mobile phone detectors. Along with some heroin, valium and cannabis. Lucky,' he adds.

I quickly do the maths. The haul of drugs has a prison value of £1,600. Someone's going to be pissed. I roll the tube around in my hand. The blade's about five inches long. Serrated.

'Someone is going to be upset they've lost their stuff,' I say.

Victor agrees. But I can't help but feel upset that this amount of drugs, the knife, has come into the prison without me being aware of it. Only a member of staff could've left the articles up there. And it's my job to find out who, and about all the other subversive activity that's going on.

Whoever Scout is – he's good. Because it has to be linked to Scout, right?

A hundred different scenarios fill my head, and I meticulously discount them. Victor sits quietly drinking his coffee. This isn't the biggest find of his career, but it's the biggest find of mine. I fidget with the sharps tube, tapping it against the table. Another clue, I think. Another step forward to identifying Scout.

'What are you thinking?' I eventually ask. And thankfully, this time we're on the same page.

'Is this the work of Scout?'

I let out a deep sigh. *Scout.* He believes me. I'm still at risk. I press the palm of my hand against my stinging eyes. 'Do you think the knife was for me?'

'It's possible. Kennedy, I don't want you going anywhere on your own. Stay in the IMU. Don't leave without an escort.'

'I can meet you in the car park in the morning. Chum you in,' Jacob offers. Victor nods. 'That's a good idea,

Jacob. Chum her out, too,' he adds, like I'm not sitting there.

I can't help but feel like I'm the one being punished here.

He turns to me. 'I'll phone my contact in the police. Pass this on. Tell them they have to act on it this time. Get them to put a flag on your home address. Your registration number.'

'Ellie drives the car too. Should I warn her?'

'Yes. You have to let her know what's been going on. Considering what happened before, we have to take these threats seriously. If 999 is called from your house, the police will treat it as a priority. Take a different route home if you can. If you think someone is following you from the staff car park, drive straight to the nearest police station.'

'Fuck, Victor. I thought I was being paranoid. You've made me feel worse.'

'Do you want to go home? I can sign you off on compassionate leave.'

'No, I think I'll be safer here. But I need to speak to Ellie.'

It's not just my safety I'm worried about now. The threat from Scout is real.

'Who's your money on? I can think of a few names,' I add, eyebrow raised, trying to defuse the tension.

'You can't make the intelligence fit the people you don't like, Kennedy. We have to let the intel guide us. No one is safe from our scrutiny. Not until we can develop the intelligence further. Rule people out. Until then, everyone is a suspect.'

'Do you want this reported to police?'

'Yes. We have a rogue member of staff. No one else can access the loft space. We need all the help we can get.

Security has taken pictures. I'll make sure they send you copies. Everything up there was covered in dust, bar the illicit articles. They haven't been up there long.'

'CCTV?'

Victor shakes his head. 'There're no cameras at the stairwell up to the access space. And the stairwell to the space is accessed by the staff room in every wing of the hall.'

My head drops. There's no CCTV in the staff rooms either. In other words, it *could* be anybody.

'What about fingerprints? In the dust?'

'I'm thinking the perpetrator would've worn gloves,' Victor adds. Nitrile gloves are accessible from every part of the prison. Officers need to be able to grab a pair at short notice. For touching bodily fluids. For area searches. To help preserve a crime scene. But what if the perp had a short time to access the loft space and wearing gloves hadn't entered their mind?

'I've done some investigating with the Estates team.'

My head snaps up.

'Apparently, anybody who draws a set of keys can access the loft space.'

'You're kidding?'

'Nope. Although' – he looks at his watch – 'that should be rectified as we speak.'

Not all puzzles are solved, but I'm determined to get to the bottom of this one.

'We have to catch this dirty bastard,' I spit.

'Estates are pulling off a list of every key bunch that's accessed the loft space over the last two weeks. It's the only way we can try to narrow it down.'

'When will the report be ready?'

'Well, I emphasized the importance as much as I could.

147

I delicately pointed out there might be a dirty Estates worker.'

Could it really be someone from Estates? After all, they're the only people who have a justified reason for being in there. I don't have many dealings with the group, other than when they annually test the electric and the smoke detectors. I wouldn't recognize one of them if they came after me out of their blue coveralls.

'So,' Victor says, 'if anybody asks you about a big find in the loft space . . .'

'Play dumb?'

'Exactly. I know that'll be easy for you.'

'Ha. Funny.'

He slurps the rest of his coffee. 'Anything else happening I should know?'

He stares into my eyes and, for a scary moment, I think he knows about me and Molly. But that's silly. There is no me and Molly.

'No, I'm working on this 12 chart for Fred Filan. Bit pointless though, since he's been moved to the hall without them knowing all the information.'

'You don't make the decisions, remember. You only provide the information.'

'That's my point, though. They didn't bother to wait for the information. That Crawford Docherty needs to be told. He can't make decisions when it's not his area.'

'It was Tim, actually. He deemed he wasn't at risk and decided to take him up on the threes. Plus, we needed to create a space in the Seg unit after the riot at exercise.'

'Oh.' Victor's words suck all the air from my body. I hate it when it isn't Crawford Docherty.

'I haven't heard much about the night out on Saturday. You went though, eh?'

I stutter, words failing me. In the end, I nod. Unable to trust myself to speak.

'There's nothing to tell. I only stayed for a couple of drinks and then left. I'm not really interested in anything that happened afterwards, to be honest with you.'

'Wasn't there a scuffle?'

'That must've been after I left,' I lie. It'd completely left my mind.

'I'm waiting for someone to put it in writing for me. Apparently, someone filmed it and it's being shared online. If that's the case, we may be looking at a suspension.'

'I'll let you know right away if anything comes into me.'

'OK.' Victor drains his mug. Sighs. 'The security officers have been told to carry out hourly perimeter checks over the next few days. And I'll task the nightshift officers to keep an ear out too.'

'We have to highlight the rise in violence, Victor. The senior managers need to listen to us if we're recommending transfers and time in segregation.'

'Leave it with me.' Victor looks towards the door. 'I better go – I need to brief the Boss on this find. I don't want him hearing about it from someone else.'

I flick my eyes over to Jacob, who appears engrossed in a report. I want to speak to Victor in private about him, but I don't want to come across as a bitch.

'Can you trust him to keep it quiet?' I say, observing Jacob to gauge his reaction.

'I have to tell him, Kennedy. He's the Governor. It's his ball, remember. We all play to his rules.' He leaves his dirty mug by the kettle and picks up the productions to take with him to show the Governor.

'Before you go, is there an update on Darren North?'

'He was kept in overnight for observation. Bad

concussion. But he was discharged. They won't know if his nose is broken until the swelling goes down.'

I close my eyes against the flashbacks. I know first hand about broken noses. The bump in my own nose vibrates in sympathy.

He steps closer. Lowers his voice. 'Are you sure you don't want me to sign you off until all this is resolved?'

I shake my head.

'No one will think any less of you, Kennedy.'

'There're cameras here,' I say, teeth clenched. 'And I have my babysitter,' I add, jerking my head at Jacob. 'I'll be fine.'

But neither of us believes it.

'That sounds exciting,' Jacob says, without looking up from his monitor.

I expect him to ask a hundred questions, but he continues to stare at his computer screen. His fingers no longer working.

'Not really.' I reel at his insensitivity.

'But . . . the . . .'

'Maybe if you were the one being targeted, you wouldn't find it so exciting.'

15. Kennedy

Since you don't have the balls to message first, I'll be the bigger person ;) How are you. Up to anything exciting? xx

When the message flashes up on my iPhone, I nearly fall off my seat.

'Is everything OK? Is it about the knife find?'

Ellie and I couldn't be arsed to cook. The message comes through while we're waiting on our Chinese to come.

'Um, yeah. It's work,' I lie.

I switch my phone off and go for a shower so I don't seem too keen by replying eagerly. What even is the relationship etiquette these days?

I stay under the spray of hot water, mentally composing witty responses in my head. As soon as I wrap a towel around my body, my phone's in my hands and I'm typing back.

Hey you. Just had the most amazing shower. Had you on my mind the whole time . . . x

I squeeze my eyes shut as I hit send. It's more forward than I'm used to, but I know it's what a girl like Molly expects. The phone makes its swoosh sound and it's too late to take back. My insides squirm. Is it too far?

Her response is immediate. She's not the type to play games.

Meet me for dinner tomorrow. My treat. I can't stop thinking about you xx

When the Chinese comes, I've lost my appetite.

After the first couple of messages, I don't care about appearing too keen. For she's making all the moves.

'Just work, yeah?' Ellie scoffs, but I ignore her. I'm too busy giggling at my phone. She makes a point of banging about in the kitchen, throwing the dishes into the sink. But all I can focus on is Molly. Everything else diminishes around me.

My hands are curled into a numb claw. We've been texting for hours.

I have to go to sleep. I'm up in five hours for my early shift xx

I check the time. Rub my eyes. Tiredness has been chased away by her. I haven't thought about Scout, or knives, for hours.

I keep thinking of the way she asked me if I wanted to kiss her. How her words hit me deep in my core. And how I wish I had been brave enough to accept.

I feel like a dick when Ellie offers to drive me into town the next night, but it doesn't stop me accepting. She knows I'm going out on a date, but it's not serious enough for me to give her any other details.

'Are you sure it's safe for you to go out?' she asks when we climb into the car. 'You still don't know who has it in for you.'

'A few different people have it in for me,' I confess. 'It's a consequence of the job. We're getting closer, though.'

I'm touched at her concern, but my need to spend time with Molly outweighs the concerns for my safety.

'I'm not convinced going out for food is a good idea,' she sniffs, and I can't tell if it's genuine concern or jealousy that I'm not on a date with her.

'It's a busy restaurant. I'll get an Uber home.'

'It was a busy supermarket.'

I swallow.

'Sorry, but I'm worried about you,' she goes on. 'I've

half convinced myself to wait in the car until you're ready to come home.'

'Thanks, love. But that's not necessary.'

'You could've invited her to the flat. I would've made myself scarce.'

'It's a bit soon for that, Ells. But I appreciate the offer.'

She drops me off as close to the front door as she can. I wait there, under the CCTV and the security lights, until she drives off. I don't want her waiting outside in the car, but I couldn't tell if she was serious or not.

Once the car disappears, I let myself into the restaurant, rubbing my hands against the cold.

Molly's waiting at the table, scrolling through her phone. I take a moment to drink her in before I hurry over.

'Sorry I'm late. Traffic.'

'Hey, babe, you look stunning.' She stands to kiss me on the cheek. Her lips linger. She must be able to hear my heart.

The restaurant she's chosen is quiet, with only a few other couples whispering over candlelit tables.

'I got you something,' she says after we've ordered. She places a wrapped box on the table.

'Go on. Open it.'

Her smile is wide as I pull the box closer to me. Curiosity superseding any manners, I pull at the pink bow and carefully lift the lid of the box. The smell of pomegranate overpowers the chicken curry on the table to my right.

'Oh, wow. You shouldn't have,' I say as I gently place the candle next to my dessert spoon.

She really shouldn't. This was too expensive for a first date. Should I have brought her a gift? I make a mental note to google the price later so I know what I should spend in future. Or am I being paranoid again? Could she have regifted this to me? But still. My face heats up at the shame.

'Don't be silly. I wanted to get you something nice.'

'Thank you.' I squirm under her scrutiny. Would she expect the same gesture? Christmas was on the horizon so I'd soon have to start saving for that. The price of the Jo Malone candle was about my budget for Ellie, far less having to spend the same or more on Molly.

'You're welcome, babe. When you light it, I want you to think of me.'

Light it? It was too expensive to ever light.

'And when I light mine, I'll think of you.'

Her forwardness throws me. She reaches over, stroking my arm. 'You really are beautiful, and you deserve beautiful things.'

I swallow. I'm saved from answering by the arrival of our food. I'm nervous to eat in front of her and pick at my food instead. She doesn't have the same bother as she spoons mushroom risotto into her mouth.

'Do you know him?'

'I'm sorry?'

'That guy over there. The *Peaky Blinders* reject. I think he's trying to get your attention.'

Scanning over where she means, I spot him immediately. Wearing a brown shirt, braces around his shoulders and a familiar tweed flat cap. It takes a moment to place him, for I know I've seen him before. Recently. He was in the bar the other night. I frown. Turn round to my girl.

'No. I don't know him.' I swallow. My senses on alert. Has he come here to target me? Should I ask to leave? Go somewhere else?

She looks at me funny, like she thinks I might be lying. It kills whatever mood was between us.

'He's staring at you.' A shrug. 'Not that I blame him. I can hardly keep my eyes off you either.'

The thought of his presence cowers after her words. There's no denying it. The way she stares at me makes me forget how to breathe. My heart pummels. My head is hot and light.

'You'll jump in if he tries anything.' I play it off as a joke, but she merely nods. Takes a drink. Maintains eye contact, which I'm the first to break.

We order more drinks when our plates are taken away. 'Tell me about yourself,' she says, and my mind goes blank.

'Like what?'

'I don't care. I want to know everything about you.'

'That's a lot of information.' I beam. 'Be more specific.'

'When's the last time you had sex?'

'What?'

'It's OK. I won't judge.'

I scratch the back of my neck. 'Um . . .'

She cackles. 'Are you blushing?'

'Yes.' Because I can't be anything other than truthful.

'Have you always wanted to work for the Prison Service?'

I'm relieved and disappointed in equal measure with her change in direction. But it's better to be on safer ground.

She plays with the ends of her hair while she waits on my answer.

'No.'

'Really?'

'Yeah. It's a long story.'

'We have time.'

I look down at my glass of wine. 'That's a third-date kind of question.'

'If you wanted to talk about sex, you just had to say,' she smirks, and I stop myself from grabbing her face. Kissing her.

Her forwardness is alluring. She picks up her own drink and downs the dregs of her Southern Comfort.

'OK,' she says. 'Tell me about your parents.'

'Ugh. That's a third-date question too.'

'You already see us on a third date? That's reassuring. Look at you blush.'

I giggle then cringe.

'I don't speak to my parents,' I say. 'They're homophobes. Kicked me out when I was fifteen.'

'Oh my God, that's disgusting.'

'Yep.'

'What did you do?'

'I moved in with my girlfriend, Ellie, and her parents.' Parents who'd always been the complete opposite of mine.

'I'm sorry I brought it up. That must be painful for you.' Her eyes shine in a way that makes me think she's about to cry.

'It was. But I don't think about it any more.'

She clucks in sympathy.

'Actually. That's a lie.' There's something about her that wants me to open up about everything. Good or bad.

'I do think about them. Christmas. Their birthdays. My birthday. But they made their choice, and it makes my heart ache, even ten years later. That they chose their own ignorance over their own daughter.'

'No wonder you don't want kids.'

'They don't deserve grandkids. Children don't deserve them. Anyway, please tell me a nicer story about your parents. Please.'

'My dad,' she begins, using her fingers for inverted

commas, 'put the boot down and boosted when mum was pregnant with me. He didn't want to know. But when I was five, she met a wonderful man who's more of a dad to me than the one I've never met. They're the best and I'm very lucky.'

She plays with a scrap of food that has escaped from her plate. 'I'd do anything for him, my dad. He literally saved Mum's life.'

My eyes smart, and I quickly wipe a finger under my eye. 'Is your stepdad a friend of Bruce's? I think he told me they play golf together.'

She nods before changing the subject.

'Shall we get the bill?' she says as she waves for the waitress.

'Sure. Jeez, this got a little emotional, huh,' I joke.

She pays with her credit card.

'Are you ready, my love?'

I nod. 'Do you want to go elsewhere. For a drink?'

'Nah. Sorry. I'm on early shift tomorrow.' She pulls a face. 'Need to get home for my beauty sleep.'

I pull on my coat. Mask my disappointment. Have I done the wrong thing? Been too reserved?

'Thanks, guys,' shouts the waitress as we head for the exit. No wonder. Molly left a healthy tip.

We step out into the crisp night. I zip my coat as she starts to speak.

'I'm sorry,' she whispers. 'I have to kiss you, or I might die.'

My mouth doesn't open in preparation for the caress of her lips but at the shock of her words.

She takes it as a sign of consent, and we kiss. I clutch at her shoulders. The kiss deepens. All thoughts vanish. My grip loosens; I rest against her chest. Bubbles fizz and pop in my head. Fireworks.

The kiss I've fantasized about for a long time is finally happening. I'm kissing Molly. She's kissing me back.

I'm the first to pull away, to maintain control of the situation. Then we're kissing again and my mind goes blank. Her hands stroke my face; I run my fingers through her hair.

I can't think of anything. Or anywhere else I'd rather be. To think I nearly gave up on this. That I almost let my insecurities win. I didn't, and this is my reward.

We break free. Both panting. Wanting more. Time's stopped. My head's scrambled. My heart wrenches.

'Are you OK?'

Incapable of speech, I nod.

'I feel like I should apologize,' she adds. 'I've thought about kissing you every minute since the other night.'

My heart darts over to the right side of my chest before returning. The movement sudden. My legs flop.

'That's OK,' I stammer.

'Is this OK?' She reaches over and kisses my cheek. My nose. My eye.

I can't breathe with want. Anyone can see us, and I don't care. She pushes me against the brick wall. My coat soaks up the earlier raindrops. It cools me down.

Her cold fingers caress my neck, my legs melt. She could ask anything of me in this moment and I'd agree.

The taxi pulls up beside us, the driver tooting its horn. 'Time to go,' she pouts. She opens the car door for me and I climb inside.

'Actually, mate, can you do two drop-offs?'

I swallow my disappointment. I'm not the type to go home with someone the first night, but Molly makes me feel things I've never experienced with anyone else.

'As long as you have the money.'

She winks at me and scrambles inside, grabbing my hand and squeezing.

'Don't you live the opposite side of town from me?'

'I don't care. If it means I get to spend another ten minutes in your company.'

I give the driver my address. She doesn't try anything on other than a simple caress of my hand. Our legs press together.

'Can I see you tomorrow?' Molly asks as I get out.

'I'll message you,' I say, kissing her goodbye.

Only when the lights of the taxi disappear do I let myself into the flat.

'How was it then?'

It takes a minute to compose myself. I can't let Ellie see me this happy.

'It was' – *magical* – 'good.'

Ellie licks her lips. 'Are you seeing her again?'

'Maybe,' I say, aiming for nonchalance. The thought of Molly changing her mind is not one my brain can process.

The half-bottle of wine grabs my attention. I pick it up while contemplating whether there's enough to dirty a glass or to stick in a straw. I'm deliberating when Ellie speaks again, determined not to let the subject drop.

'When do I get to meet her?'

I bite down my anger. She introduced me to Kym on their fifth date, against my desire. Kym, who had a toddler son I'd somehow still managed to avoid meeting.

'I'm just looking out for you, Kennedy. I don't want to see you get hurt.'

I bang the bottle of wine down on the kitchen counter. 'I'm a big girl, mate. And it's not as if I haven't already got the experience.' I stare at her until she retreats to her own room.

I take the wine to my single bed, but there's no point in trying to sleep. I'm staring at the ceiling when a shadow flits past outside my bedroom window.

I jolt up. Switch on the bedside lamp. My bedroom window looks on to the small piece of land we were mistakenly sold as a garden. Beyond that, it's fields. I slide out of bed, heart racing. But when I get to the window there's nothing out there in the dark.

By morning, my subconscious has explained it away. But I kept the light on for the rest of the night.

16. Kennedy

My eyes are gritty from lack of sleep, and I can't focus on my screen. It must have been a bird, I think. A wing. Not a person watching from the dark. My body is screaming out for sleep, but I'm only two hours into an eight-hour shift.

The only time I felt safe last night was the time I was with Molly. I phone the flat, my anxiety increasing with each unanswered ring.

I'm about to hang up when Ellie answers, sounding breathless.

'Is the front door locked?' I ask.

'I think so.'

'Please go and check.'

'I'm trying to clean the bathroom.'

'Please.'

My breathing exercises come in handy until she returns to the phone. 'It's locked.'

'Good. Keep it that way.'

I hang up before she can speak then phone back five seconds later.

'What?' she answers.

'The windows.'

'Babes, we've lived here for years without ever opening the windows. You know I don't like beasties to get in.'

'OK. Thank you,' I say before gently replacing the receiver.

Sensing this might be his chance, Jacob attacks with the question he's been too scared to ask me for the last hour.

'Can I ask you a question about this incident?'

'Of course.'

He gets up and hands me the report. 'It's the prisoner-on-staff assault from the other night. I'm updating the confirmed injuries on the system, but I don't know if I need to record another prisoner's involvement.'

I take the report from him and scan the details. Details I'd only skimmed over so far. Kyle McGregor attacked Officer Darren 'Bloodhound' North seemingly out of the blue. I discard the details regarding medical intervention and use of restraint.

'Adrian Maddox was seen deep in a hushed conversation with the perp before the assault. Should I link him to the incident? That's my question.'

I read on. Adrian Maddox and Caleb Dyer were also restrained due to their behaviour. Pool balls missing from the table were found down Dyer's boxers after a strip search.

'Let's double-check with the CCTV,' I say.

It takes a moment for the system to boot up, but it gives me the chance to show Jacob how it works. Selecting the date, time and area, we press play.

'That's interesting,' I say.

'How so?'

I point at Adrian Maddox on the monitor. Confer with his picture on the system to make sure it's definitely him.

'Look at the interactions here. Tell me what you see.'

I give Jacob a few moments to gather his thoughts.

'He's talking to him. It's suspicious?'

'Exactly. Do you see McGregor's face? He's wary of him.'

'Yes.' Jacob peers closer to the screen. 'Wait a minute . . .'

He leaves me hanging as he rewinds the footage.

'There. Do you see it?'

'Slow the footage down,' I command. And then I see it.

Right before McGregor attacks the Bloodhound, Maddox gives him something. A payment?

'Drugs?' Jacob says.

'Definitely.'

We watch the footage through again three times. Mr Maddox's just moved himself to the top of my priority list.

'Link them both to the incident.'

My gut is telling me there's a reason why the Bloodhound was attacked. And it looks like Maddox had a hand in it. He must be worth looking at further. It must be connected to everything else going on. But the question I need answered as a matter of priority is whether Maddox is the muscle or the brains?

Maddox's profile on the prison records system doesn't tell me much. Nothing recent on his intelligence record. The last time he'd been in custody, he'd been attacked a few times. No known obvious links. I make a note to dip into his phone calls. See if he's stupid enough to discuss anything over them.

'I'll be back in a minute,' I say. 'Stick out a tasking to the managers asking them for a list of associates of all three, please.'

My bladder requires my immediate attention. I dry my hands and step out of the ladies. Wondering what Molly's up to. Is she thinking about last night too? Has she been able to go longer than three minutes without thinking about me? Because I haven't stopped thinking about her. It's having an impact on my duties. I don't want to be here. I want to be with her. My thoughts are full of her, replaying every second of last night, compiling a message to her in my head that doesn't seem too keen, too eager, but at the same time letting her know I'm interested. If she is too.

But then, by associating with me, am I putting her at

risk? Molly works on Hayworth three too. Could she be next to be assaulted? I can't let that happen.

Molly might be able to give me a better insight into Maddox's capabilities. Who he associates with in the hall.

Neil Sparks from the Estates department walks out of the lift directly opposite the ladies, wearing the same blue Estates overalls he's worn his whole service – all faint paint splatters and frayed elbows. I ignore the spanner that hangs from his back pocket.

'You've saved me a trip, Kennedy.'

'Really?'

He clutches paperwork with both hands, like he's scared he's going to drop it.

'I have the report Victor asked for.'

'Report?'

He takes a step closer to me so he can whisper. 'A report of everyone who's accessed the roof space above Hayworth Hall over the last two weeks.'

'Oh.' The pages quiver as I accept them. The person who wants to hurt me will be in this report.

'Thanks, Neil, that's brilliant. I'll make sure Victor gets a copy.'

'No bother. If you need anything else, just let me know.' He taps the side of his nose and I purse my lips to stop from laughing.

'Mind, don't tell anybody about this,' I say, half serious.

'I won't – I value my job,' he says as he strolls back towards the lift.

I clutch the report like it's a buoy in the sea and I have no lifejacket. Even though I'm not in a safe space, I can't stop myself from casting an eye over the names. Disappointment floors me. There're no names – only user numbers. Five A4 pages of numbers.

'Fuck,' I mutter. 'Why is nothing ever simple?'

I march back to the office with renewed determination.

'I have another question,' announces Jacob when I let myself into the unit.

The trust between us is still non-existent. I don't want him to know about the report before I've had a chance to share it with Victor. I slip it under my keyboard and turn my attention to him.

My fake smile hurts my jaw as I patiently explain the process to him. Once he's busy with his own work, I slip the report from under my keyboard and set about locating the missing information. The first name is an Estates electrician. The one who found the stash. I cross-reference with the Estate's rosters. There were contractors in that day. Justified reason for being in the loft space. The next number I identify belongs to the Estates manager.

The next number is u0525. I look through the list of Estates workers. The plumbers. The electricians. The joiners. It's not one of them.

Electricity buzzes in the tips of my fingers. This is it. Another clue?

Consulting the staff list, I find the first number that corresponds with the one on Neil's report. I'll have the name soon. I'm already itching to phone Victor with the news.

I squint. Find the number. The name. The first non-Estates staff member.

The sound of the radio dwindles, the colours sucked from the room. User number u0525 doesn't belong to anyone I want it to.

Officer Molly RANA: u0525

Fuck.

17. Adrian

'We've got a problem,' murmurs the screw.

Four words that make my stomach drop.

'What?'

I glance around the wing. Rampage is arguing with McCredie over whose turn it is to clean the floor. Spence is at a bonding visit with his kid.

'I can't access the area.'

My brow puckers, not understanding.

'The area. Where I left the stuff.'

'Come here,' I say, marching into the servery where we can't be seen. Or overheard.

'*Your* stuff?' I clarify.

'It's not my fault.'

'*Your. Stuff?*'

'Aye, obviously. The lock's been changed or something.'

'That sounds like a you problem.'

'You don't get it, Adrian. If they've changed the locks, then they've . . . found it. It's probably already with intel.'

I stand straighter. 'Tell me you're joking.' I clench my fists. Fighting the urge to knock the glaiket expression off her face.

'Obviously I'm not joking. I'm fucked here.'

I grind my teeth. 'You were supposed to keep it safe. I expected you to keep it in your locker. It would've been safer if I'd kept it myself, you stupid bitch.'

'Adrian . . .'

'Get the fuck away from me and sort this out. I want

166

everything replaced. No. I want fucking double for the stress.'

'I can't. You know I can't. Think about it. I don't know what they know. They might be watching.'

'Then you better find out. Do what you were paid to. And get me more stuff in. A mobile. One of those small beat-the-boss ones that don't set off the metal detector. In black. Pronto.'

I walk away before I lose it completely. I blink against the blurry vision, like I've stared at a bright light for too long. Another fuck-up? Or has she betrayed me? There'll be more money for her if one less person's involved.

The quicker she brings me the phone, the more secure I'll be at the top. I'm not about to be stopped. Not by some girl.

I've lost the second weapon given to me by Bar to take out Filan. And now I can't even sweeten him up with the money I would've made by punting the drugs.

And if Molly knows, then everyone will, and Scout will go running to him before I have the chance to tell him myself.

18. Kennedy

I trudge back to the IMU. A headache swirling behind my eyes.

Most of the people who have accessed the loft space have a credible reason for being up there. All except four of them. Docherty. McCredie. Clive. And Molly. The information enters my head and roughs up my brain, mixing it around like mince in a pot.

And then, behind everything: Scout. Motives? End games. Was Scout the one snooping outside my flat? Has Scout already smuggled another knife into the prison to replace the one we've found? I didn't have a clue about the last one, so what's to say there isn't something else lurking somewhere?

It has to be all connected. It has to. I rip a page out of my notebook and start a chart. SCOUT written in a circle in the middle, with separate strands for Docherty. McCredie. Clive. Molly. Maddox. Rampage. There's a reason these names keep cropping up. I have to find a way to discount them. One by one.

'Are you OK?' Jacob's voice intrudes. 'You look weird. Kennedy? Hello?'

'Hmm?'

'Is everything OK?'

'Yeah. Just peachy.'

I can't make eye contact. I'm annoyed at him for keeping secrets with the Governor. But aren't I just as guilty? Keeping secrets with Molly? With Victor?

If someone discovers the connection between me and Molly, will it make me just as culpable? It's hard to remind myself I've done nothing wrong. But it eats away at me all the same. And I want to be clean.

'I think I'm going to pop out for some fresh air.'

The last thing I need is his grating voice in my head. I amble around the perimeter of the prison's concrete wall, my thoughts unable to focus on any one thing. Shock makes my heart pound fast in my chest. My veins throb. I lean against the fence, fearful I might fall in the canal that runs parallel to the establishment. The cold metal digs into my skin.

Have I mistaken butterflies for warning signs?

The smell of fresh-cut grass catches in my throat. I kick at the unraked tufts as I attempt to regulate my blood pressure.

'What do I do now?'

There's no one around to answer me. No one I can talk to. I've never felt more alone.

Am I jumping to the wrong conclusions? Or am I right to be wary?

Maybe someone from Estates asked her to open the loft space for them. Or maybe she'd done an overtime shift escorting contractors. If there's a shortage of operations officers, they'll pay anyone to do it.

My training comes back to me. Question everything. Trust no one. Believe no one. No wonder I find it hard to have a normal relationship.

There's only one thing I can do. Grill Molly. See if she's loyal to me, or the colleagues on her division. Only then can I make an informed decision. And until I have all the facts, can I really go to Victor and potentially make us all look silly when a plausible reason reveals itself? Because it has to, right?

I can figure this out on my own. I'll meet Molly and find out. Then, and only then, if it's still suspicious – *then* I'll take it to Victor.

I'll have to act quick. Because someone will want their stash back sooner or later. And I want the element of surprise. To be on the front foot instead of being reactive.

The tension eases off my shoulders, but only slightly. The gnawing sensation's still there in the pit of my stomach.

I return to the prison, keeping my head down. My fob lets me into the officers' area, and I march towards my locker, where I keep my phone during office hours. It's not permitted to have it in the office with me, despite my lack of prisoner contact.

The vivid pink scar on my abdomen itches and I rub at it absent-mindedly. Try not to think of the knife in the sharps tube. It might do more than leave a scar next time.

I open my text messages and cue one up to send to Molly.

I can't stop thinking about you. Meet me tonight?

I hope the message is enough to ignite an appetite I know exists within her. That my judgement of her hasn't been totally skewed by sexual attraction.

Deceit. The slippery way it makes me feel. Like a thousand tiny insects are crawling over my skin.

I need my smartphone for two reasons: to contact Molly. And to stalk her social media. I can access the internet at work, but not any social media site.

With a heavy heart, I slump out of the locker room. Molly's early shift will finish in an hour. I can come back down then. Hang around in the hope that I'll see her, however fleetingly. Maybe I'll know in our interactions if she's able to look me in the eye.

Tina's working on the front desk. I wait until she's finished flirting before I hold up my metal key chain.

'I don't have anything else on me,' I say.

'Fine.'

I walk through the metal detector. It beeps and I keep my eyes straight ahead. Keep on walking until I'm past the secure line. Past the warning poster.

Any Personal Communication Device taken beyond this point can result in a £2,000 fine and a two-year custodial sentence.

My breathing hitches as I wait at the secure door for the control officers to click open. I hold the handle of the door, fearful that I might pass out if I don't have something to grab on to. When the door clicks open, I scurry to the IMU. My tell-tale heart beating in my trouser pocket.

There's a thrill, I'm shocked to understand, in breaking the rules.

Making sure the phone is safe in my trouser pocket, I hurry along to the accessible toilet, locking myself inside. I pull on the light cord and sit on the lid of the loo.

She mentioned being on TikTok. Technically, any open-source research on social media should be conducted by the National Intelligence Bureau at HQ.

Thank God for mobile data, I think as the icon loads up. I'm not a huge social media fan, but I have fake accounts exactly for this reason.

I'm disappointed how easy it is to find her account. She uses her real name – not mixing it up with extra numbers and letters like most. Also, it's not private. Anyone can glance into her private world.

Changing my avatar on the app to an Arsenal flag so as not to arouse suspicion, I lurk through her account, starting with her friends. I nearly drop the phone when someone rattles the door, trying to access the toilet.

They curse before storming away, and I know I have to hurry.

Molly's TikTok account appears to follow mostly Arsenal fans and LGBT+ protesters. She has over five thousand followers but only follows eighty-nine accounts. She has TikTok rewards activated, and I make a mental note to look into that further. Could that be why she can afford such expensive gifts?

She has hundreds of videos. I don't have the time to go through them all. I quickly log into Twitter, but her account has been dormant since early 2014. Her Facebook is private, as is her Insta.

Whatever I was trying to achieve has been inconclusive. I put the phone away, give my hands a quick wash and slip out of the accessible toilet.

19. Kennedy

Victor is distracted. Jacob is quiet. Neither knows my phone's in my pocket, which adds to my jittery demeanour.

Jacob leaves the room as Victor shuffles through the daily papers. I'm supposed to go through them first thing in the morning to make sure there are no articles about prisoners or officers, but I never have the time. Unless I know to expect something. But, by then, Communications branch at HQ has already briefed the Governor.

'Didn't take them long, eh? Bloody vultures.' Victor holds up the latest edition of *NEDitorial*. The death in custody hasn't made the front page, but it takes up half of the fifth page. A picture of Kalvin Jones's poor mum holding a candle and his primary-school photo.

'What's it saying?'

'How prison officers are to blame. How he should've been placed on protection and how he was being bullied.'

'She has a point.'

'True, but it's easy for outside influences like these so-called journalists to make bold statements. They don't have the first clue of how a prison's run. And as for the mother . . .'

'I take it the article doesn't mention how he was born in HMP Cornton Vale, in the Mums and Tums? After Mum was serving a sentence for fraud?'

'Does it fuck.'

Victor's swearing is a clear sign the article's annoyed him. His distraction gives me the chance to remove my phone from my pocket and slip it into my top drawer. I watch him out of my peripheral vision as I press the side button to switch it off.

Jacob comes back in and I jump from my seat. Pretend to flick the kettle switch. Use my forearm to wipe the perspiration from my forehead.

'Would you like me to take a copy through to the Governor?' Jacob pipes up. My eyes widen. I can't look at anyone.

'No need. He's already been briefed by Comms branch,' Victor replies without looking up.

The magazine will rehash the story whenever there's a slow news day. If the mother's persistent enough, it might even make it into the red tops. The six p.m. news.

When Jacob leaves the unit, I feel like I can breathe.

'What's going on?'

'With what?' Victor answers, playing dumb.

'With Jacob. And the Governor.'

'I don't know what you're talking about.'

'You do know; you just don't want to tell me.'

'Maybe it's not my news to tell.'

'There is news?'

Victor shrugs. Turns another page.

'You're asking the wrong person. Maybe you should ask him.'

'I don't want to get involved.'

'I can't help you out there. Sorry.'

Victor lives on mystery and intrigue. Sometimes, like today, I find it more annoying than anything else. If he doesn't think he can trust me, then he shouldn't have me in his IMU. I've more than proved myself over the years, after all. I can be discreet.

My relationship with Molly is evidence of that. Not that I can point this out to Victor.

174

I cast my eye over the intelligence reports, but there's nothing pressing. All I can concentrate on is the potential unread message on my phone. It's been almost twenty minutes since I last checked it. Focusing on my drawer, I don't hear Victor.

'KENNEDY!' I lift my head. 'Three times there I said your name. Are you going deaf?'

'Nope. I'm just concentrating hard on my work,' I lie.

'I asked if all the witness statements are in for the staff assault.'

Jacob, coming back in through the door, saves me. 'All bar Officer North's. CID are arranging for a statement to be taken at his home.'

'I better get going. I want to take a walk up to Hayworth Hall and test the atmosphere. Some of the officers have been to the union.' He grimaces.

'I could've bet on that.'

'It wouldn't have bothered me if they'd run with the truth instead of embellishments and lies.'

He doesn't ask me to go with him, so I seize an opportunity.

'Before you go, can I take some TOIL? I forgot to mention I've got the doctor's this afternoon.'

The smile vanishes from Victor's face. 'Do what you have to,' he mumbles, uncomfortable.

Almost five years we'd worked together, and I've lied to him twice in one week and broken the rules I've been so proud to have previously adhered to. And all because I need to know whether I can trust Molly before I can take my concerns to him. A small part of me is scared by the thought that I don't want to.

Victor leaves the office. I wait until Jacob's concentrating on his screen before I swipe the phone from my

175

drawer – anxiety making me double-check it's switched off anytime Jacob leaves the IMU.

There's no point in me staying here much longer. I'm making mistakes. My concentration's shot to shit.

But there's one thing I can do before I leave.

20. Kennedy

I call up the profile of Adrian Maddox on the prison records system. His prison picture speaks volumes, an expression of utter contempt on his face. His swaggered stance. His curled lip. The North Face jumper immaculate – the clothing of choice of all plastic gangsters.

I click on to his visitors list and quickly scan the names. But none of them jumps out at me. I send Stan at Prison Intel an email asking for an intelligence package.

His personal officer narratives all say the same thing. Quiet and polite to staff. Keeps clean room and kit. Nothing juicy. But sometimes, it's the quiet ones you have to watch.

His last Governor's report prior to last night was from the day I came back to work. Placed on report by the Bloodhound for being disrespectful and abusive. I can only imagine what's gone on there.

I click a separate part of the records system to find out who his known associates are and am surprised there's none in custody. I chew on my bottom lip. On the surface, Maddox seems to be a complete nobody.

But my gut is telling me this guy is involved. I just have to develop him. Build the jigsaw.

I queue up the PIN system and log on. He doesn't make many long calls, which helps.

I pull on my noise-cancelling headphones and press play on the most recent call, fast-forwarding the fifteen-second warning message.

'Hello? Helloooo.'

'Sorry. It's me.'

'Well, I don't know anybody else that's in prison.'

'Listen.'

'How are you?'

'On my arse a wee bit. Did you see what happened in here the other day?'

'Aye. Another suicide?'

Maddox giggles. 'Who knows?'

'A wee bit of excitement for you all,' chuckles the female.

'I need to get a message to B. There's been another fuck-up. Not my fault.'

I pause the call. Write 'B' in my notebook with two question marks. Play the call.

'He knows. He's spoken to Sc—'

My eyes widen. Is she about to say it? To confirm what I'm thinking?

'Don't say any names over the phone, ya stupid cow. Can you come to a visit?'

He stops her right before she says the name. My insides fizz and I can only hope she'll slip up again. Reveal a clue.

'When?'

'Same time, same place.'

'Sure.'

'Will you do me proud?'

'I thought you said you didn't need me any more.'

'Aye, well, desperate times.'

'I suppose so.'

'What would I do without you?'

His voice drips sarcasm.

'Waste away in that shithole, probably.'

'Aye, probably. Look, I'm going to try and get a dog.'

'A dog? Like a Labrador or something? In your cell?'

'You're a fucking idiot. Dog and bone. Think about it.'

'I hate when you talk like that. I don't know what you're saying.'

'Don't be so thick then. Look, I need to help with the bins. I'll see you soon. Remember. Same time. Same place. Do your wee brother proud?'

'Yes, Adrian. See you then.'

'Get the stuff from Uncle B, but don't tell him it's for me.'

'What am I supposed to say to him?'

'You have a brain. Figure it out.'

As soon as the call ends, I investigate the female. Ashleigh, his sister. The more digging I do, I discover he doesn't have a dad and his mum passed away a few years before.

He can blame his criminal career on his upbringing. He'd been in and out of the care system since the age of eight.

Ashleigh is his next of kin.

I check our records for the sister, but she's never spent a night in prison before.

Maddox has promoted himself on to my list of things to uncover, along with the identity of Scout. And now I know he's arranging the introduction of a mobile phone. Interesting. There's only one reason for someone like him to need an illicit phone. To arrange drugs, and other criminality, undetected.

Scout. The name buzzes around my head. I finish writing my notes and lock my pad away in my drawer. Is this the breakthrough I've waited for? Or another dead end?

Am I closer to feeling any safer?

Maddox has no uncle as a listed visitor, B or otherwise. I add it to my chart. Too many names and not enough answers.

I print off his picture and stick it on the wall by my desk.

That way, I'll have to look at the bastard every day until I solve the puzzle he's given me.

I click on to his upcoming visits, but nothing's been booked yet. Not that it means anything; you can book a visit right up until twenty-four hours before the start of the session. If an officer likes you, you might get it booked for you even closer. I write myself a Post-it note and stick it to the corner of my monitor.

As soon as the visit's confirmed, I'll request assistance from the national search team.

I make a final check of the intel folder, ensuring nothing important has come in. Satisfied I'm OK to leave, I say goodbye to Jacob and hurry from the unit. My TOIL kicked in half an hour ago.

I hold my phone in place in my pocket until I'm safely out the building.

It's time to devote my detective skills to Molly.

21. Kennedy

I shake the rainwater from my yellow umbrella as I make my way into the restaurant.

Molly's sitting at the bar. I pretend not to notice her as I give the booking details to the server. Molly's wearing a black dress and no tights. Her glossy hair styled wavy.

'Right this way, please,' the server says as I follow her to the back of the restaurant, away from the small bar area.

'Can I get you a drink while you wait?'

'Diet Coke. Please.'

There are two reasons I've brought the car. I'm not sure how the night is going to go and having the car parked right outside makes for an easy getaway. And secondly, not having to rely on public transport makes me feel safer.

Ellie's working a backshift at the hospital. I don't have to worry about her – she'll get a lift home from a colleague.

I peer over my menu, watching as Molly picks up her pint and checks her watch.

My blood buzzes like electricity at seeing the back of her head. Any minute now, she'll turn around, glance over the restaurant and find me waiting. She'll smile and I'll melt when I need to stay strong.

It was Molly's suggestion to come out for dinner again, almost as if she'd sensed I had something serious to talk to her about and wanted to be in a public place to avoid it.

It'd be so easy to walk back out before she sees me. As

much as I know I need to challenge her, I'm fearful of what she might say. The truth is, I want her in my life. I've been strong all afternoon. Determined to question her. But now we're sharing the same space, my resolve weakens.

I want to run my fingers through her glossy hair. Kiss her. Smell her. Charm oozes from her. And I'm not the only one who thinks so, not by the way the barman belly-laughs at whatever she's saying. An unexpected wave of jealousy overwhelms me.

When she checks her watch again, I send her a message.

'Have I to sit at the table by myself all night?' I add a smiley face, so she knows I'm not being serious.

She turns around, her eyes squinting as she seeks me out. When she finally sees me, she gives me a little wave before slipping off the barstool. She grabs her pint and stumbles towards me.

'Hey,' she says as she reaches over and kisses me on the cheek. 'Thank God. I thought you were standing me up. How are you?' she asks as she makes herself comfortable.

I snatch my hand back from the middle of the table. My desire to see her has suppressed my common sense.

'Are you OK, Kennedy?'

'Sorry, it's been a long couple of days.'

'It must be tough.'

'I'm sorry?'

She scrutinizes me over the rim of her tumbler. 'Shouldn't you be on some sort of return-to-work programme? A phased return.'

'I patched it. I just wanted back.'

'No offence, but was that wise? I mean, you don't want to push yourself too hard and do more damage. Maybe you should go off sick – you know, take it easy.'

I sit straighter. My gut hisses. Her eyes flit around the restaurant, like she can't calm herself.

Paranoia or justified?

'My injuries have healed. Why would I be off work?'

Molly begins to stutter. 'I think maybe we should start again. Thank you for coming out on this miserable night. It's good to see you.'

'It's good to see you too.' And I realize it's not a lie. 'How's life on Hayworth three?'

Molly winces. 'Do you really want to talk about work? I hoped we'd have the night off.'

'Sorry, I'm not thinking.' I pick up my menu to hide my blushing face.

'It's OK. I didn't mean to sound like a dick. I could do with a few days off myself. It's hard, you know. You don't ever think it'll happen to you.'

'I'm sorry?'

'Finding a dead body.' She shivers. 'I used to panic about it when I first started. But then I got complacent.' She shudders, reliving the memory.

My heart pangs for her. I place my sweaty palm on hers.

'I'm sorry that happened to you, Molly, I—'

The server appears, ruining the moment.

'Are you ready for me to take your order or would you like a few more minutes?' She places my Diet Coke down on the coaster in front of me.

'I know what I'm having,' says Molly. 'How about you?'

I've been looking at the menu without really seeing it.

'What are you having?'

'Steak and chips. Best meal ever.' She grins.

'Sounds good. I'll have the same, please.' The server takes our orders, our preference on how we like the steaks to be cooked and our sides. I fidget with my cutlery and hope she'll leave.

'I love a good steak,' says Molly, plucking at conversation starters.

I haven't seen her like this before. Normally she's so confident. Like the alcohol is having the opposite effect to what it's supposed to.

'Yeah,' I say, my mind blank. Her presence is so bright, it steals all my words.

'It's good to see you. Best part of my day . . . Until now.' She reaches across the table to grab my hand. I recoil like she's burnt me.

'Is everything OK, babe?'

I've ordered a meal I'm not hungry for. And Molly's tipsy. I can tell by the glazed look in her eyes. I clench my teeth and grip the edge of the table. I can't have a serious conversation with her now.

Or am I self-sabotaging again by thinking the worst? Picking up on small, inconsequential things to prove she's a bad one. Avoiding a difficult conversation. The truth is, I've lost my confidence to ask.

'Sorry. I'm fine.' I plaster a smile on my face to ward off any more questions.

'I feel like I've pissed you off,' she slurs. 'Have I done something?'

'You haven't. I'm not used to public displays of affection.'

'Shit, sorry. How did you manage with your other girlfriends?'

'There's only ever been the one.' I shrug. 'I don't want to talk about it. Not tonight.'

'It's our second date. I should've come and picked you up.'

'I drove myself. It's fine.'

'It's not fine. You deserve to be treated like a princess.' She scratches her head before continuing to talk shite. 'You intimidate me, Kennedy. I needed to have some Dutch courage.' She holds up her pint glass.

'I intimidate you?'

'Yeah. You're so aloof. I can't tell what you're thinking. I wanted this date to go well, but I fear I've ruined it.'

'You haven't ruined anything. I'm nervous too. I deliberately brought the car so I couldn't drink. Say anything stupid.'

'Are you just saying that?'

'I'm not a liar.'

'I'm not going to have another drink. I'll have a Coke too.'

'Don't feel like you have to.'

'I do, babe. I do.'

I take a sip of my drink to lubricate my tongue. 'Do you have any hobbies outside of work?'

It's better I keep the questions about her. People love to talk about themselves. Molly's no different.

'Just the usual stuff. Going to the pub with my mates. Watching the football.'

'Do you support any Scottish teams, or is it just Arsenal?'

She grins. 'It's always been Arsenal. I go with my dad. Just us. Not every weekend, obviously. But for our birthdays. Christmas.'

The conversation remains neutral until the food comes, which we eat in silence

'Can we have two coffees, please?' she asks the server when she comes to clear the plates away. Her eyes sparkle in response.

Molly reaches over and grabs my hands, pulling them across the table. 'I've had fun tonight. Have you?'

'Yes,' I answer too quickly. 'Although, I still don't feel like I know you very well.'

The food's helped sober her. She hasn't ordered another drink.

She frowns. 'Ask away. Anything you want to know. I'm an open book.'

My mind goes blank. Think fast.

'Have you ever been in love?'

'Of course. What about you? Do you have exes buried in the garden?'

'Doesn't everyone?'

'But not enough to get married?'

'Never even been proposed to.'

It's more honest than I intended. Ellie had dropped enough hints, but how can you get engaged when you want different things? Another example of her forcing something I'm not comfortable with. She didn't possess the patience to give me time to get used to myself. To love myself.

'That's a shame.'

'Not really. I've never thought about it much. It's not something I'm looking to cross off a list anytime soon.'

'You haven't met the right person.'

I groan. 'If I had a pound for every time I've heard that . . .'

We linger over our coffees. It's on the tip of my tongue to ask about the loft space, now I feel more comfortable, but every time I open my mouth a different question emerges. And when a group of loud males enter, the moment vanishes completely.

'Do you fancy going for a drink?' she asks after insisting on paying the bill.

'I have the car, remember.'

'I didn't mean tonight, silly? Maybe you'll leave the car behind next time?' she adds with a wink. 'However, since you have the car – can I be cheeky and ask for a lift home?'

And just like that, she's handed me the opportunity to interrogate her in private. But privacy can be an ambiguous thing.

I must not sleep with her.

22. Kennedy

'Is that your car?' I say when I pull up in front of her house.

I'm surprised when she directs me in front of an end-of-terrace property in an affluent area. But the sight of the sleek Subaru Impreza punches me in the gut. The colour of the alloys matches her eyes.

I'd be lucky to afford the toy version.

'Yeah, that's my baby.'

My mouth dries. 'How did you manage to afford that on an officer's salary?' I don't mean it to come out as sharp as it does, but it hasn't escaped my notice that Molly appears to live beyond her means. Another black mark against her. She must be up to no good.

'It was a present. From my parents.'

I keep my thoughts to myself as she unlocks the door. They seem to like buying her expensive gifts. Or is that what loving parents do? I wouldn't know.

Taking a deep breath, I enter her property. If my flat is decorated in cheap Ikea, Molly's is all from John Lewis. Extravagant candles. Framed prints cover the walls.

'Your house is beautiful.' I can't help but try to figure out what the rent might be.

'Thanks. It's taken me a while to get it how I want it to look. Can I get you a cup of tea?'

'Peppermint, if you have it?'

'Sure.'

She directs me to the living room while she makes the drinks. It gives me a minute to have a quick look around.

The walls are painted a pale grey. A large L-shaped velour sofa takes up most of the room. A sofa I have on my dream wishlist that costs £4,000. A large TV is pinned to the wall, with no obvious cabling destroying the look. A crystal floor lamp is already on, giving the room an ample glow.

'Something's definitely up,' she says when she returns with two mugs.

'There's not,' I answer. 'It's just been a weird week.'

I take the peppermint tea and fake a smile. Scrutinize her. She sits, tucking her long legs under her. At ease. She doesn't know what's coming.

'Sorry if I'm prying. But . . . I care about you, babe.'

'Would you like me to lie and pretend I'm fine?'

'No, I don't ever want you to lie to me. Just as I'll never lie to you.'

'Do you mean that? Honesty is important to me.' I maintain eye contact and it pains me when she looks away first.

'Of course. I'd be lying otherwise.' She chuckles again and my heart races. This is it. My chance to say something. I have to get it out.

'Can I ask you some questions about work? It might help me with something that's bothering me.'

She pauses to take a drink. The colour leaches from her face. 'Sure.' Sometimes in life, you have to be direct.

'Do you have any other duties than working in the hall?'

'Like . . . ?'

'Do you ever do any escorting, external contractors, or that?'

She takes another gulp, almost like she's buying herself time. Paranoid or valid?

'No. Why do you ask?'

'I can't tell you.'

189

'Secret-squirrel stuff? From the jail polis.'

Her four words penetrate my heart and crack it.

'Don't call me that.' That's what they call me. McCredie. Docherty. Others.

'Sorry.'

'It's about an intelligence report I received today,' I lie. 'About residential officers escorting contractors about. But I thought it was rubbish because they don't escort contractors. Unless I'm wrong?'

'No. You're not wrong. We don't do that unless the prison's completely short-staffed and they've no other option. But it's normally the work party officers they poach first.'

'Is it something you've ever experienced?'

Another gulp. 'No.'

I struggle to ask more questions without giving everything away.

'It might not be rubbish then?'

'I wouldn't say that. I've not heard anybody moan that they've had to do ops work.'

'Is that something they'd normally moan about?'

'The warders? Definitely. Some folks don't like change. Some folks aren't happy unless they're moaning. You know what Ray's like.'

'When I need the mobile-phone detectors up in the loft space . . . Is that something hall officers do?'

It's out there now. I can't suck the words back into my mouth.

'What? Go up into the loft space?' Another gulp of her tea. 'Not unless there's an operational requirement to. Where are you going with this, Kennedy?'

'Uh? Nowhere. I told you, it's something I read, and I want to get my facts right before I make an informed decision. Sorry if my questions have made you feel uncomfortable.'

We stare at each other. An impasse. She picks up her mug then gently sets it back down. My head is spinning. I want to believe her. But. I've been an analyst too long. And my gut isn't satisfied.

I set my mug on the coffee table. The atmosphere's strained. I'm about to make my excuses to leave when she speaks.

'You know, now you mention it, we officers do go up to the loft space.'

My ears prick up, as does my intrigue. 'Why?'

She clears her throat, buying more time. 'I don't know if I should say. I don't want to get anybody into trouble.'

Words that always make me fear the worst.

'Do you think I'll stick you in? Remember, the first rule of intel is you don't reveal your sources.'

She continues to pause. Then it dawns on me.

'You don't trust me?'

'No-oo,' she replies, dragging the word out.

'No?' My blood turns to ice.

'I mean, no, I do trust you.'

'Then what?'

She sighs dramatically, rubs a hand through her glossy locks. Oh my God. She really doesn't trust me.

'Just forget it then.' I stand, look for my car keys. As much as I want to know what she's about to say, I'm not going to beg.

'Come here,' she says, enveloping me in her arms. She pulls me closer, and I bite down harder as my eyes water.

'Of course I trust you. And I hope you trust me too.'

'I want to.'

'We go up there to smoke, babe. We take it in turns. I'm

sure, if the area's searched, old fag butts and lighters will be found. It's an open secret. Even the managers go up there, sometimes.'

It's always been a bone of contention among the staff group, since smoking was outlawed inside. The prisoners can smoke, but staff aren't allowed to. I've heard of prison staff smoking in empty cells, but not in the loft space.

I rub my nose; it tingles like I'm about to sneeze. My heartbeat accelerates at the news.

I gaze up at her sincere face.

'That's your big secret.'

'You already knew, didn't you?'

'Not really.' I chew on my bottom lip. Rub at my eye. She pulls my hand away. I want to believe her so badly.

'Why do you do that?'

'Do what?' I rub my eye.

'Play with your lashes like that?'

I lick my lips. 'It's a bad habit. From childhood. You know, make a wish. I used to pull them out to wish my life was better. It's kinda stuck.'

'Jeez, babe. That's harsh.'

My honesty has shocked me. Not even Ellie knows that. Anytime she's seen me at it, she's looked away.

Molly gently grabs my wrists. Pulls my hands to her lips. 'Stop it. For me?' She kisses me on the cheek. The tip of my nose.

My body reacts to her touch. I feel my resolve weakening. I allow myself to pretend that there's no fear, only an excitement for a future. We sit like that for a minute, neither of us having the need to break the silence.

'Will you pass it on? What I've said? About the loft?'

I pull my hands away from her.

'What managers?' I ask. A test. Is her loyalty to me, or to them?

'The one that runs Morton Hall. Somebody Docherty.'

It's against the rules for any staff to take smoking materials into the prison. If they want to smoke, they've the leisure to do so on their breaks. The thing is, knowing the SPS, if everyone's doing it, nothing more will happen than a slap on the wrist. But if it's only one or two, they'll be suspended.

I can get Crawford Docherty suspended. And now I have a valid piece of intel to begin an investigation.

'Why would he go up there? That's not his hall.'

Molly shrugs. 'Probably football chat and a smoke break with the others. He probably does it in his own hall too. You've gone all quiet,' she says, kissing my hand. 'What are you thinking about?'

I shrug. I must be careful. Not give too much away.

'Are you going to report it?' she persists.

'Why would I tell? It's not exactly corruption.'

Maybe it'd reduce the violence? A lot of the incidents occur because the prisoners are short-tempered, brought on by lack of nicotine when they don't have the money in their canteen to buy any. Officers' attitudes too. If they're deprived of their tobacco for several hours. Especially the heavy smokers.

'Good.' She kisses my temple. 'Although,' she adds after another pause, 'it's kind of dodgy in a way.'

Stop talking, I think. I no longer want to hear what she has to say.

'How come?'

'Well . . . Not all officers have keys to access the loft space. Not in the halls.'

Anxiety bubbles in my stomach. I want to kiss her, purely to stop the words coming out of her mouth.

Don't tell me, I silently urge. *Don't tell me.*

She continues, oblivious. 'So, they pass keys about.'

And there it is. I close my eyes. This I can't ignore. Gross misconduct. There are fucking rules for a reason. As soon as you accept a set of keys, you are responsible for them. Passing them to someone else is a breach of security. If anything happened to those keys, if someone else took them so far as an inch out the main door, every single lock, every single key would have to be replaced, at a cost of £30,000 – money they can afford since they won't be paying an officer's wages any more. It's drummed into you from the start. Don't remove your keys.

I turn around in her arms to look directly at her face. 'Be honest with me,' I urge. 'Have you shared your keys with anyone?'

She doesn't have to answer. I can tell by her pale complexion, the sad look on her face, the way her teeth gnaw at her bottom lip.

'You silly idiot,' I whisper.

The feeling's a bittersweet one. Molly might be in the clear for planting the drugs and weapon. But at the same time, she's shared a secret with me that I'm duty bound to report.

Just as I solve one problem, another one pops up to take its place.

23. Kennedy

Soon after her confession, I leave. I can't stay there and let her hold me in her arms while my head is so knotted. I need time to myself to process what she's said.

I let her kiss me goodbye and get lost in the moment.

'Please stay,' she begs.

'Not tonight. I'm working this weekend. Soon.'

'Me too. On Sunday anyway.'

I remind myself, if she is Scout, she's had the opportunity to do something to me. And hasn't. But still. *Trust your gut* has also been drummed into me, and my gut isn't happy. Is my desire for her to be innocent clouding something sinister?

My stomach cramps as soon as I get into my car. I focus on starting the engine, pulling out on to the road. Because as much as I need space from her to think, I'm too tempted to take her up on her offer to stay the night.

'You're home early.' My heart stutters at the sight of Ellie lying on the couch under the weight of her knitted blanket.

'I'm not feeling too good.'

'Same. Do you want me to get you a hot-water bottle? Some painkillers? A glass of wine?'

Ellie always knows exactly what I need when I need it, with no thought for herself.

'All three.'

I go straight to bed, stripping off as soon as I enter my bedroom. Ellie comes up with the things five minutes later.

'I didn't realize you were going out tonight.'

'I didn't realize I had to report my movements.'

'Don't be like that, Kennedy. I'm just making conversation.'

'I'm sorry. Rough night.'

'Do you want to talk about it?'

I shake my head.

'Do you need a hug?'

Before I have the chance to answer, her arms are wrapped around me. The familiar smell of vanilla; a comfort. She turns her head a fraction, towards my neck. I push back when I feel her lips on my skin.

'What are you doing?'

'Nothing.'

We stare at each other, trying to figure the other out. There was a time not all that long ago, I'd have been more responsive to her touch.

'How's Kym?'

Ellie jumps from the bed like I've electrocuted her. 'You know where I am if you need me.'

My skin crawls as soon as she slams my bedroom door. I've no right taking my black mood out on her.

I lie in the dark, watching the illuminated time on my alarm clock as it hits every hour. At some point, I doze, but jolt awake soon after. I've kept the blinds open. The moonlight lights up the room.

I get up three times to check the front door is locked. It's just after four when I creep through to the kitchen. Fill the kettle. Flick the switch. Less than two hours until the prison opens for the day. I drink cup after cup of coffee until it's a more reasonable time for a shower.

Is it Molly that's keeping me awake, or the upcoming

operation to intercept Maddox's drug delivery? After all, the last time we ran it, I almost died.

It's early when I leave the flat, unable to keep reading the last message Molly sent me last night.

I'm falling for you x♥x♥x

I've yet to reply. But that hasn't stopped me from re-reading it every two minutes. It should be easier than this, I can't help but think.

I'm falling for her too, but can I trust her?

A thick frost covers our ageing Ford. The door creaks open, and that's when I see him. By the bin, two hundred yards from the streetlamp. If he hadn't lit his cigarette, I wouldn't have noticed. It's the glowing tip that catches my attention.

My body stiffens. He's looking in my direction. My heartbeat quickens. I dive into the car and lock the doors. Switch on the engine. The windscreen heater to dissolve the ice.

Is it him? The guy that was lurking behind the flat? There's no reason for someone to be out this early. He's nowhere near a bus stop. He's not dressed like he's going to work. He doesn't have a rucksack.

'Come on,' I mutter, my hand clutching my phone, 999 ready to be dialled. The biting cold makes my eyes water. Other than the lamp posts, my car is the only light in the dark street. It's too early for nosy neighbours to be witnesses.

Wipe the condensation from the rear-view mirror. My face is pale. My gritty eyes drag. The heated screen gradually melts the ice from the window.

And he's there. In touching distance of the boot. Face covered by a balaclava.

I cry out. Drop my phone. The belt stops me from leaning forward to get it from the footwell.

I click it off. Reach down. I'm ready to call the police. Ellie. Anybody.

But he's gone.

With ice coated on the side windows, I put the car in reverse and screech out of the space, not caring if I knock the bastard down.

When I'm out of my street, on the main road and feeling safer, I roll down the windows so I don't have an accident. Wanting the police to stop me for careless driving. I get to work in less than five minutes, breaking the speed limit the whole time.

I abandon the car in the space closest to the streetlight. My legs judder as I emerge. I go to the boot to grab my fleece, and that's when I see it. With fumbling fingers, I take a picture on my phone.

On the back of the car, scratched in melting ice, two words: *Die Bitch*.

A warning?

Scout says goodnight.

I dash beneath the streetlights that line the path down to the entry of the prison.

The knife.

A few of the nightshift officers are already making their way to their cars. I keep my head down as I walk the path to the main entrance. I don't want to be seen.

Balaclava man.

It's another twenty minutes before the early shift turns up. By the time I reach the main doors, I can barely breathe. I rest against the empty front desk until I catch my breath. Only when I feel like I've regained my own body do I move past the front desk.

Cheap fluorescent lights and CCTV cameras are now the only things that make me feel safe.

There's no one in the key-vend room. I grab a personal alarm and my set of keys. Once I've attached them to my belt, I leave the sterile area, marching out into the cold corridor. The lights are off, only turning on the further I step. Something scutters to my right, but I ignore it. Every prison has an ongoing issue with vermin. When it gets too bad, they adopt cats to take care of business.

My heart beats in time to my footsteps, hurried and quick.

'Morning, ma'am,' says one of the new recruits I pass, escorting a prisoner down to reception.

I smile back, ignoring the prisoner. The way he's clutching two clear bags tells me he's a straight court. Not expected to return. I feel a pang of jealousy. Sometimes I wish I could be released in the hope of never having to return.

I keep going, determined it won't take up too much of my morning. I stop at the T-junction between the two halls and the digger. I take a left and head towards Hayworth Hall, pulling out my keys to fob open my access.

The warmth hits me as soon as I enter. Protocol dictates I should announce my arrival to the first line manager on duty. But the fewer people that know I'm here, the better.

The quietness unnerves me as I climb up the stairs to the threes. There's no one awake this early. I creep into the darkened hall, the motion-activated lights turning on as I hurry over to the staff office.

If it's locked, then this has been for nothing. But I have to know. My heart thuds when I depress the handle and the door squeaks open.

The office is filthy. Dirty mugs line the table. Paperwork is strewn over the small desk. But I ignore that as I locate the door to the loft space. Another stairwell to climb.

At the top of the stairs, I pull my fob. The roof space is dark, with the churning noise of the boilers. Despite being a floor above, I hear the muffled shouts of the officers talking to each other down below. The early shift's arrived.

I step into the gloomy room. It smells of stale cigarette smoke and body odour. The dust makes my nose twitch and I jump when something flashes to my right. It's only a mobile-phone detector.

Sweat pools under my arms and on my top lip. It's like all the heat in the building is released from up here. I run my hand down my hairline to stem the sweat.

I crouch down. The dust's been interrupted around where the articles were found. Whoever put the stuff up here, it wasn't there for long.

My knees creak as I stand up. I've seen enough. Squinting in the darkness, I see them. The ground is littered with many cigarette ends, like the room's been treated as a giant ashtray. I move around carefully, not wanting to stand on anything, and breathe out of my mouth.

One thing is clear. Molly was telling the truth. About the smoking, at least.

I let myself out of the loft space and head down the back exit to avoid the officers that are now on duty. By the time I'm outside, the world isn't as dark. The sun is rising on the horizon, and I feel like I can relax.

But when the item lands at my feet, I startle. Step back. The fresh stench hits me. Someone's awake. I hurry along, anticipating the arrival of another shite bomb. It's how they get their kicks, the prisoners. Shitting on to a bit of newspaper, wrapping it up and waiting for an unsuspecting officer to walk close enough past the outside of the hall.

I peer up at the cell windows, but there's no lights on. It could've come from anywhere.

I press my back against the concrete wall and walk sideways up the side of the corridor, feeling like an idiot. Someone will be dining out on this story for weeks.

When I'm in the corridor and the motion-sensor lights activate, I look at my shoes to see if there's any splatter. I can still smell the shite, but my shoes are clean. I rush towards the comfort of my IMU, breathing in lungfuls of fresh air to cleanse my nostrils.

My thoughts return to Molly. I need to reply to her message. She didn't lie.

She needs to know that I'm falling for her too.

But when I get to my car, safe in the emerging light, I check the photo first. Dismayed, I find the picture is blurry. Can I make out the 'e'? Part of the 't'? The car is clear.

My proof is gone. If it ever existed in the first place.

24. Adrian

'Where's my stuff, wee man?' growls one of the cons. 'I paid for it; I better get it.'

I look around for Rampage for back-up, but he's behind his door at the other side of the hall.

'Relax. It's coming.'

'So is Christmas.'

I walk away and join the queue going to the visit room, fighting the urge not to look back at the goon. I can feel his stare boring into the back of my neck.

'This your first visit?' I ask Filan, uninterested in the answer.

Filan nods once, not in the mood for small talk. There are only a few others booked on to my visit session. One's in the corner, ironing his top. Something he should've done earlier, along with the rest of us.

I flex my jaw and keep my mouth shut. The screws huddle over the centre console watching the computer screen intently. I make a bet with myself that it's sport-related. Sport, or porn.

Filan slowly prises away from the rest of the group and walks over to the exit. He places his back against it, gripping the door handle with his right hand. Doesn't he know the doors lock electronically?

I pace around the console, keeping near the screws so the goon doesn't have any bright ideas of attacking me. The next forty-five minutes of my life are crucial. I need the drugs that Ashleigh better have brought in. I don't want to think about the consequences if she's let me down.

Sneaking glances at Filan, I know I'm going to have to take him out. And soon.

It's imperative that I speak to Uncle Bar sooner still. Would he be happy with me delegating the task to Rampage – who would do anything for drugs? Or does it have to be me?

Filan looks up to see me frowning at him before I saunter over.

'What are you doing?' I ask out of the corner of my mouth.

'Nothing. Just bored.'

'Remember there're cameras everywhere. There's nowhere for you to go. Especially in these bright tangerine visit tops.'

He saunters away at the sound of footsteps echoing on the other side of the door. A screw comes through and shouts for the visits. I rub my nose and pretend to fasten my shoes. One of the screws comes over with a clipboard and shouts out our surnames, checking them off his board.

We file up before we're escorted from the hall. It's not until the hall door's locked behind us that I sense him walking beside me.

'Who's visiting you?' I ask as our feet pound the concrete walkway. Will it be someone that recognizes me? Will there be a square go in the visit room after all?

'A friend. Yourself?'

'My big sister. She better have brought something . . . For the vending machine,' I add with a wink.

I bite at my thumbnail as we walk along the gloomy, cold corridor. The rain's been relentless all day, giving the appearance of night-time.

But being in the corridor is the first time I feel fresh air blow at my skin for days.

We march the route in silence, grateful for the heat of the admin building where the visit room's located on the second floor. We climb the stairs.

This building's different to the residential blocks. For a start, it smells cleaner. Warmer.

The visit room's large and empty. My hall the first to arrive. To the left-hand side are a couple of vending machines selling chocolate, crisps and bottled juice. At the top-left corner of the room is a children's play area. Inflatable toys and a ball pool. Some dog-eared kids' books. And if you're lucky, the WRVS shop will be open for a hot drink. A wider variety of confectionery. But the screws depend on volunteers from a nearby church to keep it open. Today, it's closed.

The visit screw directs me to a table, and I sit. The table's lower than my knees, to make it harder for contraband to be passed. My back's to the wall, giving me a clear view of both doors. The prisoner entrance and the visitor entrance. If an enemy comes in, either prisoner or visitor, they can't sneak up on me. I'll have the upper hand.

Once all the prisoners arrive, then they'll let in the visitors. I sit forward in my seat as the prisoners filter in from the other hall. I scrutinize every face before I can relax.

If your visitor doesn't turn up, you must wait in the visit room along with everyone else, watching everyone's visit and cursing the folk that don't turn up for an excruciatingly long fifteen minutes. Then you're taken back to the hall. If anyone did that to me, I'd cut their balls off. There's nothing more humiliating to endure in the prison than being patched for a visit.

The door opens and prisoners from Morton Hall file in.

The prisoners shout across the room to each other. I close my eyes. Feel old.

Eventually, the doors open and the visitors stream in. Young kids push past their elders and run towards their daddies, their brothers. Their role models.

And then he's there. Wearing his trademark jeans and tight white top. He's added to the ink on his arm since I saw him last.

Junior Green. Filan's right-hand man. If anyone's going to recognize me, it'll be that cunt. I slink further into my seat. Luckily, he only has eyes for his leader.

'Fred, mate, how are you doing?' Junior shouts.

'Fine,' Fred answers as they hug. A screw's right over, making sure nothing's been passed.

They sit.

'Hello-oooo.'

I look up. Ashleigh's standing in front of me, arms crossed over her fake tits.

'All right.'

She sits. Pulls the chair closer to the small table. 'Seen someone you fancy?'

'Shut the fuck up.'

If the Valley boys look over, they'll recognize her too.

'What you been up to?'

She looks back at me.

'It's not like you to bother with small talk. Do you want the usual from the vending machine?'

I look over her shoulder to see where Junior is. I give her permission to go for chocolate and full-fat juice as Junior's deep in conversation with Filan.

I'm on the edge of my seat when Junior stands up. Checks the change in his pocket and joins the queue. My sister's three people in front of him. I look between

Filan and the vending machine as Ashleigh takes a step closer.

'What the fuck took you so long?' I say when she returns. Ashleigh drops the goods on the table.

'Don't start your shite or I'll just go. And you really need to hear what I have to tell you.'

At no point do Junior or Filan look over.

'Adrian.'

'What?' I grunt, distracted.

'I have something important to tell you.'

We cover our mouths with our hands as we speak. That way, no one can tell what we're saying should someone try to lip-read on the cameras.

I glance around the room. Four screws are on duty, huddled together and having a joke. It's never been this easy to get shit passed in here.

'There was an issue downstairs.'

I freeze. Wait for her to continue.

'They have the dogs in. Downstairs.'

'Fuck sake,' I growl.

'Let me finish.' She scowls. 'I managed to leave the stuff in the female toilets. But it spooked me. I don't want to do it again.'

I relax. A minor setback. I'll get Flakes to collect it when he's cleaning down there.

'If you managed to drop the stuff then you didn't get caught. What are you bitching about? If I need more next week, then you'll be here dropping it off.'

'Adrian . . .'

'Adrian nothing. We keep going.'

'Have you managed to speak to him?'

I swallow down my rage. Who does she think she is?

'Nah. He won't answer a call from here. Not on the PIN phone. And I haven't got my hand on the mobile yet.'

'You must be losing your touch.'

A glare from me is enough to make her flinch. She busies herself opening a bottle of Coke.

'You better not be making jokes about me out there. I'm running this place. Ask anyone.'

'I've spoken to Uncle Bar,' she says, ignoring me.

'And?'

'He isn't giving you any more stuff, Adrian. You've lost him too much. I didn't want to say anything, but if I'm to come visit you next week, I won't have anything, even if I wanted to.'

'He's cut me off?'

I'm fucked. Everything handed to me on a plate, and I've fucked it.

'He's unhappy with how much you've let him down.'

'It's. Not. My. Fault,' I spit through clenched teeth.

'He's sick of you saying that. He told me to tell you' – she pauses to take a drink – 'you've to do that thing and it'll wipe out all your debt. He'll get you anything you need. But you have to do it.'

'And if I don't?'

If I don't kill Filan for Bar, then I'll be the dead one.

'It's business with him, bro. It always has been. Business before blood, you know that.'

Before I can process her words, I smack all the confectionery from the table. Mars bars and a bottle of Coke go flying. Ash stands up. 'Fuck sake, Adrian.'

The screws are over in an instant.

'Lovers' tiff?' smirks one.

'Shut the fuck up, ya baldy prick.'

I'm drawing the attention of the others, but I can't help myself. The red mist's descended.

'Right, that's a misconduct report for using threatening and abusive language. Want to make it two?'

'Calm down,' hisses my sister. 'This is why you can't be trusted.'

'Get the fuck out of my face,' I say, holding up my hand to block her view.

'Visit terminated,' announces the screw.

I stand and they're on me immediately. Ash jumps back before she's knocked over. Filan's looking over, but the screws are already pushing my sister towards the exit.

'Back to the hall for you,' sings the screw. They're lying on top of me and, once more screws arrive, I'm turkeyed up. Carted back to the hall. When we get into the corridor, I fight against their restraint and they flatten me against the concrete floor. It tears at my face, leaving redness and scratches.

Unshed tears of anger burn at my eyeballs as I try to sustain the pain. My hands stretched tighter, my thumb in a peculiar position. Just as it's on the point of snapping, I give up.

I let them drag me back.

I'll get the digger for this, I think as I'm dragged into my gaff. Made to put my hands against the far wall so I can't go toe to toe with the screws as they make their exit.

Flakes comes to my gaff when I shout on him through my hatch.

'I need a favour, wee man,' I say.

'Aye?' His eyes widen in excitement that he's being trusted to do something for the top dog.

'There's a parcel. In the female visitor toilets. I need you to grab it for me. Bank it and bring it back.'

'Righto, bro. That's sound.'

'Get off that door,' orders McCredie, who has re-appeared with the misconduct report paperwork.

Flakes nods and the hatch closes.

When I'm alone, I let the tears fall. Frustration. Anger. Disappointment. The three emotions I've had most practice with all my life.

25. Kennedy

Some might call it entrapment. I call it an opportunity. I can't live like this any more, fearing every person, every shadow.

Catching Maddox is my best shot at uncovering Scout. At least then I'll know who I should be afraid of.

I didn't have time to meet with Stevo from the National Search Team prior to the visit session. I wasted time, checking and double-checking that Zac Boward wasn't booked on to the same visit session. That I'm not going to run into *her*.

Stevo's training a new Patterdale terrier called Oscar but insists the dog's just as good as Tyson, if a little more immature. Police Scotland aren't available to assist at such short notice.

Ashleigh Maddox sits by herself. It's hard to see if she's nervous, due to the amount of fake tan and make-up on her face. It makes her look older than we have her recorded as. Her trout lips make it look like she's asking for a kiss. I can't help but stare. How can that be comfortable?

The colour of her face doesn't match that of her hands. Fake lashes make it look like she's squinting.

I start off with a compliment.

'I like your necklace.'

I don't. It's a gaudy yellow-gold letter 'A'. Cheap.

'Aw, cheers. It was a present from my boyfriend,' she says, stroking it affectionately. 'Thirty carats,' she adds, which I'm pretty sure doesn't exist.

'You been with him long?'

'Nearly two months,' she gushes.

'Nice. I've been with my man for a year.'

'It must be hard, him being in here.'

I fake a sniff. 'It is. But it'll only bring us closer when he gets out. You here to see yours?'

'Nah.' She exhales in relief. 'I'm here to see my wee brother. The wee dick.'

'Oh, that must be hard.'

'Not really. You get used to it – not his first time.'

She turns in her chair to face me. She thinks I'm just like her. I look around, making sure the staff are still distracted. I'm not supposed to be here, after all.

'Mine has only been in a few weeks. This is the first time I've been to see him.'

She reaches out and strokes my arm. 'It's OK. We're all in this together.'

I sigh. 'Thank you, that means a lot.'

I chew on my bottom lip. 'He's struggling,' I confide.

'Struggling.' She nods.

'It's the family contact. His mum's in a bad way. Terminal. Is there anywhere he can . . . You know . . . Make a call . . . During the night?'

I leave the rest unsaid and hope she'll fill the silence. Ashleigh doesn't disappoint.

'Look, I can't say too much down here, but I can speak to my brother, see if he can help. He has . . . friends in high places.'

'I don't understand.'

She's so close she must hear my hoof-beat heart.

Security officer Maria Collins enters the waiting area. Frowns at me.

Ashleigh nods her head in Maria's direction.

'What? A screw?' I say.

'Aye, mate. Not her. One in the hall. I'll speak to my brother. Meet me outside after the visit, yeah? It's not just that he'll be able to help your man out with.' She winks.

'A dodgy screw in the hall?'

My hands clutch the armrests of my chair so I don't fall off the edge of the seat. Scout? Molly? McCredie? Or a new player I haven't discovered yet?

A slight nod. 'Meet me after. I'll hook you up.'

I want to ask her outright, but I know it'll spook her.

The moment is taken from me when, two minutes before the start of the visit session, Ashleigh Maddox stands. She pulls her sleeves down and marches towards the toilet. I try not to whip my head around to watch. Instead, I stand and flex my joints – as if sitting too long has left me stiff.

I move my neck from side to side. Stretch my legs. But she's still in the ladies. I contemplate going to use the facilities too. But there's only the one cubicle.

Maria Collins catches my eye. I raise my eyebrows. She frowns. I look away before anyone notices. It's time for the visit to start. I dash over to her before she gives the game away.

'You shouldn't be in here.'

'How much longer do we have to wait, Officer?' I moan.

She looks at me like I'm drunk. 'Um, just one more minute.'

At that point, Ashleigh Maddox emerges from the ladies. If it's possible, she's wearing even more make-up on her face. I nod once and walk back to my seat.

'Maddox. Simmons. Filan. Roberts. Nguyen,' shouts Maria.

The group of visitors pulls themselves from their seats

and files through to the search area, unaware of the National Search Team's presence.

I want to follow them, but I stay where I am. Maria closes the secure door and I dig my fingernails into my thighs. Try not to think about the last time we ran this operation. The consequences.

My heart rattles in my chest. I practise my breathing.

McCredie.

Surprisingly, Maria comes back for the next batch of visitors too soon. The dog screens everyone, but there's no indications. As soon as the last visitors are escorted to the visit room, Stevo and Oscar enter the waiting room.

'No indication?'

Stevo shakes his head. 'It's not the dog, before you say anything.'

'I wouldn't dream of it.' But it had to be.

'She has something on her. I know it,' I add, trying to keep my tone calm. 'Did you offer her a closed visit?' I direct my question to Maria.

'But the dog never indicated.'

'It doesn't matter. She should've still been placed on closed visits because of the intel.'

'No one told me.'

'Fuck,' I mutter. 'Radio the visit and control-room officers and tell them to keep an eye on the visit. I want him strip-searched as soon as it's finished.'

Maria storms out of the waiting room. Irate she has to take orders from me.

'The intel isn't right all the time, Kennedy. You know that.'

I turn to Stevo. He's never been condescending before, and I don't know how to take it. 'Can you check the toilet?'

'I'm sorry?'

'Check. The toilet. She was in there ages.'

'Kennedy . . .'

'Humour me. Please.'

'Fine.'

I storm over to the toilet door and knock loudly three times. Satisfied there's no one in, I push the door open, allowing Stevo and Oscar to follow.

Oscar bounds into the toilet, sniffing every area. When he goes into the cubicle and fails to return after a few seconds, a frisson of excitement flares in my stomach. 'What's he doing?'

'His job. Give him a minute.'

'Is he giving any kind of indication, though?'

'Um. Yeah. But you're not going to like it.'

I frown. Slink over to the cubicle and peer inside. Oscar's sitting at the sanitary bin, his tail thumping against the floor.

Stevo sighs, pulling on his fresh pair of nitrile gloves. 'You owe me big time for this.'

There's nothing linking the find to Maddox, except gut instinct.

The recovered stash has a prison value of nearly £3,000. The police agree to remove the drugs, but they can't take it any further than as intel, unless the sister has left her prints on the bags.

Combined with the prison value of the stash within the loft space, that means someone's seriously out of pocket. Although there's no corroboration to link the loft-space find with Maddox either.

And if he is working with a corrupt officer, why does he need his sister to smuggle in drugs?

There must be more to this than we know. Just because

he doesn't have many visitors doesn't mean he isn't linked to the local criminal underworld. He must be getting the drugs from somewhere, after all. Especially at this level.

I log on to the PIN system and run his code through the system. He hasn't made any calls since the last.

I quickly type an email to Stan at the Prison Intel team in Gartcosh to chase up the intelligence package I asked for.

Next, I type a tasking to the Security group. If Maddox has a way of contacting the outside world for other prisoners, he must be in possession of a mobile phone. Security will make sure a phone detector is placed directly above Maddox's cell.

I check Maddox's personal cash and his wages from being employed as hall pass man. It's not that he doesn't have any money to put on his phone either. On the last canteen day, he received £20 worth of treats and toiletries, without putting a single penny towards using the phone.

If he has a phone, I'll find it. And if he's it banked up his arse, then he can spend the next three months in the digger until he gives it up. But there's no way of knowing what he's up to if he isn't using the bloody PIN phone for me to listen to. And I'm still not getting intel reports from the hall. My head's bashed in from repeatedly hitting it across a brick wall.

And even if I do recover a phone from him, legally, I'm not allowed to look at it. Despite there being intel on it that might only mean something to me. Or further planned criminality I'd be able to prevent.

With the taskings issued, I return to the PIN system and type in Filan's details. There's a solitary three-minute call for me to sink my teeth into.

But I'm distracted when an email pops into my inbox

from Molly. Logging out of the PIN system, I open the email.

Are you free tonight? Would be good to see you. I can pick you up at six. We can do anything you want. Let me know xx

I don't have to think about it. I hit the reply button.

Six sounds perfect xx

It's time to confront her. About everything.

26. Kennedy

'Isn't it a bit early for wine?'

I jolt. Clutch my chest. 'Fuck's sake, Ellie. Did you creep up on me deliberately?'

'I didn't realize I needed to announce my arrival in my own home.' Her right eyebrow is raised. 'What are you up to?'

I jut out my chin. 'I have a date.'

'With the same girl from last night?'

'It's early days.' I press my lips together to stop them trembling. There's a time not so long ago I'd have felt this way getting dressed up for her.

I contemplate pouring myself another small drink, followed by a piece of chewing gum, but it's five to six and Molly's due any minute.

'Where you off to? You can share that, at least.'

'I don't know.' I stand taller. 'It's a surprise?'

'Since when did you like surprises?'

When they aren't followed by heartache, I think, but don't have the courage to say. I don't want Ellie to put me in this mood, the one she's so adept at.

'What's her name anyway? Where did you meet?'

I chew on the inside of my cheek, debating on how much to tell her. 'Molly. We . . . met in a bar.'

'Lovely.' It doesn't sound like she means it.

'She's picking me up any minute, so . . .'

'Are you going to bring her in? Introduce us?'

'I don't think so.'

I clench my teeth. She doesn't have the right to be jealous. She'd had all this time to tell me she'd made a mistake, but never has.

'Are you sure she's right for you?'

I put down my glass. Clench my teeth.

'It's early days.'

She gives a pointed look at the Jo Malone candle I left on top of the mantel. 'It's a bit much, Kennedy. Don't you think? The love-bombing?'

'You don't know her.'

'Oh, I think I do.'

We stare at each other until I remind myself she's not the enemy here. I relax. Change the subject. 'I think I'm getting closer to identifying Scout.'

'Oh, really?'

'Yeah. I got some intel this afternoon.' I fight the urge to tell her what's really happening. If I thought she was at risk, I would confide in her. But doing so would make me feel like a failure.

'Not the Crawford guy you've always hated?'

I wipe smeared lipstick from my teeth. 'Nah, but I got other intel in about him doing something he knows he shouldn't. I might get to see him squirm, after all.'

'Good. I'm pleased for you.'

'I just want this over, Ells. I want whoever it is locked up a million miles away, along with all those involved. And then I can live happily ever after.'

'With Molly?'

I stiffen. 'Maybe.'

'I'll leave you to it then. Don't want to get in your way.'

I place my palms down on the kitchen counter. Concentrate on my breathing. All the excitement I felt is gone. I shake it off, but the feeling of disappointment lingers.

The closer it gets to leaving the house, the more trepidation I feel.

No sign of Molly. I switch my music off and sit on the armchair. The best seat for looking outside. A part of me is wary, that I'll see the bloke in the balaclava. He's the type to only come out in the dark of night.

6.05.

I could've painted my nails and had another drink at this rate, I think as I perch on the end of the armchair, my leg jittering.

6.10.

When I see approaching headlights, my heart stops in my chest. But the car's black, not blue.

6.15.

I pick up my phone. Switch it off. Switch it back on again. Still nothing.

My contact lenses nip my eyes. I've had them in for over twelve hours. But I don't want to wear my glasses on our date.

I trudge through to the kitchen and pour myself a half-glass of wine.

6.30.

'Are you still here? What happened to your big date?'

'Running late.' I swallow. 'She'll be here.'

6.45.

The wine's finished. I can't drink any more on an empty stomach. I don't want to be half pissed when she turns up. If she turns up? Is she standing me up? Come to her senses?

An hour late, with no phone call or text. I look down at my body, the effort I've made. Humiliation overwhelms me.

This is karma for being a bitch to the only person who has ever been there for me.

'I'm sorry, Ells,' I say, hoping it will reverse any bad luck. 'I have a lot on just now. It's cunty of me to take it out on you.'

Maybe the email said seven. It's not like I can log on and check. But I know, deep in my gut, it was six.

'Do you want to order some food?' Ellie asks. 'I'm starved.' Her tone softens.

'I'm not hungry. But thanks.' I clench my jaw. I want her to disappear. I don't want her to witness what's happening.

'Have you heard from her?' The concern in Ellie's tone spooks me. Because I've been silently wondering if something bad has happened. I can't stop my mind from catastrophizing. A car accident. A hit and run. An assailant stabbing her because they can't get to me. Or has my incessant questioning put her off? Spooked her?

'No. Should I, do you think?'

'Why don't you message her?' Ellie suggests. 'Maybe she's been held up. Or had bad news.' Ellie's always been able to see through my bullshit. The girl knows me better than I know myself.

'Yeah.' But the thought of sending the message makes me squirm. Ellie stands over my shoulder as I type.

Hey, are we still doing something tonight? X

I don't have to wait long before I have my answer, but I hold off from reading it until I drink more wine. Then maybe it'll not hurt as bad.

'Is that her?'

'Yes. Can you give me some privacy?'

'Sure. I'll be in my room. Ordering Chinese food for one.'

Molly and I haven't had the exclusivity talk. She's quite within her right to be on another date with another person. I've never been the type to date multiple people. Too much of a headache.

I guzzle the wine. Licking my lips, I pick up my phone and open the message.

Bit of a nightmare. I'll explain when I see you.

I note the no kisses. Her messages always end in kisses. Even the first one she sent, before we knew what we were.

Disappointment weighs down on me like a rock, my shoulders drooping. Haven't I been expecting something like this?

I contemplate opening Ellie's other bottle of wine. I want to get out of my fancy jeans and my sparkly top. I'm dressed for a night in the pub, a romantic meal in a restaurant – not for sitting in my living room with my gloating ex.

When the doorbell rings, I almost don't answer. Anger fills my chest, and it's about to be unleashed.

I steam over and pull the door open. I'm taken aback to see Molly. There's no smile on her face. No sign of any sheepishness. Her face is red, her mouth set in a firm line. She's angry.

'Hey,' she says. 'Can I come in?'

I pull the door wider to allow her access. I don't say anything. It should be me that's angry. What gives her the right?

'Did you know?' she demands as she barges her way into the living room.

'Know what?'

'I've just been interrogated by the police for the last two hours.'

'About what?' My gut begins to tingle.

'About the death in custody. You must've known. Because I was the last person to see him alive. You could've edged me up. I feel like a fucking criminal. Violated. In my own home.'

'I didn't know, honest.'

Not that I would have warned her if I had. It concerns me that she assumes I would.

'Why were you the last to see him?'

'Because he needed toilet paper. I'm absolutely disgusted with them. Coming to my house unannounced' – she points at her chest – 'treating me like a criminal . . .'

'Calm down. They're only doing their job. It's not like you have something to hide.'

Molly exhales deeply. 'You really didn't know?'

'How would I? I don't work for the police.'

'I thought they'd let you know who they'd need to speak to.'

'Not all the time. It depends on what CID officer it is.'

'I don't want the prisoners knowing about this. Or the other officers.'

I lick at my sticky lips. 'It'll be fine.' It isn't that she's been interviewed by the police, it's the fact she assumed I'd have warned her. And it confuses me.

'No one needs to know. Everyone else will be inter-viewed too.'

Her reaction's so over the top it makes me nervous. Has she not been interviewed by the police before? It's starting to make her look guilty. But of what? What does she have to hide? And what did the police need to ask her that wasn't covered in her original witness statement? Has she lied? Been caught out by the CCTV?

The sizzle in my gut intensifies. The threatening stiffy, Scout, the knife? In that moment, I know – my gut's telling me it's not a suicide.

'I'm sorry.' She pulls me into a hug and kisses me. 'I feel better now.'

But I don't.

'I can't tell you what I don't know. And I can't share

anything with you that relates to my work. Not unless you need to know. You understand that, right?'

'Of course, babe.' She brightens. 'It just threw me. I'd never put you in a compromising position. I know how important your job is to you. They could've interviewed me at work, is all. They could've given me the heads-up.'

Confusion consumes me. I've had to give a statement at home. It didn't bother me. Not like this.

'How are you anyway?' she asks as she leans over and kisses me again.

'Fine,' I chirp, deciding to play along.

Ellie's bedroom door opens. Her face appears. And I realize my night is going to go from bad to worse.

'Is everything OK?'

Molly turns around. Squints at Ellie, who has her arms defensively across her chest. She's changed out of her grey jogging bottoms and put on her skinny jeans. The ones she knows I like her in.

'Hey,' Molly says.

'Uh, this is Ellie, my . . . flatmate.'

Ellie raises her eyebrows. 'Flatmate?'

'Hey, I'm Molly.'

'You're an officer? At the prison?'

'Yeah, that's how we met.'

I close my eyes as my face contorts in shame.

'Interesting. I thought you'd met in a bar or something?'

'Technically, we did, but we worked together first.'

I open my mouth to elaborate, to clarify, but there's no point. Ellie stamps back to her bedroom.

'She seems nice.'

'Yeah. She is.'

And now I have another fire to put out.

Molly looks good, in a long-sleeved white top and

stonewashed ripped jeans down to her black Timberland shoes. She's wearing Obsession by Calvin Klein – an intoxicating aroma.

'Are you hungry?' she asks.

'I could eat.'

'I'm thinking we can pick up a Chinese from the restaurant down from my house. I'm not in the mood to go out any more.'

'Sounds good,' I say, and head towards the front door.

'Aren't you going to say goodbye to your friend?'

I glance towards her bedroom. 'Nah. She's a big girl. She'll figure it out.'

We leave the property, walking closely together. My fingers touch hers. I feel a deep want for her.

Now that we're together, there's no more procrastinating. The fact that she wants to stay in with a Chinese is a sign from the universe that I must challenge her and it must be tonight.

I buckle my seatbelt and try to think happy thoughts. She starts the engine and pulls out into the main road.

I wait in the car while she nips in for the food. It gives me fifteen minutes to process what's happened. How to frame the questions I want to ask her. Molly's reaction to being interviewed by the police unnerves me.

My phone beeps in my hand. I don't want to look at it, but I'm compelled to.

I never thought you'd hurt me. But you have. What's so different about Molly, eh? You're happy to be OUT with her, but not with me? And from your work too? Am I such an awful person? Do you know how embarrassing that is for me? My heart's shattered.

Ellie thinks that because her dad's a retired governor everyone he used to work beside is still there, when the truth is most of them have moved on. She'd hardly know any of the staff these days.

There's no point in replying. I've nothing to say that isn't a lie. My head throbs as I slide the phone back into my pocket. Ellie's feelings will need to wait. There's nothing I can say that'll change things tonight. She needs time to calm down. It isn't like this is the first time I've hurt her. I'm the awful person.

Molly emerges from the Chinese, looks over at the car and smiles. I smile back.

A car, a white Audi, steams up the street doing about 50 mph. My mouth opens, warning Molly to watch.

She steps out on to the street. The car misses her by an inch.

I'm out of the car in seconds. 'Ohmygod, are you OK?'

'Yeah. Fucking idiot,' she says, staring off into the distance.

'Did you get the reg plate?'

'No,' she says. 'It sped by too fast.'

'That car could've killed you.'

'It didn't. Try not to think about it.' Her face has paled, and she's clutching at her heart. Trying to be brave for my sake.

The thought of eating makes me queasy. 'We need to phone the police.'

'No,' Molly says firmly, planting the food on the foot-rest of the passenger side. 'I've had enough of police tonight.'

'But. The car.'

'What can we tell them, huh? There's no CCTV in this street. We don't know the reg. It's probably stolen.'

'But . . .'

'Leave it, Kennedy. Please. I just want to get home and relax.'

How can I relax when the car could have balaclava man behind the wheel? Could knock down a child trying to get to me?

'You'll stay at mine tonight, right?' Molly suggests. And, I'm ashamed to say, all thoughts of Ellie, the car, work, evaporate from my mind.

27. Adrian

I pace the gaff. It doesn't calm me down; if anything, being cooped up in here makes me feel worse.

They let me apologize to the visit screws and I get a caution in the orderly room. The screws in the hall stuck up for me, like I knew they would. I'm put on probation on the pass. One more wrong move and I'll be sacked.

Three grands' worth of drugs – missing for over a week. I punch the TV. Knock all my coloured shower gels from the shelf. And as they fall to the floor, I kick them away.

Almost ten shitting grand in debt. With no way out.

I'll have to make an example. Save myself. Especially now I'm in debt to too many people. My hand's been forced.

I do push-ups in my room until it's time to be unlocked. I pull on two pairs of jogging bottoms and an old prison top over my good one.

I bounce out of my gaff and head over to Rampage, who is doing a bit cleaning, for once.

'What's happening?' Rampage asks.

'Do you still have that blade?'

Rampage nods. 'Do you need me to get it for you?'

'In a minute.'

'Who's the target?' He's overdue a bit of madness.

'Gaff 68.'

Rampage's eyes widen. 'Flakes? I thought he was one of us?'

'Same. Prick's stolen my stash. From the visits.'

Rampage whistles. 'Dirty scumbag. How much?'

'Enough that it would've made me around ten grands' worth,' I embellish. 'And now I can't pay my bills.'

'Thieving bastard. I'll stab him for you. Right in his crook heart. I'll chop his fucking hand off too, dirty bastard.'

I suppress a smile. Rampage reacts in exactly the way I'd hoped.

I find Spence and motion him over. He's having a discussion with Filan, but I don't want him involved. Spence give his apologies and jogs over.

'What's up?'

'I need you to be lookout.'

'Where?'

'Gaff 68.'

He frowns but doesn't question it.

'When?'

Spence doesn't bother himself with the details. That's why he's one of my loyal acquaintances in this shithole.

Rampage returns with the blade concealed in the waistband of his joggers. Nods. Taps his side.

A toothbrush with melted razorblades on the tip. Laces from a pair of busted shoes wrapped around to give a better grip.

Not wanting to be caught with it, I trust Rampage to keep it safe for me in exchange for a couple of grams of hash. Nothing's free in here, not even for your pals.

Rampage begins bouncing on the spot.

'What are you doing?' Spence asks.

'Psyching myself up. I'm going to slice that cunt up.'

'Come on then,' I order.

Spence grabs a mop pole and pretends to clean the floor outside gaff 68, and his own, 69.

Filan's watching from the other side of the hall, leaning against his gaff door. I give him a smile. He glares back.

Does he know who I am yet? He's about to find out. For he's next on my shitlist.

With one last look around to see where the screws are, I push the gaff door open.

'Flakes!' I yell.

The wee cunt springs off his bed. It's frightening enough me walking in, but having Rampage backing me up?

'Adrian,' he stammers.

'You owe me ten grand.'

'Adrian, mate, there was nothing there. I promise.'

I turn to Rampage. 'Search his gaff.' I turn back to Flakes. 'And I'm not your fucking mate.'

Rampage doesn't search quietly. Toiletries are knocked to the floor. The TV smashes to the ground. He rips bedding from the mattress, chucking it away.

Flakes presses himself against his window. He knows what comes next. Knows there's no way out. That's why they give the pass to the strongest. The rest are just victims.

'There's nothing here,' Flakes wheezes.

I stare at him for several seconds, ramping up the fear. 'Strip,' I command.

'What?'

Rampage is on him like a hungry locust, tugging at his top and pulling down his prison-issue jogging bottoms.

'I don't have anything, I swear!' Flakes cries. Shitebag. I want to stab him in the heart. End his misery.

'He doesn't fucking believe you,' Rampage says, punching him in the mouth.

My reputation's in question. I can't have this getting out. It must be managed now. And my reputation will blow up. Cemented as top dog.

Rampage holds his arms while Flakes slumps in between them.

'Stand straighter,' I order.

He's sobbing. He's every right to be scared. Still. Take it like a man, for fuck's sake.

I take a step closer. 'Bend him over the bed.'

'No,' he wails. 'Please. Not this.'

I ignore his pleas. Even if he promised to have fifty grand plus interest transferred into a bank account of my choice, this hasn't gone far enough. The cons need to know who I am. An example needs to be made.

We press him against the bed, hooking his legs so he can't move. The mattress muffles his cries as I plunge the blade, wiggle it about. Flakes screams, resulting in another punch from Rampage.

There's no resistance. He's clean. Slowly, I withdraw the tool. The boy squirms beneath me. Roars into the balled-up blanket that's been stuffed in his mouth. Rampage laughs like this is a comedy sketch made especially for him. Flakes won't be able to take a shit without thinking about me for months.

'He's clean,' I sigh.

Rampage drops his arms. Flakes slinks to the floor, naked and bleeding, sobbing on to the hard concrete.

'You owe me the money,' I say, grimacing at the particles of shit on the end of my weapon. He continues to cry so I boot him in the ribs.

Blood pours from his nose down to his chin and on to his chest. Snot travels down like tiny boats on a stream.

'He's pissed himself,' Rampage screeches. 'Look.'

We chuckle as the concrete darkens beneath him.

'I'll finish him off,' says Rampage.

'Nah, he's had enough.'

But Rampage takes the blade to the lad's face. I flinch at his brutality. I look away, unable to watch.

'Mate, that's enough,' I say, pulling at his arm.

Behind me, Flakes begins to scream. If I don't stop this now, Rampage will commit murder.

'Screws,' I hiss. The only word I know that will make him stop.

I can't be caught in the gaff by the screws. I leave the cell and notice Filan in another conversation with Spence. If he's annoyed, I can't tell by his face. Anger flares up in me. Spence's supposed to be watching out for the screws, not kissing ass with his new boyfriend.

We head back to our own gaffs. Now the weapon's been used, it'll need to be disposed of – same as the extra clothing I've worn over my good clothes. I have no blood on me and no lacerations on my hands, since I used my feet rather than my fists. I'm all good.

I remove the excess clothes and stuff them out the window. Grab my toiletries and towel and head for a rushed shower. The stench of blood and shit clings to me.

I'm staying on top now. No one's brave enough to cross me.

28. Kennedy

Molly's calmed down by the time we finish eating. I'm jumpy. Can't escape from the thought I'm being followed. It makes me itch. Persistent. The not knowing.

I allow my mind to wander. To the cause of death. The identity of Scout. And Ellie. I know I've hurt her. I'll find out how much in the morning.

'Will I put on a film?' Molly suggests.

'Sure,' I say, distracted.

I'm surprised she's chosen a romcom, but all becomes clear five minutes into the film when she leans down and begins to nibble my ear.

'I think you should take me to bed,' she suggests. And because I'm desperate for the voices in my head to disappear, to forget everything, just for a moment – I stand and reach for her hand.

'Come on then,' I say.

She's up keenly, like she can't believe I've agreed. She grabs at my face, kissing me deeply as her hands swarm over my body.

'I want you right now,' she whispers, her breath tickling my face.

Desire shoots through my body.

'Take me to bed then,' I whisper.

She pulls me along, switching off the living-room light as she walks through the hall to her bedroom. She switches on the bedside lamp. Dust motes dance in the glare.

'I'm going to powder my nose,' I whisper between kisses.

'Second door on the right.'

I smooth down my hair as I make my way to the bathroom, squeezing past the clothes horse, my heart fluttering wildly.

My legs stop working when I see it. On top of the radiator. And immediately wish I hadn't. It's out of place next to her underwear. Running tights. Work shirts. I reach out to pick it up but draw my hand back at the last second.

I flush the toilet and wash my hands. My face is red when I see my reflection in her mirror. I look away.

'What's the matter?' she asks softly when I force myself to return to the room.

Regret consumes me. There are now way too many more questions than answers.

'Hurry up and get into bed,' she pants. And in an ideal world, I would. She's lying there, in nothing but cream lace lingerie and a smile.

'Bad news,' I say, thinking on my feet.

She frowns. 'What's wrong?'

'Time of the month.' I blush.

I can't sleep with her now. All the concerns I've had about her return tenfold. Alarm bells and spinning fireworks. Why the fuck does she need a balaclava?

I slide over to the empty side of the bed and climb in. 'Is it OK if we just cuddle?'

'Sure. I mean, do you need anything?'

I shake my head.

She kisses me once then spoons me, lights off.

I wait until she's asleep, the whole time unable to shake the image of the looming balaclava-clad face in my rear mirror. Taking a deep breath, I psych myself up to find something that might break my heart. It's better to find out now before I fall any deeper.

Molly's a shady character. It's time to stop glossing over that.

The easiest thing to do is wake her up and ask. But I won't be satisfied she's telling the truth. A balaclava? There's no explaining that.

I go through to the kitchen. Pour myself a glass of water with shaking fingers. The water chills my hands through the glass. A gulp lubricates my dry mouth.

I take a long drink of water and contemplate my options. I could phone a taxi. Return to the safety of my own home. Or I could use this time to snoop.

But as the decision percolates in my head, I'm not convinced I'm doing the right thing.

I stop. Listen out. I can't hear anything.

I rub at my weary eyes. So exhausted my teeth start to ache. With no other possibility, I head back to bed.

The balaclava mocks me with its presence. It's still there, heating itself next to the radiator.

Molly's asleep on her back. Mouth open. Snoring gently. I observe her for several seconds. A part of me wants to wake her up and demand answers. But at the same time, the coward part of me won't. It sucks, being so pathetic. I cross my arms and continue to watch her. I'm not brave enough to hear the truth.

I step towards the bed. My muscles are screaming out for rest. Her phone illuminates in the darkness, immobilizing me.

Unable to stop myself, I skulk over. It's an email from Groupon offering deals in the local area. I take a step closer. Click on the phone, expecting to find it password-protected. It's not.

Stealing another look at her; satisfied she's still asleep.

Drying my damp hands on the duvet, I unplug the phone from its charger. The heat from it burns my hands.

Before I can stop myself, I clutch the phone to my chest. Slip out of the bedroom.

The living room's in darkness as I root for my own phone. A banging sound stops me. I stand up straight. Creep into the hall. Don't breathe until I hear a clear snore. Count ten seconds. Another five.

When there's no further sound, I continue.

A picture of Molly's Arsenal team stares back at me. I chew on my lip. Decide. I've committed now. Caress my lashes as I click into the messages.

I go through the phone. It's the one she uses to message me. Her mum. Her friends. Our last texts are at the top. It's the one she uses to access social media. But she hasn't left herself logged in and I can't access it. It's not her social media that interests me. In an instant, I've become one of those women.

I creep back through to the bedroom, sneaking glances at her. Still asleep. My fingers are slick with sweat. There's no defending this if she opens her eyes and catches me.

Molly doesn't stir. It makes me bolder. Biting at my lower lip and flickering my eyes at her to make sure she's still asleep, I click on the home button again, making sure there's nothing I've missed.

Molly's lying in the same position, snoring gently and cocooned in the covers. But when I go to find the charger cable, it's gone.

Shit.

Drop to my knees. Pat the floor. The blackout blind prevents any light entering the room. But I've been awake so long my eyes have adjusted to the darkness. But it doesn't help me to find the cable.

It's slipped behind the bedside table.

Fuck. Fuck.

Molly's hand flops out of the bed, touching my shoulder. I nearly scream. Scramble away from the bed, bumping my shoulder off the bedside table. A dull thump reverberates around the room.

The snoring stops. I freeze. Wait for her to sit up. Hold my breath.

Count to ten. To fifteen. Twenty.

Only when she doesn't move do I continue my search for the cable. The back of the bedside table scrapes my forearm. I clench my teeth to block me from crying out against the sting.

I find the cable. Recharge the phone. Wipe the sweat from my body. Place the phone back where I found it.

In the kitchen, I go through her drawers. The back of her freezer. The medicine cabinet in the bathroom gives me no clues. The desk in the hall is full of paperwork, but I don't find the bank statements I'm looking for. It was a long shot anyway. Who gets paper statements in 2018?

She's still asleep when I climb into bed beside her.

My heart's thudding the mattress so hard it might wake her up; it rattles the headboard against the wall. But she remains asleep. I turn on my side. Away from her. Unlock my phone and stare at the number until sleep claims me.

Molly's 5.45 a.m. alarm wakes me. When I feel the pressure of her lips on mine, she's already showered and made my morning coffee.

'Morning, gorgeous,' she announces.

'Morning.'

The light from the lamp is fiery bright against my tired eyes.

'Here,' she says, handing me a coffee. 'You look like you need it.'

'Yeah,' I yawn, wishing I could have at least another two hours.

'Was it my snoring?' She pouts.

'Yeah,' I answer. 'It's your fault.'

'Sorry, baby,' she says as she leans over and kisses me on the tip of my nose. Her touch elicits a repulsed shiver.

She's brushed her teeth, her mouth smelling of Listerine.

'Do you want a shower?'

'Um, I'll get one when I'm home.'

Guilt pervades my body.

I take a sip of the drink I don't want.

'I hope you don't regret staying over?'

Another sip disguises my pause. Do I regret staying over? It's not a question I've allowed myself to consider.

'It's not something I normally do. This soon, I mean,' I confess.

'I can tell that about you. It's partly why I like you. You're a good girl, Kennedy.'

I blush at her words.

'Drink your coffee – it might make you feel better. Wake you up.'

I do as she says to keep the equilibrium. She stares at me, and there's something different. It takes me a moment to figure it out.

'Your eyes? They're green?'

She laughs like it's hilarious. 'Yeah, biologically, I suppose.'

'But . . .'

'I wear coloured contacts, babe. I like to be different.'

Is anything about her real?

'Be ready to leave soon, OK?' she says gently, prodding me to get up and get dressed.

For the first time, I feel uneasy in her presence. I

drink more coffee as I watch her pull a brush through her hair. I turn my head to check the time against her alarm clock.

'I could get used to seeing you in my bed in the mornings,' she says with a grin, watching me in her mirror.

I offer a grin back that's more of a grimace. Take another sip. Does she know what I saw? Does she suspect?

I peer at her through my fringe. From her gold eyes, her athletic body to her sleeve of tattoos. I'm attracted to her. There's no denying it. But I can't listen to my heart when my head is screaming warnings at me.

'You're not a morning person, are you?' She giggles.

I sip at the coffee. It tastes like copper: blood and betrayal. 'Not really.'

'Do you need any painkillers?'

'Painkillers?'

'For your cramps?'

'Oh. No. I'm fine, thanks.'

Leaving the rest of the coffee, I spring out of bed. It feels grim, putting last night's clothes on. Matching how I feel on the inside. Dirty. Used.

When I go to the bathroom, my heart jolts. She must've realized her mistake and removed it while I slept. The bitch. My eyes feel heavy with unshed tears. Sometimes, I hate being right.

'You're doing it again.'

'Doing what?'

'Pulling at your lashes.'

We maintain eye contact. 'It's a habit. I can't help it.'

'What do you want to wish about this moment?'

Tears threaten to spill. I swat my eyes. Of course this was too good to be true.

Molly grabs me in an embrace. 'Aw, babe. Don't get

upset.' Her perfume makes my body betray me. I purse my lips, trying to forget how much I want her.

She plants a kiss on my forehead and I leave the bedroom, away from her. The pull of her.

I glance at my Fitbit. We should be leaving soon.

As if my thoughts make her appear, she's there in the living room, wearing her jacket and slinging her bag over her shoulder.

'Are you ready?'

I nod, picking up my bag. She slaps my arse as I walk past her, gritting my teeth, and fighting the urge to slap her back.

It's cold outside. The pavement's glistening with ice.

'Cold, eh?' she says, stating the obvious. I nod; the cold robs me of speech.

'Thanks for letting me stay last night.'

'I was hardly going to kick you out. And anyway. Your flat's closer to work. Maybe you'll let me stay overnight next time.' She winks.

Shame engulfs me. 'Yeah. I bought it last year. Well, me and Ellie did.'

'What? You don't rent?'

'No. We were lucky to be able to buy when we did.'

She glances down at her fleece. Picks at something only she can see. It hadn't dawned on her last night, but now, the penny's dropped.

'Nice one. You and Ellie, eh?'

'We're just friends. Now, I mean. Good friends. There isn't anything there, you know.'

'Cool.' But she doesn't look in my direction. Annoyed at herself for missing the obvious.

I turn to face her, my eyes letting me down and focusing directly on those lips. 'We better get going,' I say, unable to tear my gaze away.

Her presence is suffocating. It seems to take for ever for the car windows to demist. She drives me home in silence.

'When can I see you again?'

'Um, I'm not sure.' The heat melts my face enough for my lips to work.

'OK, cool. You can let me know then?'

'Sure.'

I scurry from the car, almost getting tangled in the seat-belt. I don't look back as I make my way up the path to what should be my sanctuary.

My heart's heavy as I let myself into the flat. I don't want to wake up Ellie. I creep into my own house, lock the door behind me. I place my keys in the bowl on top of the bookshelf and tiptoe down the corridor into the kitchen. But when I switch the light on, I startle when I see Ellie sitting at the small dining table.

'Why are you sitting in the dark?'

'Couldn't sleep. Got up to make some warm milk a few hours ago.'

I swallow. I should say more. But I can't. 'I'm just about to make myself a coffee. Do you want one?'

'No.'

I pick up the kettle. Check if it needs water. Click it on.

'Good night?'

My back's still turned to her, for which I'm grateful. She can't see the look on my face.

'It was OK.'

'Must have been better than OK if you stayed out all night.'

'Ellie . . .'

'We ended it because we wanted different things, Kennedy. Not because I stopped loving you.'

'Ellie . . .'

I turn round. But she flees the room.

I hover too long outside Ellie's room. Her words have penetrated my heart. I loved her too, but not like that. Not any more. I place my hand against the wood but can't bring myself to knock.

'I know you're out there,' she huffs.

'Can I come in? We need to sort this. Please.'

'Can you just give me some space? We'll talk later, I promise.'

I keep the shower water cold in order to wake me up. I can pretend to myself I'm not crying as the water from the shower cleans my face.

I don't want to go to work. I want to climb under my duvet and stay there for at least twenty-four hours. For a brief second, I consider it. It'd be too easy to phone in and take the day off sick. But the professional side of me won't allow myself to make the call. Nor does the thought of being trapped home all day with Ellie. We will speak at some point, but for now it's too raw.

Plus, I'm close to figuring it all out. My home isn't safe, not with me in it. Which makes Ellie unsafe. If I don't solve it soon, something might happen to her. The innocent one, and I can't let that rest on my conscience.

I can no longer kid myself that Molly isn't in too deep. Is she Scout? The person who's wanted me harmed? Or is she a different entity entirely? She *can't* be Scout. She had access to me all night. If she wanted me harmed that badly, then why am I still breathing?

Did I ask too many questions? Have I spooked her? Is she a danger to me? I desperately don't want her to be. But even I can't explain the appearance of the balaclava-clad stranger after I'd interrogated her about the loft space.

Without bothering to dry my hair properly, I tie it back

in a bobble and some Kirby grips to keep it out of my eyes. I brush my teeth until my mouth feels clean.

That's as much energy as I have. I allow myself to lie down on my bed for thirty minutes, looking at the number I saved during the night. My finger hovers over the delete button. But I can't bring myself to get rid of it.

My eyes burn as it overwhelms me, all the feelings. Towards her. Towards Ellie. Towards myself. I want to feel nothing.

I forward the suspicious number to my work email. Maybe Stan at Gartcosh will be able to help me out? My mind always bolts to the dark side. It could be innocent.

But to find out finally, I'm going to have to be anything but innocent.

29. Kennedy

'Is there anything I can do to help?' Jacob offers.

There is. But I don't trust him to do it. I play the CCTV footage back, but there's nothing to be seen, except Kai Spencer pretending to mop the floor before he moseys over to confer with Fred Filan.

Then Rampage and Maddox enter the cell of Jack 'Flakes' Doyle. Both come out approximately three minutes later and head to their own rooms. Before Doyle is seen crawling from his room covered in blood.

'The violence is completely insane,' I say, not expecting him to answer. 'We need more intel coming in from the hall.' Maddox again, I think. Does this mean Scout is involved too? At least I was with Molly last night. I know from personal experience she isn't involved in this.

'I could listen to calls for you,' he continues.

I fight the urge to roll my eyes. 'It's fine. I have a system in place. If you record the incident on the system and report it to the police, that'll be great.'

'Sure, of course.'

Caleb 'Rampage' Dyer. And Adrian Maddox. Both are refusing to speak. As is the victim.

'Is that the worst injuries you've seen? I mean, all those stitches to his . . .'

The cell searches were all fruitless. No weapon recovered. Not even the clothes they were seen wearing on the CCTV were found in their rooms before the two men were separately moved to the digger.

'No offence, Jacob. But I need to get these calls listened to.'

Without waiting for a reply, I stick my headphones on, cutting off the conversation. Fred Filan's used the PIN phone. I queue up the call. Press play.

'Fred?'

'It's me, aye.'

'How are things?'

'Bonkers. Someone just got their arsehole slashed.'

'Fuck off.'

'I'm telling you.'

'What happened?'

'I'll tell you at the visit. I'm not saying anything over this. Did you check that name for me?'

'Name?'

'Aye. Him at the visit. A M.'

'Fuck, mate. I forgot. I'll get right on to it.'

'Do. Thinks he's a wee hard man. Can't fight with his fists, know what I mean?'

'One of those ones.'

'I'll see you at the visit, yeah?'

'Sound.'

A M? Adrian Maddox? It had to be.

I try Kai Spencer next. Cue up his call.

'Babe, don't be mad.'

'What have you done now?'

'Nothing, babe. I swear.'

'Go on.'

'There's been a bad slashing in the hall. They're saying I'm involved, but I swear down on Mila's life that I'm not.'

'Fuck sake, Kai. You promised.'

'They've taken me off children's visits, babe. As a punishment.'

'How can they punish you if you weren't involved? You

said you'd stop lying to me. You said you'd keep the head down.'

'I am, I swear. I was outside the room. When it happened ... Cleaning the floor. I'm going to get my lawyer involved. They can't punish me for this. Punish us.'

'Kai ...'

'Don't leave me, babe. I'll do whatever I can to get these visits back. You know how much they mean to me. And I've been offered work when I get out. Legit work.'

'Aye,' she sobs. 'Where?'

'Driving a taxi. For Fred Filan, but I swear, babe. That's all it is.'

'I can't do this, Kai.'

The calls beeps, indicating he's been hung up on. He's tried to phone her back a few times, but she's been unable, or unwilling, to answer.

The victim hasn't returned from the hospital. The extent of his injuries is unknown. But according to the witness statements, the amount of blood over the floor made the officers think he was dead.

The violence is getting worse. I type an update and send it to the senior management team with a recommendation that all alleged perpetrators should stay in the digger for a month to allow further investigation.

One of them will talk. No one likes it down the digger. It's just a matter of time.

30. Adrian

With hindsight, it's obvious I'd be dragged down the digger thanks to the invention of CCTV – the biggest grass going. Things are slipping from me, and I can only blame myself.

The gaff's sparse. No TV. No kettle. Just a mattress on the floor so I can't wreck the place. Or kill myself.

There's a button on the wall where I can listen to Radio Forth Valley, but since it's run by the beasts, I'd rather pull my fingers off and stuff them in my ears.

The screws have changed down here since my last visit. Warned me I'm looking at a month rule. It's imperative that doesn't happen. It's hard enough doing three nights, far less a full moon.

Maybe I have gone too far this time. But then, I'm a big believer that everything happens for a reason. I can't physically kill Filan from the digger. But at the same time, my hold over the hall will weaken.

With nothing to do but read and think, I'll go insane. At least Rampage is next to me. If we go to the windows and scream at each other, we can keep up a conversation.

Word has got to me Flakes needed eighteen stitches in his cheek. Rampage did a decent job. People will look at him and think of me. What I'm capable of. Not that I'll see him. We'll be linked as enemies, even though the chicken's requested protection. Put in with the other beasts. He had to, after the gaffers reported it to Police Scotland. They'll be up to civvie-charge us any day now, the scumbags.

But it's my word against his, thanks to there being no CCTV in the gaffs. There's nothing worse than a grass. The truth is, I've fucked it. Deep down, I know it. I've given Filan the opportunity to take over. It's time I started to think before acting.

I pray something happens in the hall, so I'm flushed out the digger, like what happened to Filan when he arrived. There's only one empty gaff down here. It could happen.

I yell up to the lads in the hall until my voice is strained. Order them to riot. But they ignore me. Would be different if I had gear. They'd do anything for me then.

The nurse comes to the hatch with a screw, hands me the anti-psychotic medication I've been on since I turned eighteen and a small plastic cup filled with water.

'When can I get out of here? I done fuck all?'

'I'll ask the Governor the next time he's doing his rounds,' says the screw, bored.

I throw the beaker away. That's not the answer I want, although it's the one I expect.

I get down on the floor and complete another two hundred push-ups. Anything to keep my brain calm.

'Boward,' I shout. 'Boward the coward needs his mammy to fight his battles.'

After a beat, he responds. 'Shut it, Maddox. At least my family done what had to be done.'

'Really? The bitch's back at work – your maw didn't understand the assignment.'

'She was supposed to be taken off the numbers, coward,' Rampage shouts.

'I'd like to see you two try,' he cries.

The rest of the digger laugh at the wee pussy. The cunt should be on protection for what he did, but Uncle Bar said we had to look after him. Scout's orders. The Bowards are nothing but plastic gangsters.

'Look at him being a digger warrior, opening his gub cos he knows he's protected by the door,' another con laughs.

'The Boward family are bacteria, mate. A different breed. Shag his sister and your knob will fall clean off. Happened to someone I know,' I shout.

We wind the wee cunt up until he cries, then the game becomes boring. I've been down here two hours. How am I supposed to last a full month?

There's only one thing I can do to get out of the digger and back to the hall. But it goes against everything I was brought up to believe in.

Another hour and I lose all my principles.

'Here, Rampage, you there?'

A pause. 'Aye, man.'

'You all good?'

'Aye.' A chuckle. 'I told the screws I was going to kill myself, so they give me a telly. I'm sound, mate.'

Different rules for different fools. No one else down here has a telly.

I press the in-cell button and request a cup of tea from the screws. They aren't allowed to refuse me. When you're in the digger, you aren't trusted to possess a kettle in case you fill it full of boiling water and sugar and pour it over their heads. Napalm time. One psychotic nut job ruined it for the rest of us. Chickens.

Bang. Bang. Bang. He kicks his cell door purely to wind up the digger screws. He seems to be doing all right without me. The digger's like a second home to Rampage; he's never away from the place for too long.

A knock on my door quietens him down.

'What are you doing down here?' I ask as she enters my gaff with my plastic beaker of tea.

'Staff shortages. I've been deployed down here for my shift.'

'Is it true Rampage has a telly?'

'You know I can't discuss other prisoners with you.'

'You're not supposed to bring in drugs and blades either, are you?'

'Making false allegations against officers can lead you into getting a longer time in the digger.'

I smirk. 'Your face has gone a bit red. You feeling the heat?'

'Adrian . . .'

'So, you'll get me a TV then? We understand each other?'

'I'll see what I can do.'

'Not good enough. I know all about you, remember. The things you've done for me. For my uncle. For Scout.'

'Watch what you're saying, son. That mouth of yours can get you into a lot of trouble.'

'That sounds like a threat. I want that phone. The one you wanted £2,000 to smuggle in. For free. For your cheek.'

'I never . . .'

'The Governor will be doing his rounds soon. Maybe I'll see if he knows how you supplement your wages. And that's just for starters.' I maintain eye contact until I'm not the first to break it.

She brings me a TV within the hour.

'Remember, if anyone asks, you're feeling suicidal.'

I roll my eyes. 'Whatever. I need to see the Governor.'

'Crawford Docherty is on duty. He'll be doing his rounds later.'

'I need to see him now. I want to tell him what happened.

To the visits pass man. How he ended up with all those stitches.'

'How you cut him up, you mean? Tore his arsehole to shreds.'

I laugh. 'I'm innocent. And the Governor needs to know that. Make it happen.'

'I'll see what I can do.' She sighs.

'How are you getting on with the other thing?'

She chews her cheek. Reluctant to answer.

'Get to fuck. Don't come back unless you have something I want to hear.'

I stew for the Governor longer than I did for the TV, which is just a back-up plan. It's after teatime when the Governor does his rounds. He leaves me until last, as if on purpose.

'I need to speak to you in private,' I whisper as he opens my observation hatch.

The screws have had a vendetta against Rampage ever since he put one in hospital with busted ribs and a broken eye socket. They're always looking for a reason to get rid of him. And this time, I'm happy to oblige them if it gets me out of the digger.

I'm escorted from my cell by three screws and taken to the closed visit area. I'm on one side of the glass with three screws while the duty governor is on the other. It makes me feel like I'm Charles Bronson or some shit.

'Talk,' he says, not interested in taking any shite.

'It was Rampage that assaulted the lad in his gaff. I tried to talk him out of it, but you know the mad bastard. There's no talking him down.'

'Why are you telling me this?' The Governor sounds bored. Maybe I'm keeping him away from the football or something.

'I don't deserve to be down here. I've done nothing wrong. I want to go back to the threes.'

The Governor sighs. 'That's not my decision to make. As far as I'm concerned, three of you were in the cell and only one person has injuries. In my book, that makes you both guilty.'

I glare up at the Hayworth screw.

Fix this, I silently urge.

'If I can just say, Governor, I know Adrian from up on the threes. This is out of character for him. But Rampage – I mean, Mr Dyer – I firmly believe he's capable of inflicting the injuries sustained by the victim.'

The Governor taps his pen against his bottom lip. 'A decision will be made at the end of your three-day punishment whether you return to the hall or not. You're not going back up tonight.'

With that, he stands, pushing his chair back and exiting the room without saying goodbye.

'Are you going to walk back to your room, or will we have to deck you?' growls a short screw. I want to take him up on his offer, but my desire to return to the hall is greater.

I hold my hands up. 'Don't fucking touch me.' They cover me as we walk the short distance back to the gaff. At least I have the TV.

'I tried,' whispers the screw before the gaff's locked up for the night.

'I'll be back up the hall in a couple of days. Make sure the mobile phone's brought to me or I'll be having a different conversation with the Governor. I have money to make back because of your fuck-ups and your smart ideas. Someone will be in touch to drop off more drugs to you.'

There's one more person on the outside I can rely on.

I can only hope they'll dig me out of the hole I've got myself in.

'Not at my house,' the screw stammers.

I cross my arms and stare through the observation hatch. 'When are you going to learn you're not the one in charge here? You'll bring in what I want you to bring in and you'll collect it where I tell you to collect it. Are we clear?'

'I told you about being greedy. I told you about being stupid. Why should I do anything else for you?'

The hatch slams closed.

31. Kennedy

'You've to report straight to the head of operations,' announces Tina with an excited glint in her eye.

I've barely removed my jacket.

'Has something happened?'

She shrugs. 'I haven't heard anything.'

Immediately, my palms coat in sweat.

Victor is tapping away at his computer and, for a second, I don't want to interrupt him. Taking a deep breath to steady the nerves, I knock on his door before rambling in. Head up, chest out.

'Morning,' I announce, breezily.

He finishes typing his sentence before he stops. Turns around. Keeping me hanging.

'Morning.'

I sit at the table and wait for him to begin.

'Two things. The assault on Hayworth three. The victim doesn't want it reported to Police Scotland but, since we have a duty of care, it needs to be reported.'

'I already asked Jacob to report the incident to the police. We don't need the victim's consent on account of the injuries and the use of a weapon.'

'Can you get him to fire me over the police reference number? I need it for the serious incident report. Officers suspect it involved the drugs we recovered. He needed eighteen stitches to keep the left side of his face together. He's in surgery this morning to repair the damage to his colon.'

'Are we looking at transferring him to another establishment?'

'I've already had that conversation with the population manager, but nowhere will take him. We're the only place with room, allegedly. And you know the Governor likes to consume his own smoke. He won't ask for a favour.'

'How do we protect him when he's discharged from hospital? Can they keep a room for him on protection?'

'You know it's not that simple. We'll need to cross that bridge when he gets released.'

I grimace. 'I'm sure there'll be plenty of intel reports,' I say, rolling my eyes. 'Will the victim talk?' I go on. It'll be worse than a permanent scar for him if he does. If the police don't take a statement from him soon, his arse will collapse a second time.

Victor nods. 'He's been asked twice. And both times he seemed eager to pretend he fell in the shower.'

My eyebrows raise. 'You remember his dad? He won't have been brought up to grass,' I say.

'CID are dispatching someone to the hospital to take a statement. He's more likely to provide one there than when he comes back to reality here,' Victor says, as if he's read my mind.

'I'll dip into his phone calls. See if I can find out anything.'

'Good idea. If you can disseminate the intelligence to the team at Gartcosh, let them know we're linking it to the find.'

To Adrian Maddox.

'Secondly,' Victor says as he pushes his glasses up his nose, 'we finally have the PM results.'

I pick at a loose bit of skin on my thumb. 'How did he

die then? Kalvin Jones?' My stomach churns. For some weird reason, I don't want to hear the answer.

'It's an interesting one. He was found to have consumed cocaine that'd been mixed with fentanyl. In fact, there was more fentanyl than cocaine.'

'Fentanyl?'

Victor nods. 'The police are working on the hypothesis, as far-fetched as it sounds, that it was deliberate. Someone wanted someone else out of the picture.'

A flash of shock. I was right.

'But Kalvin Jones was a nobody. Who'd want him dead? Unless it's the relatives of the female he's alleged to have raped?'

Scout says goodnight.

The knife.

Victor licks at the corner of his mouth before he continues. 'The police think Jones might have been holding the drugs for someone else. Got a little bit greedy.'

'What are you saying, Victor? Do you think someone's tried to commit murder here? Accidentally killed the wrong person?'

He shrugs. 'That's what it looks like. To the police, anyway.'

'Fuck sake,' I say. Stunned. The stiffy I found makes sense now. The one scrunched up in Jones's bin.

Scout. It has to be.

'Can we initiate any CHIS meetings? See if we can corroborate?'

'That's for the police to investigate. We've handed everything over to them and now it's up to them to do their job.'

I normally struggle to find sympathy for prisoners. But this one strikes me as sad.

I swear again. 'Can you imagine if that'd been passed around? It could've wiped out the whole hall.'

Ignoring my profanity, Victor continues, 'I need you to look into all the drug dealers on the threes. And this time, we can't discount Fred Filan. His movements since the day of admission will have to be scrutinized on the CCTV. I want to know everyone who speaks to him. Who's hanging around his cell. Who as much as glances at him.'

'But the timing's off.'

'Who's to say Filan didn't organize the route of introduction for him to use on someone else before he even got to the hall?'

He has a point, but I'm not convinced. But then, Fred Filan has the financial backing and psychopathic tendencies to execute a murder in this chilling way.

'I'll look into it straight away.'

Someone is at risk in the hall. Maybe the knife wasn't for me? And even if they are a prisoner, no one deserves to be murdered. I have to find out who. Despite what Victor says.

'What about the other drugs?'

'What do you mean?'

'Shouldn't we get the police to analyse those too? The other recent finds. See if they contain lethal doses of fentanyl?'

'The police will be up at some point this morning. Mention it to them. They'll want a copy of the deceased's movements from the minute he was unlocked in the morning until the minute his body was found. But I want to know the information first. Before they get it. The union have already been on the phone. They've started taking statements from officers without giving us the heads-up first. That's not on.'

I rearrange my expression to look shocked. 'They already have the footage; Security signed it out to them the other day.'

I saved the CCTV footage on the system, knowing it could be requested at any moment.

'We can't rule out staff corruption here, Kennedy.'

If someone's hidden drugs in the loft space for a prisoner, they could also be responsible for this.

'Scout,' I whisper. *Molly?* I remember the balaclava, drying in her house. I can't go on like this. I need to confront her, and get to the truth.

'There is a third thing,' he adds, 'but you're not going to like it.' He puts the paper on the table, pushing it towards me with his index finger.

Restricted: Confidential

HMP Forth Valley
5 x 5 Intelligence Report

REPORTING PERSON: (Person receiving the information from the source)	Crawford Docherty	PAY REF NO: u0272
SOURCE NAME: (Person providing the information)	Adrian Maddox	
PROVENANCE OF INFORMATION:	1. How did you come by this information? Witnessed it. 2. Where the source is a prisoner, what's their motivation for passing this on to officers? Innocence 3. Who else knows this information? Other prisoners in the section. 4. As a result of this information, do you feel at risk? No.	

DATE & TIME OF REPORT:	Tuesday 16 October 2018 @ 18:52 hours				
SUBJECT OF REPORT:	Incident				
SOURCE EVALUATION	A Always reliable	B Mostly reliable	C Sometimes reliable	D Unreliable	E Untested source
INTELLIGENCE EVALUATION	1 Known to be true without reservation	2 Known personally to the source but not to the officer	3 Not known personally to the source, but corroborated	4 Cannot be judged	5 Suspected to be false

Reporting Person's Evaluation

Source Evaluation	A
Intelligence Evaluation	1

Intelligence:

The above prisoner claims the assault was perpetrated by Caleb Dyer and wishes to return to the hall. Seems plausible.

32. Adrian

The gaff feels more claustrophobic by the minute. It's been madness down here. Rampage is in the middle of a dirty protest. He thinks I'm joining in once I get the need to go for a shite.

'I've covered my hatch,' he shouts, cackling. 'I've written my name on the wall.' Rampage's running commentary of where he's spread his own shite drives me round the bend. I feel like I can smell it, even though we're in concrete coffins. Not even the small window opens.

I get on fine with the guys up the hall, but I can't take another hour of them shouting shit to each other.

I clench my teeth hard until they hurt. Someone has to save me from this. I don't have any scoobs to make the time go faster or easier either. And the Governor's disappeared without a trace.

It's too late now, anyway. The nightshift screws are on. Giving up, I press the emergency buzzer.

'What?'

'I need a glass of water. Please.' It's hard for me to sound sincere, but I think I manage.

When he comes to my door, I'm ready. 'How we doing, boss?'

'Fine. Here's your water.'

It's as simple as that. The nightshift screw isn't allowed to pass us anything. Our needs should've been met by the backshift before they left their post. That's how easy it is to get them round to my way of thinking.

I grab the glass and down the water. 'I bet you get paid shitty money to put up with these clowns, eh?'

The screw shrugs as I peer at his name badge. 'I have a dog called Benjamin,' I continue.

The screw softens up. 'I've got two German shepherds. Right thugs they are. My missus wants a cockapoo.'

'I bet they set you back a bit. My cousin's a breeder. I could set you up. Get you a wee discount?'

'Really, like, ten per cent? Or higher? They're expensive wee bastards.'

I rub the stubble on my top lip. Hide my smirk. Sometimes, it's too easy.

'Much higher, mate. I'll give you a number if you're interested?'

'Yeah, that would be great. In time for Valentine's Day?'

It doesn't hurt to have too many special friends in here. Especially when that stupid cow's doing my head in.

33. Kennedy

It's funny how you can only look at things objectively in the end. The realization quickens my resolve, and my steps, and I'm soon in front of her red front door. Red for danger. I shiver as I press down on her doorbell.

I have to be quick. I only have forty-five minutes for lunch.

She opens the door quick, like she's expecting me. Or someone. Surprise filters her face.

'Kennedy? Hi. What are you doing here? Not that it isn't a pleasant surprise. But I'm expecting a friend over.'

'We need to talk. Can I come in?'

She holds the door open for me. I swoop under her arm, dodging the kiss she tries to plant. If that doesn't convey a certain type of message, then I'm screwed.

'Can I get you a drink?' she asks. And just to prolong the inevitable, I nod. Suddenly needing a caffeine rush. Suddenly feeling weak. She looks so good in her maroon joggers. Her grey vest-top.

'Have I caught you at a bad time?'

'No, babe. I'm just home from the gym. I need a shower,' she adds, wiggling her eyebrows. The question left unasked. I look away, and the moment's gone.

'Come through to the kitchen.'

I follow her through with trembling fingers. Struggle to put one foot in front of the other.

'Two sweeteners, no milk,' I say. We haven't even known each other long enough for her to know my hot-drink order.

She flicks on the kettle and tries to open the canister of coffee at the same time.

'Take a seat,' she says as she operates a fancy coffee machine. Like the rest of the place, it looks expensive. Sleek. I rest my back against the breakfast bar. Furtive glance around at the luxury kitchen goods. The overbearing American-style fridge freezer. Built-in double oven. Everything looks so new it's hard to believe it's been used.

'It's good to see you,' she says and, again, tries to kiss me on the lips.

'Molly, don't.'

'What's the matter?'

I look down at the coffee mug she places in front of me.

'Let's grab the drinks and go through to the living room.'

She frowns at me but complies. Stirs the coffees for longer than necessary.

The plant on her windowsill has begun to droop, its petals wilting. A ten-day romance.

I look down at the floor, choosing to sit on the couch nearest the door. Easy for a quick exit.

'How's work?' asks Molly when she walks through with the coffees. 'Is Maddox behaving himself yet?'

I take a hit of the coffee.

'I take it you haven't come over because you're missing me?' Her tone turns cold. Does she know what's coming?

'I really like you . . .'

'But.'

I lick my lips.

'Don't say, *It's not me, it's you*. I fucking . . . hate it when girls say that.'

'It's complicated, Molly.'

'It didn't look too complicated when you were almost fucking me the other night.'

I continue as if she hasn't spoken. 'Don't shit where you eat. It's what I was told my very first day.'

'But we're good together. I know we can be. Or are you just running away from something good? Running back to the safety of her? Your flatmate.'

I raise my eyebrows. Carefully put down my mug before I bounce it off her head. 'Really? That's how low we're stooping?'

She rubs her hand over her hair. 'Look, I'm sorry. I don't take being rejected very well.'

'I'm not rejecting you . . . I have – trust issues.'

'Trust issues? You don't trust me?'

'No. I don't.'

'You haven't given me a chance.'

'I don't need to.'

'Kennedy. Please. Don't do this. I think about you all the time. Even when I'm brushing my teeth, I think, *What's she up to? Is she thinking about me?* Don't say there isn't something there. We can get past this.'

'We can't. Not until you tell me this life you lead is because your parents are wealthy. The car, the jewellery, the fancy presents. Tell me I'm wrong. Tell me . . .'

'Kennedy.' She chuckles through nerves and I see the real her. 'My finances are nothing to do with you. I don't have to explain anything to you. We like each other. A lot. Why can't we leave it at that?'

It hits me suddenly. There's no denial. I've got the answer I came looking for. This has to be over.

'We can't be together. I have to put myself first.' I can't

be connected to her, and the pain of the realization nearly rips me in two. 'This is a mistake. Me and you. I'm sorry.'

'Kennedy, don't go.'

But I rush from her house, tears blurring my vision.

I'm sick of thinking about what happened to me that day in the supermarket. Has it really only been a few months since I was attacked? The ruminating – it's exhausting. But the memory takes hold of me again as I clutch the car door and gag.

I can still smell the faint trace of stale alcohol on her breath, competing with the cheap perfume sprayed liberally to mask her smell. The leather of her wrinkled skin, her brassy yellow hair. *Scout says goodnight.*

I pull open the car door, only feeling safe when I'm locked inside. But it's too late.

I stay where I am and cry until all the water's out of my system. I didn't expect her to be so – uncaring.

As soon as I'm home from work, I head straight to bed. It's still there in my mind. The incident. The pain. Intermingled.

I hear footsteps outside my bedroom door. The shift of light under the doorframe. But if Ellie planned to see if I'm OK, she changes her mind and tiptoes away. We still aren't speaking. And I don't want to give her the satisfaction of knowing she was right – not when I'm hurting so badly.

I used to be so strong. What's happened to me?

Disliked that much at work that someone is trying to kill me when all I ever strived for was to keep everyone safe. Staff and prisoners. Betrayed all my principles for a woman who's, at best, a liar. And I've hurt my relationship with the only person who's ever truly been there for me. The only one who's ever truly loved me. I'm broken.

My hand inadvertently strokes the box of antidepressants as I adjust my pillow. The box is as bashed in as my heart. Biting my lip, I tear off the lid and peer inside.

Nothing can get any worse, I think, using my thumbnail to burst the foil packet. The white rectangle pill is smaller than my pinkie nail. Without a second thought, I swallow it down dry, wincing at the bitter taste.

34. Kennedy

I understand it now. Something that I haven't before. How you can be so close to the edge, it's easier to end it all. I can't see myself making it to the end of the week. It would be so easy to just – stop existing. No more pain. No more let-downs. No more humiliation.

At work, a song comes on the radio and sets me off. 'Unchained Melody'. The song McCredie sang the first time Molly and I met. But in my haste to leave the IMU, I don't notice the time, and now I'm stuck. Frozen. Unable to move.

I've made a point of avoiding the front-desk area around visiting times. And now I've fucked up. Because they're here. Fanning themselves against the heat. Complaining about the queue. I can smell their perfume. Their sweat. Last night's liquor.

The Bowards.

My vision blurs and I struggle to draw air into my lungs. I can't move forward, yet I can't move back.

And the worst thing? There's nowhere for me to go. Her large body blocks the exit. She doesn't see me as she whispers to a young male who must be her other son.

My breathing hitches. I fight to get air into my lungs. My vision blurs. My head swims. I'm frozen. Back pressed against the cold wall.

'Are you OK, Kennedy?' someone asks. But I can't tell if the voice belongs to a male or a female. My head's woolly, and everything diminishes around me. Far away. My scar itches, my brain working against me to replay memories I try too hard to forget.

The feel of her clammy skin on mine. The intense pain in my face. I reach out, and my hand connects with the lockers. I press my back against the wall, sweat dripping from the end of my nose. But it's my heart, beating away far too fast. I can't catch my breath. Is this a heart attack? Am I dying? I slide down the lockers until I'm on the ground. All I hear is white noise.

Scout says goodnight.

I close my eyes. Because I can't see them if I can't see.

Someone grabs me and I shriek. They put their hands around my shoulders, trying to calm me down.

I have no recollection of being pulled into the staff room, but that's where I find myself when I come to. It's not a place I frequent often, and initially I don't realize where I am.

The pool table to my right is new. The smell of someone's lunch lingers in the air. Something fishy. A nearby bookshelf contains magazines and books. Plastic flowers are dotted around the room.

'Are you OK, Kennedy?'

A plastic cup filled with water is on the table in front of me, dribbling condensation on to the table.

My cheeks are hot, but due to shame rather than heat. 'I'm fine,' I mutter. Of all the people, they called Jacob.

'You gave the front-desk officers a bit of a fright there. Do you want me to give you a lift home? I'll sort it with the Governor.'

I close my eyes against his voice. 'What an idiot. I take it they're all talking about me?' Something else for them to gloat about. Kennedy finally got hers.

The officers who monitor the CCTV cameras in the

control room are probably watching my meltdown on repeat. Jacob keeps quiet. He knows better than to bolster my paranoia.

'I can take you home, it's not a problem. I can come back for you in the morning. Your car will be fine in the car park overnight.'

I don't say anything. The last thing I want is to be stuck in a car with him. The truth is, I don't want to go any-where. Because there are officers on the other side of the door. And I don't want to see them. I'll just stay here. In the muster room. Indefinitely.

Then, unexpected, he says the thing I'm sick of hearing. 'Maybe you came back to work too soon?'

I bite my tongue. What does he know? He didn't know me before the incident, and he sure as hell doesn't know me now. But does he have a point? If I hadn't come back, I wouldn't now be a laughing stock. I wouldn't have met Molly. My heart wouldn't be fractured. I wouldn't have lied to Victor.

'Are you after my job too?'

Deep down, I know he's trying to help, but it's from him, and I don't like him enough to appreciate the senti-ment. I don't trust him.

'No, I'm just worried about you. I don't think the Ken-nedy I've met is the Kennedy you were. I want to see you get better.'

I grunt. Pick up the water. Put it back down.

'Is there someone I can call for you, if you aren't com-fortable with me? I can speak to HR.'

Can he read minds?

'No. Thanks. I'm fine.'

I pick up the water and take a sip. My mouth incredibly dry. Who would HR phone? Ellie? Will that make her speak to me again? To repair the damage between us? The damage I caused.

'I don't have anyone to phone.'

He chews on a thumbnail as his face reddens. 'I'm sorry about that.'

'Why are you always so nice to me? I'm not always nice to you.'

He shrugs. 'If you can bring anything to your day, it should always be kindness. We're all fighting our own demons, you know. Everyone should remember that.'

I press my lips into a tight line to prevent myself from laughing. I've tried kindness. But this job has ruined me. I'm cynical of everything. I trust no one. It's not working.

'I used to be so miserable. Then I got put on sertraline and, after six weeks, I woke up feeling like a different person. Maybe that's something for you to consider?'

Maybe I should never have come back at all. Maybe this isn't the job for me, after all.

'That's why you always get me in the same mood. I don't care what other people think of me. That's what ruined my childhood.'

I glance at him. For the first time, I'm interested in something he has to say.

'I was bullied all the way through school. Lost so many hours of my life worrying about things I couldn't change. What I could do to be accepted. How I could harm myself.' A sniff. 'It's my only regret in life.'

'What's the script with you and the Governor?' I blurt, needing to think about something other than myself.

Jacob blinks, then smiles. 'Sebastian? He's my uncle. He's doing a favour for my mum. Giving me a job. That's why I'm here. What's the point in being at the top if you can't pull in any family favours, right?'

My bottom lip drops to my chest. They aren't lovers. I was wrong. But I knew there must have been a reason for his sudden employment here. A familial reason. What else have I been wrong about? My cynicism making me jump to conclusions that aren't there.

'I flunked uni,' he continues. 'I didn't fit in. I didn't want to lose any more of my life. But at the same time, I just want to make my family proud.' He sighs. 'This will do for now. Until I decide what I want to do with my life.'

'Thanks for being honest with me. It means a lot. I have them too. The sertraline. But I haven't taken any.'

He shrugs. 'I haven't kept anything from you, Kennedy. If you'd have asked, I'd have said. I don't think Victor likes me much, but I'm here to do a job. A respectable job. His feelings towards me are his issue.'

For the first time in what feels like ages, I laugh.

'Keep taking the tablets, Kennedy. Six weeks from now, you might feel differently. It certainly helped me deal with things completely differently to how I would have before.'

Lumps form in my throat. It's time to get a move on. 'I'll think about it. I promise. And don't worry about Victor. Keep doing a decent job and he'll thaw towards you. He doesn't like not being in control. He doesn't like when the Governor pulls rank and fiddles with his areas of responsibility.'

'You don't like him, do you?'

'Victor?'

'No. My uncle.'

'Ah.' I suck on my bottom lip. 'No. He's out of his depth. This isn't the place for him. I'm sorry.'

'Don't be. We're all entitled to our own opinions. He's just trying to do the best job, as he sees it. Trying to make a difference. But don't think I'll pick sides. You told me the

IMU is a place of trust. Anything said in there, stays in there, right. Don't think you can't trust me.'

I drain the water. Wait for a minute to make sure it's not going to make a reappearance. Maybe it's time to give counselling another go. There isn't any shame in admitting I need help. I can't live like this any more.

Letting my negative feelings win. Pushing people away. The perpetual mistrust.

'I started taking the pills last night. I should've started taking them weeks ago. But I saw it as weakness.'

'I'm not a doctor, but you do have all the classical signs of depression. There's no shame in admitting you need help. I was on them for two years.'

'Do they ever let you sleep?'

He laughs. 'Yeah, after a couple of days. But you need to keep taking them. Trust me. They help a lot.'

I nod. I know he's right. I've never thought about harming myself until recently. That's not right. But I keep that part to myself.

'Let's get back to work,' I announce.

'Are you sure?'

I glare at him.

He gets the message. 'Come on then.'

Jacob holds the door open for me like I don't have the strength to do it myself. Maybe I don't.

I take the steps slowly, delaying my eventual appearance at the front desk. I pause at the controlled door.

'Take your time,' Jacob says. 'There's no rush.'

And I do. I stand there so long Jacob saunters over to the large noticeboard on the wall. Staff selling concert tickets. Staff looking for roommates. Staff advertising their trades.

'Huh,' he says.

'What?'

'I've been looking for a new mechanic.' He taps his finger on a business card tacked to the board. 'Is this Ray McCredie reliable?'

His face is innocent as he waits for an answer.

'Come on. I'm ready.'

Walking past the front desk is easier than answering that question.

Tina's pitying face makes me want to cry. The visitors have dispersed to the visit room. I keep my head high and walk through the turnstile without being stopped, despite setting off the metal detector.

Jacob's hand is on my lower back as he guides me through to the key-vending area, where we each retrieve our keys. In a way, I'm glad it's Jacob they called. It would've been more awkward had it been Victor. My scar continues to throb. I surprise myself by giving a thumbs-up to the cameras. Let them analyse that.

Jacob holds the doors open for me as we make our way back to the IMU. If people heard what happened, no one mentions it.

Except Crawford Docherty. He's sitting at a desk with that smug smirk on his face. His usual expression for me. I give him a winning smile as I step past. Let the bastard choke on that.

As soon as we're back in the IMU, Jacob locks the door and makes sweet tea. I accept the mug gratefully.

He stops suggesting things to me. It's not his fault I dislike him. He's an annoying pain in my arse. But. I've thawed.

'Is there anything I can do for you to help you out?' he asks. He sees the hesitation on my face. 'I know I'm clumsy, but I'm not stupid. Give me the chance to prove myself to you. As soon as the right job comes along, I'll be gone.

You won't have to put up with me for ever, Kennedy, but my God, make use of me while I'm still here.'

I look at him. He isn't out to score points. To set me up. He's being genuine. Sincere.

I could be more like him.

We all could.

'Come here. I'll show you how to dip into phone calls.'

I see Jacob in a new light. We can be an ally for each other. 'I have to tell you something,' I blurt. And before I can stop myself, I confess everything about Molly. Our relationship. My suspicions.

'I don't think you're being paranoid,' he whispers.

35. Adrian

Prisoners kick their doors. Shout threats to the screws when I'm walked back into the section with three screws dressed in riot gear.

As soon as they told me I was returning to the hall, my arse collapsed. Have they kept it a secret, what I did to get back to the hall? Or does everyone know? I kicked off, deciding I was better off in the digger. Be careful what you wish for, right?

This was supposed to be a canter. But everything's gone downhill since Fred fucking Filan came into my hall.

'Calm the fuck down!' roars one of the screws, feeling the big man because he's in his riot gear. A masked warrior.

Tim Reilly waits for me outside my new gaff.

'I didn't have to bring you back,' he begins. I hurry into my new gaff, not wanting to have this chat in the earshot of others. 'If you so much as fart without asking permission, I'll make sure you're dragged back to the digger for three months.'

When did he grow a backbone?

'Put your arms on the far wall,' they order. Not wanting to compromise my position, I comply with their instructions, and they leave me alone.

My posters lie ripped on my new bed. My row of coloured shower gels are empty and abandoned on the floor. Contents squeezed out in the search for contraband. The cunts. The only thing in my new gaff is the stink of pish.

I smirk. But the smile is wiped off my face when I notice I've no TV.

I bang on the door.

'What are you doing?' asks Tim. 'Are you ready to go back to the digger already?'

'Where's my TV?'

'You're still on punishment. If anything else happens in this hall, I'm holding you personally accountable. You'll be back in the digger. I'm sticking my neck out for you here. Don't let me down.'

I boot the door again.

'OK, Mr Maddox. I'm extending your prescribed rule. Which means you'll continue to follow the digger regime. No TV. No recreation. And don't even think you'll get your pass job back this side of Christmas. Do you understand? Bang the door again and I'll extend it until the end of the month.'

The urge to hurt someone is real. The cunts stitched me right up.

'I don't hear you.'

'Yes!' I scream, booting the door one more time. I might be back in the hall, but I've lost my pass job, my pass gaff, and the freedom to wander. At least it'll give me the opportunity to see which way the land lies.

I give the door the finger. He pretends to be decent, but he's just like all the rest.

I shout on Spence five times before he finally comes over. My hatch scratches open, but he doesn't speak.

'What?'

'Who do you think you're talking to? Get me some coffee and biscuits. Sort me out, eh?'

'When are you getting out of your cell?'

'Fuck knows. They've got it in for me, kid.'

He stands there, rubbing his hand through his hair. Playing with his glasses. 'On you go, then.'

'Right.'

'Bring me back a chunk of green. And a spare telly if there's any extra in the KIT store.'

He looks over at Filan, as if he's waiting on his permission to act.

I pace the gaff until Spence returns, shoving the stinky through the hatch. He's already pre-built the joint for me. I light up and take a hit. My shoulders involuntarily relax as soon as the drug hits my system.

'We're running low on supplies, Adro.'

I take another draw. 'Leave it with me.'

I mentally count the sums in my head. I've yet to break even. More stuff will have to come in soon.

'There's no tellies, Adro.'

I exhale a steam of smoke. 'Don't worry about it. The dog squad won't be on shift in the morning. That McCredie will get me a telly.'

'That your mole?'

I giggle as I pass the joint through the door. 'Pleading the fifth there, mate.'

'What are you doing, you madman?'

My chuckle turns into a cough.

'We need to send a message,' I say. 'A protest. Riots. Something to tell them we're not putting up with their shit any more. That we run the hall. Are you with me?'

'Always.' But he doesn't sound convincing.

'Tell the boys. Friday night. Let's ruin the screws' weekend for a change. Two free scoobs for everyone that joins in.'

It's time to remind Spence and the rest of them that Adrian Maddox is back in charge.

36. Kennedy

I dump my bag and go straight to the bathroom, where I strip off and step into the shower. The water masks the tears. My skin reddens, the longer I stay under the hot water. It's like a hug. And in this moment, I desperately need a hug.

I lay on my bed, wetting the covers, staring up at the ceiling. My body's drained. Hunger evades me. I can't even muster up the energy to make a drink.

I close my eyes, despite it being only late afternoon. I need this day to be over and the only way I'll get over it is just to get through. Second by second. Minute by minute. Hour by hour until it's tomorrow.

The earlier I sleep, the earlier I'll wake up, and another day will be over. Another one will start. And soon, I'll forget Molly Rana ever existed. My eyelids are heavy, pulling down as I'm drawn further into an exhausted sleep.

The doorbell rings. I don't open my eyes. See if Ellie will answer. I pull the duvet tighter around me. I can smell her around me, which is weird, because she's never been inside my bedroom. Every now and then, the whiff of Molly's perfume causes me distress.

Banging on the door proceeds the doorbell.

'I can see your car,' Molly shouts through the letterbox.

My eyes spring open. Have I dreamed her up, or is she here? How the fuck did she get in the building?

I dive out of bed, imagining my neighbours with their ears pressed up against their doors, listening to my private life being played out around them. Free entertainment for the night.

I pull on my dressing gown and flee across the hall.

'How did you get in the building?' I ask through the door, using the peephole to make sure she's alone.

'One of your neighbours let me in. They thought I was the police.'

She is wearing her uniform, which often gets mistaken for a police one.

'What do you want?'

'Let me in, Kennedy. I want to talk. To apologize.'

'I've nothing to say to you.'

'You'll want to hear what I have to say.'

I keep the locked door between us, debating what to do.

'Kennedy, don't be like this. Please. I'm trying to say sorry.'

I want to close the door in her face, to get the closure I need. To wake up in the morning feeling different. But a part of me needs to hear what she has to say. For I am weak.

The curtain twitches at number ten. I unlock the door, open it wider, and she barges in.

By the time the door clicks shut, I'm almost sure I've made a mistake.

'We have a connection, don't we?' she says, waiting for me in the hall.

'Look, I'm not in the mood for this.'

I'm acutely aware I'm naked under my dressing gown. Her eyes twinkle, her shiny hair inviting me to stroke it. I shake my head to clear my thoughts.

'What do you want to know, Kennedy?'

'The balaclava. I wasn't snooping; it was there for me to see. The other night.'

'Are they illegal?' she tries to joke. 'I wear it when I'm out running. It is winter.' Her explanation is seamless. 'If it was sinister, I wouldn't have had it lying around for you to see. Credit me with some intelligence. Please.'

I chew on my bottom lip, unsure of whether to believe her or not. My heart wants to reach out and embrace her, but my gut won't let me. There's still something off about her. I just don't know what.

'Someone has been hanging around me. Intimidating me. Wearing the same balaclava.'

'And you think it's me?'

'Yes.'

We stare at each other. This has to be the end.

'Are you using me?'

'Using you for what?' she wails. 'I can't believe you'd think that.'

I shrug. 'For information?'

'What information? Have I ever asked you a single thing? I wouldn't ever put you in that position. Don't you think I'd have tried to get information out of you by now?'

I think back. Has she ever tried to manipulate information from me? My head's too fried with it all. I can't think – not with her standing so close to me. I want to believe her so much, but are my years of training and experience stopping me?

'I came to see if you were OK. I heard about – what happened this afternoon. I wish you had phoned me. I'd have come and got you.'

'I had someone. Jacob. And I don't want to talk about that either.'

'Look,' she says, biting her lip. 'I'm a good officer, but you're not entirely wrong about me. There are things

I've – hidden. But I can't tell you anything. Not right now. It's not safe. I'm not safe. You need to leave it. Please.'

She pauses. My heart shudders, disintegrates in my chest like mouldy fruit. She's in front of me. Admitting it. I'm going to be sick. My hands slap against my mouth to keep everything in.

'I can't do that, Molly. I can't leave it. I'm close to figuring it all out. To finding out who's behind all this. Finding out who is after me. And if you aren't willing to be completely honest with me, then it's best that you leave.'

She takes a step towards me and pulls me into a hug. And all rational thought is gone.

'Tell me who he is.'

As she kisses me on the head, I put my arms around her. Out of habit more than anything else. A moment of weakness. Because I've needed to be held all day.

Sappy. Pathetic.

'We can leave. Right now. Let's drive into the sunset together. There's nothing keeping us here. I love you, Kennedy. Let's be safe together.'

My tears drip on to her shoulder. 'How can I, when you won't tell me the truth?'

'The truth? I wouldn't know where to start.'

'The beginning. What's the worst thing you've done? In fact. No,' I say, waving my hand. 'If you can't tell me it all, I don't want to hear anything.'

'Leave with me. Right now. And once it's safe . . . I'll tell you who he is.'

'Blackmail? You're resorting to blackmail when you won't even tell me if I'm safe from you?'

'I'll put in a transfer then.'

'I'm sorry?'

'A transfer. That's how serious I am about you. That's

the sacrifice I'll make for you. Because I believe in us,' she adds, banging her chest with her fist. 'And then. Once I've earned your trust back and when it's safe, I'll tell you everything.'

I pause. Her face sincere. Genuine. Or so it seems. I look into her eyes – her real, green eyes – and can't help but think what else is fake about her. She's done a good job of covering up so far.

'You'd do that for me?'

'I love you, Kennedy Allardyce. I'm in love with you. And I know you like me too.'

It's what I've waited to hear. But the circumstances are all wrong. My heart shatters. I can't stop the tears. But it's time for strength.

'No.'

She continues, ignoring me. 'I'll speak to HR first thing in the morning. Do you have a preference on where I go? The opposite end of the country, or will somewhere in the central belt suffice?' Her smile is weak.

'I haven't felt like this with anyone else before,' I say. 'The way I feel with you. I can't imagine being with anyone else. But there's no relationship without trust. You have to go. I don't trust you. I don't believe you.'

With the last surge of energy, I push her towards the front door and out of my life. Because if she stays for a single second longer, I'll fall under her spell even deeper. Instead, I choose to break my own heart.

37. Adrian

'Did you bring me the phone?' I yawn, annoyed at being woken so early.

The screw hesitates. I'm about to lose my shit when it's pulled from her sock and all tiredness is chased away.

'I said black.'

'They only had pink ones. I'll take it back if you don't want it.'

I snatch it from her hand.

'Be careful with this.'

'Watch your tone, bitch. Don't think I won't rip your face off cos you think we're pals. After all, you are the one that gave me the blade.'

'Take the day off, Maddox. The world doesn't revolve around you. I'm having a bad day and you're giving me a headache.'

'Like I give a fuck. What's the matter anyway? Lovers' tiff?' I cackle. 'Do you not want your cut any more?' Silence from her end. 'Did my sister come round to see you?'

'I told her not to. I've already warned you, Adrian. You're being watched. And I'm out.'

'Says who?'

She rubs her face. 'Me. I'm not doing this any more.'

'Fuck off. I say when you're out.'

'I don't work for you, remember. I work with you.' She shakes her head and scurries from the gaff.

I turn on the phone, my fat fingers pressing too many buttons. It'll be easy to bank this; it's no bigger than my thumb. But I've heard stories before about folks' bodily fluids fucking the phone. I'll need to be more creative.

I kick at the skirting boards, but none of them are loose. My last window line's been recovered, and they haven't left me any materials to make another. Fucking bams.

But when they bring me my lunch, I hide the plastic knife, and the stupid bastards don't notice.

As soon as the key turns, I relax. I need to be alert in case the screws come back. If I get caught, I'll get a one-way all-expenses paid trip back to the digger. Maybe even put on the ghost train to another prison.

I pull the plastic knife from the cheeks of my arse.

'Your da sells for Avon,' shouts some window warrior to my left.

'Go to rec tomorrow, ya daftie. I'll take you for a square go.'

I grab my lighter, ignoring the insults. I'll take them both a square go if they don't shut the fuck up.

I melt the tip of the knife, watching as the plastic bubbles. Only when it's completely melted, I thrust it into the raw plug of the plastic alarm panel beside the door.

It takes a few minutes for the knife to resemble a screwdriver. Removing the panel is an act of genius. The screws aren't as clever as me to think to search there.

I remove the plastic and rush over to the sink, running cold water over the tip of the melted plastic until it cauterizes the melted manufactured screwdriver.

Satisfied it's ready, I remove the panel from the wall. Make sure there's space for my tiny phone.

The phone switches off with difficulty. The buttons are so small I hit three at once. But I'm going to have fun with this.

But after a minute, I realize I don't have the time to

fuck about. It takes me a minute to press the buttons delicately enough that I'm not setting them all off. Fuck this. I grab a bookie pen from my desk and use the nib to press the buttons. It's the only thing I have that's small enough that'll work.

I lurch over to the door and make sure there's no one hanging about. It's a risk using it now, but I want to make sure it works. Then I'll keep it until dub-up, when the screws are away on their break. Or at night-time when they're away home.

I'm astonished to see the tiny phone has internet capabilities. It cost the screw £25 to buy down the Glasgow Barras. I'm confident I could sell it on for at least £500. If the screw brings in a few more, I can make thousands. Cheaper than drugs. Less risk. And I'll make enough to repay my debt to Uncle Bar. Get him to trust me again.

The phone buzzes in my hand and I shite myself.

'Hello?'

'You're a fucking idiot.'

'Bar, look, I trusted the wrong cunt. It won't happen again.'

'You're right it won't. I trusted the wrong cunt too.'

'Don't be like that. It would've worked. It did work. It took one clean off the numbers. It's good to hear from you. I've tried to phone a few times.'

'I need my money, wee man. I have bills to pay out here too, you know.'

'Give me another chance. I won't fuck it up this time. I was just thinking, a couple of these tiny dogs in and we could make a mint.'

'You've had enough chances. You know what needs done.'

I swallow.

'I know, I know.'

'Do the job. Your debt will be cleared and maybe then we can start again.'

'Are you going to give me some of that powder again?'

He chuckles.

'You've fucked that, wee man. You'll need to take a cosh to a square go. Use your hands. Just get it done. By the weekend, or never call me again. No more excuses.'

He ends the call. I've never heard him sound so pissed off before. Not directed at me, anyway. There's redemption there for me if I want it badly enough. And I want it.

But.

I run my hands through my hair. I don't think I have that in me. Maybe, when Rampage comes back from the digger . . . But that could be months away. And the deed needs done now.

Smoke a snout and think. If only I could go back in time. I'd do everything differently. I had this hall in a choke-hold until that prick Filan came in. I should have used Rampage against Filan, not some chicken-headed junkie.

My hatch scrapes up.

'Who's that?' I ask, hiding the phone down the waist-band of my joggers.

'Spence. What's happening?'

'I need a glove,' I say. He doesn't have to ask any further questions.

He disappears and returns a short time later. Brings me two.

'Cheers,' I shout through the door. This is going to be the uncomfortable part. I'll bank the phone during the day and hide it in the panel at night. Get one of the youngsters on the twos to hold the screwdriver.

I stick the thumb of the glove into my mouth, gagging against the chemical taste. I chew on the thumb part until it detaches in my mouth. I spit it out on to my hand, whistling as I go. I stretch the thumb part and slide the phone inside. It's tight, but it fits.

I tie the end in a knot and jog on the spot. I run the parcel under the tap for a little lubrication before I pull down my joggers and boxer shorts.

Next, I bend over the toilet bowl and slide the parcel up my arse, clenching my teeth at the discomfort. I wiggle my legs and my arse cheeks around to ensure it doesn't fall back out.

I pace the room to make sure it's secure in its own prison. It's in tight. I bend over and feel it move.

For the rest of the afternoon, I watch shitty TV under my covers. Someone needs to loan me a boxset to get my teeth into. I'm grinning when I'm handed my dinner a short time later. Back on my feet like a boss.

Spence owes me, not that he knows it. Because I told the screws it was all Rampage, it got him off the hook too. Got to keep his pass job.

A short time later, I get another visitor.

Filan.

'I want some coke. Meet me in the servery after lunch with it.'

I don't want to give him the spray off my pish, but if it means getting paid, I'd be silly to knock him back. It's the same with the beasts on the protection wing. If they want to give me their money, I'll gladly take it.

My pizza's cold, but I guzzle it down regardless, then have a smoke, content with life.

My thoughts quickly return to Filan. If I take him off the numbers, my debt will be cleared indefinitely. If I don't fuck it up this time.

After all, I've used up all but one of my lives.

38. Kennedy

The antidepressants steal my appetite. Turn my brain to sludge. I should've started them while I was still off. When I had the luxury of staying in bed all day. I stare at the computer, not doing any work.

Jacob warned me I'd feel worse before I start feeling better, but the way I feel today makes me question whether I'll take another one tonight.

Another night of no sleep makes my head feel like it's full of cotton wool. When Jacob enters the office, I could cry at the relief of seeing a familiar face.

'What do you think?' I ask when I give him my Molly update.

'I don't know.' He rubs his chin. 'It sounds like she was genuine. But I don't know her enough to say. But . . .'

'But?'

'You're still at risk, Kennedy. You're not leaving this office on your own any more. You still don't know who else is out there to get you.'

We talk it through over coffees.

After a while, it's time to get on with the day job.

'Fred Filan's used the PIN phone,' I say. 'Do you want to listen?' I unplug my earphones and press play.

'Yo.'

'It's me.'

'Uh-huh.'

'I've sent you a letter. You should get it tomorrow. Read

it. Then read it again. I'll call you back in twenty-four hours. But it must be this Friday. Do you understand?'

Hesitation. 'Sure.'

'In the meantime, say hello to Leo Price.'

Jacob studies me. 'He's planning something for Friday?'

'It sure sounds like it.'

I thought it would take him weeks to learn to listen out on phone calls. But he's picked it up surprisingly quick.

I gave him a list of code words and I think he's taken it home to study it. He knows more than I did when I first started in the IMU.

Fred Filan's an enigma. What the fuck is he planning for Friday? There isn't enough time to get to the bottom of it.

I log on to the prisoner records system and call up Filan's page. He isn't scheduled to attend court. He has no other appointments.

But then I notice it. At the bottom of the screen. A new visit's been booked with him and Junior Green, his right-hand man, according to the *NEDitorial* exposé. But there's another name booked in.

Leo Price.

I type up a quick intelligence report with the man's name and alleged address and disseminate it to the Intel team at the Gartcosh crime campus. Maybe they'll have an idea who Leo Price is.

But I already know. He won't exist. Filan's as clever as they say.

'Price rhymes with spice,' I say. Filan could be organizing a shipment of the synthetic cannabis for Friday's visit.

'Maybe he's seen a gap in the market, with all the attention Maddox is getting?'

'Or maybe Price does exist, but he's the one that'll pass drugs in the visit session?'

I sit back in my chair and smile. It's good having someone to bounce ideas off, not that I'd admit it out loud.

'Got you.'

I dial down to the security unit, but the call goes unanswered.

I open my emails and compose one. It's time for the PDA monitors to be withdrawn and analysed again. Adrian Maddox hasn't used the PIN phone since his return to the hall. He isn't smart enough to make small regular calls to detract from the assumption he's in possession of a mobile phone and avoid suspicion.

Whereas Fred Filan keeps his calls short. No longer than ninety seconds.

I switch on the CCTV monitor and check the cameras in Hayworth three. Monitor the pass men. Spence is using the phone nearest the grille gate. I'm shocked but not surprised to see Filan out on the pass. The stronger ones always rise to the top.

Maddox is locked in his cell on a prescribed rule and Rampage is still in the digger. I squint at the camera. I can't see any other prisoners out. Is this the way Filan wants it?

Molly comes into view, and I look away. I don't want to see her, I remind myself. I'm looking out for the pass men.

Spence strolls away from the PIN phone, closely followed by Fred Filan. That's an interesting development. I wouldn't have put Filan down to follow anybody.

A shiver climbs up my spine when Molly unlocks a cell and Adrian Maddox storms out. He spins around and holds up a hand to stop Molly.

What are they talking about? Neither of them looks incredibly happy. But there's a plethora of reasons for that.

It doesn't always have to be suspicious. But I can't help but think, *Isn't that the way it always turns out to be?*

There's nothing sinister in the way Maddox moves about, but I'll be able to tell better if I watch him in the hall. Close up. He grabs a fresh towel from the KIT store, and I watch as he pulls a shower gel from the pocket of his shorts.

Does he keep the phone himself or leave it with another prisoner to get caught with and take the blame?

My thoughts return to the last intel report submitted by Clive Clifford. That Kai Spencer wants to give information in exchange for a move to the top end, where he can access home leaves. Normally, I'd pass this up the chain of command. But I want to be the one to hear what Spencer has to say.

I have questions for him. Questions he might be the only one who can answer. Especially if he's desperate for a move.

Victor's rest day can't have fallen at a better time. We'll have to talk about it soon, but it doesn't have to be today. If he mentions it at all. Then there's the loft-space report. Maybe he hasn't realized I've had it for days. But Molly's highlighted name will draw questions I'm not able to answer.

'Can you go to Security and see if they've removed the phone detectors for me, please?'

'Sure.'

Racing over to my desk, I make a phone call before I change my mind. Then I watch my actions play out on the screen. A break of protocol, sure, but I need to know about Scout. I need to know if I'm safe. I don't allow myself to think of the repercussions. The career-ending repercussions. The consequences.

Only when Spencer is escorted from the hall do I make

my move. There's less travel for me, so it's normal I'm there first.

But as I'm leaving the IMU, Jacob returns.

'I've been called to a meeting,' I say. 'Continue listening to some calls and see if you can come up with anything, I shouldn't be any longer than an hour. Don't worry, I'll be fine.'

'OK. Oh, um, Security says that they haven't been asked to take out the phone detectors.'

I theatrically slap my head. 'Oh yeah, I haven't asked them yet. I must be losing it. Sorry. I better go.'

I dive away from him before he can ask any further questions. I fan my notebook against my clammy skin as I make my way to the agents' room.

The agents' visit area is clean. A warren of rooms covered in plastic Plexiglass, so the officers have full view of ongoing visits. Agents can be anything from lawyers, police, social workers and leaving care assistants. But there's only one room where the glass is frosted.

I let myself into the room without informing the officers on duty. The less they know about this appointment, the better it'll be for everyone.

I look around at the graffiti scrawled on the walls. Initials and gang signs. Even a 3D coffin. On the corner is a small TV with a built-in DVD player, so the prisoners can watch themselves on CCTV playing out the crimes of which they've been accused.

There's an unpleasant smell to the room, like long-eaten stale eggs mixed with the musty contents of an old Hoover.

Exhaling deeply when the knock comes, I quickly compose myself. It's a step closer to getting this over and done with.

'Morning. Take a seat,' I say, without looking up. 'Do you know who I am?'

A scowl of mistrust presents itself on Spence's features. He shakes his head, bemused.

'I'm your new CHIS handler. You understand what that means?'

He sniffs, attempting to look like he doesn't care. His leg shakes under the table. He taps a beat on his knee. If his peers find out he's a registered informant, a grass, he'll have a permanent reminder slashed on to his pretty face.

'You've been really helpful in providing intel, Mr Spencer. You're officially my informant. Let's work together. Help each other out.'

He doesn't have to know my knees are knocking under the table. I'm taking a risk here. This type of conversation should only take place under the direction of the head of operations and security. Victor. By a trained CHIS handler. I've crossed so many lines recently, and for what? More questions than answers.

'What do you want to know?' he asks, rubbing his nose.

'Everything . . .'

His face blooms in colour.

'In order for you to progress to open conditions, to the Training for Freedom in Larkfield unit, you are going to have to give me some decent intel.'

'I can't give you what I don't know,' he lies. Lies neither of us is in the mood for.

'OK, here's how we're going to play this. I'll ask a question and you'll nod or shake your head. Agreed?'

Hesitation. A nod.

'Think about what's really important to you, Mr Spencer, before you answer my questions. I will know if you're lying.'

He glares at me and only looks away when I ask my first question.

'Is there a mobile phone in your hall?'

He hesitates for three seconds. A nod.

'Does it belong to Adrian Maddox?'

This time, the hesitation lasts a few seconds longer before he moves his head in the affirmative.

'OK. Now I need you to talk. Does he have it in his possession, or is someone else holding it?'

'He won't trust anyone with it. Where do you think he keeps it? It's worth too much too him.'

'Good. See, this is working.' I keep my tone firm. 'I have a few more questions, and I appreciate the truth.' My mouth is suddenly dry. 'Is there a member of staff bringing in drugs for Adrian Maddox?'

I keep my eyes down at my piece of paper. But when Spence doesn't answer, I look up.

'A screw? Nope.'

He pulls his ear. Fiddles with his glasses. His leg jigs.

'Does the name Scout mean anything to you?'

'Other than the group I was in when I was a boy, no.'

'You haven't heard any member of staff being referred to as Scout?'

He shakes his head, but the colour's drained from it. He's a prisoner. It's in his nature to lie. Some things he isn't willing to share, even if it means home leaves and Christmas morning with his kid.

He's lying.

'What about Fred Filan? What's he up to?'

Spence's shoulders sag. His leg stops. 'Nothing, actually. We're all pretty surprised. We thought when he came into the hall he'd try and take over. Have stuff on him. Be violent.' A shrug. 'But he's been pretty disappointing, to be honest. Nice enough to talk to, but.'

It's the only time he's spoken where I'm a hundred per cent convinced he's telling the truth. I change tack.

'Is Scout a screw on the flat?' I ask, using slang to lure him into answering me.

'N-uh, I . . . I gave you my answer. I've told you all I know. When can I move to the top end? I have a daughter. She's my life. A chance of a new start.'

'Shame you didn't think about her when you burgled an old man and left him for dead.'

'I was young, for fuck's sake. My girl was pregnant. We had nothing.'

'And your solution was to take from other people? You could've at least phoned for an ambulance. You did pinch his phone, after all.'

He stands up with such force his chair falls to the ground. 'You're a fucking bitch. You think you know everything, but you know fuck all.'

'I've heard worse from better people than you.'

I give him my icy stare but, inside, I'm melting. I shouldn't have provoked him like that. If he complains about me, I'm fucked.

I've breached RIP(S)A in speaking to Spencer. The punishment won't be a slap on the wrist. It'll be instant dismissal. Possible criminal charges. And how many people will revel in the satisfaction of that?

'Answer me one thing, and I'll personally see to your move. I'll approve your community access. I have that power, Mr Spencer.'

He throws himself into the seat.

'What?'

'Who is Scout? Do they work for Maddox?'

He looks up to the ceiling. Closes his eyes. Clenches his jaw. My breathing stops. My body tenses.

'I don't think he's working for him, as such. I think they're in it together.'

'Who?'

'Ray McCredie.'

My heart contracts. His words feel like a punch in the gut. It takes me all my willpower not to jump from my seat and scream YES. It's taken me a few weeks, but I've got there.

My legs wriggle, I wet my lips. Need him to say it again.

'You're sure?'

'He practically confirmed it to me.'

A nod.

I blink. Surprised. But not surprised. My heart races and I try not to show any emotion, which is difficult with my heart pumping so hard.

'One more question. Please. And I'll authorize a home leave over Christmas.'

'Go on.'

I lick my top lip. Feel sweat dampen my body.

'Are there any other officers, or managers, that I should be looking at?'

He shrugs, and I fight the urge to yell.

'This is important. Are there any . . . female staff I should be concerned about?'

'No,' he says with passion. 'All the staff up there are decent, to be honest. But Ray's the one. Trust me.'

'Is there a certain time or day when drugs come in?'

'I don't know. Adro hasn't been dealing long, I guess. And his stuff keeps getting found.'

'The visits?'

A nod.

'The loft space?'

'The loft?' he puzzles.

'Never mind. Is there stuff coming in soon?'

'I'd assume so. Adro's dry.'

'Could Filan be organizing something?'

'Wouldn't surprise me. He's too switched on a fella to tell anyone his business. Total old school, him.'

It's my turn to nod.

'Last question. What do you know about the death in custody the other week?'

'No comment.'

'What do you mean, no comment?'

'I have nothing more to say to you.'

'What about your home leaves?'

He remains mute.

'Were the drugs that killed Kalvin Jones meant to harm someone else?'

Nothing.

He looks at his hands. Hangs his head. I realize I've said the wrong thing. Spooked him.

'You can go now. And remember, you don't want it to get out that you spoke to me today. Keep your fucking mouth shut. OK?'

He bangs on the Plexiglas window. Maria Collins opens the door and frowns, looking between us.

'One back to the hall,' I say, careful to keep my tone even.

She motions for him to leave the small room. 'Remember what I said,' I can't help myself but say. But he doesn't acknowledge me as he swaggers down the small corridor.

As soon as he's gone, I fall on to the chair. I've jeopardized my job, but he's told me what I needed to hear. But what am I going to do with it?

It's up to me to now prove it and end this once and for all.

39. Adrian

It's not long before I'm melted. There's something about being on this rule that's keeps me insane – like I'm dubbed-up for my own protection. Unable to leave my gaff except for appointments. It's sending the wrong message.

My hatch is pulled sharply. I squint. Sit up quick when I realize who it is.

'What do you want?'

'When can I expect the coke?'

I snigger.

'I'm surprised,' I say, the locked door between us making me bolder. 'I thought you'd have your own connections. Get your own supply route going?'

He shrugs. 'Too much of a ball-ache.'

'Good. Heard you've already stole my job. Don't want you taking my business off me too.'

'I'm not stupid enough to get my hands dirty. That's the difference between me and you.'

I giggle again. 'And yet you're doing life for triple murder.'

'For now,' he adds, menacingly.

'You can't be confident you'll win your appeal.'

'No cheek, no chance.'

'What do you want, Filan?'

'I heard about the protest. And I'm thinking . . .'

'What?'

'We'd be better doing it on Saturday. There's less screws on at the weekend. It'd cause more carnage.'

'Are you up for it? Take control of the hall, cause chaos. Show the cunts I'm in charge.'

'You only think you're in charge because I've allowed it. So far.'

'Funny.'

'I'm up for it. It's time these screw scumbags got taught a lesson.'

'Spread the word. But if anyone rats to the screws, I'll cut their ears off and stuff them up their arses.'

'No one will say anything. I can guarantee it.'

'We'll refuse to go in for dub-up,' I add.

'Why wait until dub-up? Why don't we go for it straight after lunch?'

'Fred, you're one sick pup.' I grin.

'Saturday it is, then?'

'On Saturday,' I nod, 'we tear this shit up. Spread the motherfucking word.'

I turn my back on him and my hatch closes. I suck on my bottom lip. I'm sticking to Friday. If Filan's not expecting anything, so much the better. Time to make a weapon. A balaclava. A black marker to disable the cameras.

There won't only be a riot. For Filan, it'll be his last. For I'll use a blade to poke a hole in his throat.

'When am I getting off this fucking rule?' I demand when my dinner's brought to me. I'm buzzing for the weekend, and I want out to organize it myself. A riot they'll be talking about for time.

'Calm down, Maddox.'

'I need to get out of this room. I'm feeling suicidal.'

'Fuck off.'

'I am. I don't have anything to live for.'

The screw isn't buying what I'm selling. 'I need you to source me a black marker.'

'Why?'

'That's fuck all to do with you. Just get it done. I can't exactly get one myself.'

'You should've thought of that before you started being a daftie then, eh?'

'You better watch how you talk to me. I'll bite your nose off.'

My threats don't land. The screw smirks.

'You've fucked up, Adrian. Do you honestly think anyone will listen to anything you have to say and believe it? You don't want everyone to know you're a grass now, do you? Because I can make that happen.'

Fear seizes my heart and squeezes. If this gets out . . . 'You . . . You wouldn't dare. I'll make your life miserable.'

'You don't get it, do you? There are other prisoners in here. I can get *you* done. You have no power any more. No one's scared of you.'

'And I can tell the hall Governor about the stuff you've been doing over and above the duties you're paid for.'

She tuts. 'You're pathetic, Adrian. Maybe you should do us all a favour and request a move to the beast wing, with all the other protections.'

I boot the door. Pain springs up my big toe, but I won't give the satisfaction of crying out.

'Get me out of here, or I'm telling them everything. I'll tell them you come in my gaff at night and touch me up.'

'Threaten me one more time and see what happens. I'll get Filan to drag you about like an empty tracksuit.'

'I'll tell. I'll tell them what really happened the other week. How you smuggled the dodgy gear in. To help kill . . .'

'Shut the fuck up, Maddox. You don't want to go down

that route, trust me. I don't give a fuck who your uncle is. And no one will miss you. Not even him.'

'And I don't give a fuck who your . . .'

I pause. It dawns on me. The screw's serious. Where's the cow that used to be up for anything? Then it comes to me. Clicks into place.

Fred fucking Filan. They all think their bread will be better buttered with him. With that Valley scumbag.

I knock all the contents of my shelf on to the floor. Kick the bed box until my hamstring aches.

'Are you with him now? Billy big baws in 37? Is his dick bigger than mine too? Do you suck it for him after dub-up?'

'What makes you think it's another guy?' she says before sauntering out of the gaff.

All around me, everything crumbles. My reputation. My connections. My respect. And all because of that fucking rat.

I'm going to end him. As soon as the protest is in swing, I'll end him. There's no going back. I'll end all of them.

A knife in their fucking spines.

The clock ticks closer to the weekend. Where, for Filan, it'll end.

40. Kennedy

Filan. It's taken him a few weeks to get his feet under the table. If he's going to try and take over the drug trade, it'll create a power struggle with Adrian Maddox. In turn that'll lead to more violence. Serious violence.

And with Maddox having McCredie for back-up, I don't know what intel Maddox is being fed.

I rub at my temples. They need to be split up before it comes to that. But there isn't enough intel on Filan, and the decision has already been made to keep Maddox in the hall.

It's up to me to continue applying pressure on Tim to see it from an intel perspective. Maybe I could request the staff group to be split up instead, ensuring Maddox and McCredie are kept apart.

But then, by keeping them together, Maddox might give something away in a call that I could take to Victor.

'It happened again,' Jacob says when I walk into the office.

'What did?'

'Your phone rang and the caller hung up after about ten seconds.'

'It's probably a wrong number on Gumtree or something. Written down wrong. It's a bit of a leap to make it sound suspicious.'

'But aren't you suspicious of everything?'

Jacob has a point. But it's a new me.

'Yes. But I'm trying to change.' I give him a smile.

'There's something else though,' he continues. I look up

at him and attempt to feign interest. He hands me over a piece of paper. Eleven digits.

'They forgot to withhold their number this time.'

'Oh, right.'

I stuff the piece of paper under my keyboard and promptly forget about it.

'Will you pass it to the police?' he says, his excitement palpable.

'I'll send it to my contact at Prison Intel.'

My phone rings and we both jump. Wipe my palms on my trousers. Sniff. Reach over. Pick up the phone.

'Forth Valley IMU.' I don't feel comfortable enough to offer my name. The display is listing the call as private.

'You're a smelly bitch. You're going to get done.'

I end the call as the person on the other end cackles.

41. Adrian

The cells are unlocked one by one the next morning. Friday. The prisoners assigned to work detail and education stagger out first.

Winding up and verbal abuse have been shouted out the windows until the early morning, but Filan remained suspiciously quiet. Maybe he's died in his sleep. Done us all a favour.

I remove my phone from my hidey-hole and switch it on. Wait for it to power up. There's a message from Uncle Bar.

When can I expect that done?

I type a response.

Soon! When can I get more gear?

I wait for a response for several seconds, keeping my ear to the door to listen out for approaching screws. But it gets too hot for the phone to be kept out and I put it away.

My door's eventually unlocked, and I'm allowed out to play with the others again. I have damage control to do.

Spence spends the morning packing up two years' worth of shit. As soon as he decides to take the spot on the open side, the screws want him off their numbers. One less body to look after.

'Why do you want to go over that open side?' I ask suspiciously. 'It's nothing but semi-protection.'

He eyes me warily and I wonder what Filan's told him.

'I'll get home leaves. A job outside. The chance to attend college. Why wouldn't I want to go?'

'Because it's full of the worst cunts.'

'I'm doing it for my girls, Adro. I wouldn't expect you to understand loyalty like that.'

'What's that supposed to mean?'

He scrutinizes me for a few seconds before he speaks.

'Did you grass on the others to get back up the hall?'

I blink. 'Who the fuck's saying that? I'll chop their tongues off.'

He doesn't back down. If anything, he stands taller. 'Everyone. Everyone's saying it. You're a dead man walking when Rampage comes back . . .'

'Until I give him some gear for free,' I scoff.

Spence pulls the plastic bag out his gaff, as if he's bored with the conversation and wants away from me.

'Whatever, man.' He walks over to his new friend Filan, and they shake hands. Anger flares through me as I observe their whispered conversation. Their sly glances my way.

Spence is escorted over to the open side after the morning route when the hall's quiet. He doesn't say goodbye to anyone and leaves the hall as quietly as he entered it a few years before.

What a shitebag. I'm better off without him. And once he finds his feet, he can bring me back in gear from his home leaves. He owes me after siding with Filan.

I monitor Filan's movements through my hatch. Spence's words reverberate around my head. Rampage. The big bastard will kill me. I need more scoobs from Uncle Bar before he returns to the hall. It's the only things that keeps the guy calm. My only chance of not getting a sore face.

'It's better a sore face than a red face,' Uncle Bar would say. But he hasn't met Rampage.

Today's the day. It's time to take Fred Filan off the numbers. Permanently.

42. Kennedy

Three minutes before the fire alarm rings, I get a phone call.

'Forth Valley IMU?'

'Kennedy, it's Stan at Prison Intel, Gartcosh. How are things?'

'Good. Yourself?'

'Not bad. Look, I don't have a lot of time. I'm going to ping you over a dissemination, but thought I better pass it on verbally first.'

'Go on,' I urge, getting that butterfly feeling in the pit of my stomach.

'I've been looking into this Maddox character. You know who his uncles are, right? It's just, with you having rivals in there . . .'

'I'm sorry?'

'Adrian Maddox is connected to the Shire Boys organized crime group. His uncle's Thomas Linney. Also known as Bar Linney. Second-in-command to the Shire Boys. Massive enemies with . . .'

Bar! It all clicks into place.

'Tell me you're kidding?' Although I know he's not.

'You'll be aware his other uncle, Chet Sangster, disappeared years ago. Fred Filan and the Forth Valley Soldiers are suspected of being involved in his disappearance. Nothing we've ever been able to prove though.'

He doesn't have to say any more. How could this have been missed? I end the call, slamming the receiver before

I can make another call. But the Hayworth phone rings unanswered.

'Fuck.'

'Everything OK?' Jacob asks.

'No.'

I dial a different number. The control room.

'It's Kennedy in the IMU. I need you to put out a message over the radio for me.'

'I can't. There's an ongoing incident.'

'Eh?'

But as soon as the words are out her mouth, I hear it. The fire alarm. The distant sound of an emergency vehicle. The receiver slips from my hand as I stride over to the window in time to see a fire engine squealing into the grounds.

'I need to go up the hall,' I say.

'Do you want me to come with you?'

'No. You stay here. Find out what you can about the incident.'

'Kennedy, from what you've said . . . It might not be safe for you to go up there.'

'I know. But I can't have someone else die in the hall.'

I pull on my fleece and flee from the unit. I don't wait on the lift, instead push the door to the stairwell and hurry down.

The siren grows shriller, I clench my teeth as I jog along the route towards the hall. But as I get to the entrance of Hayworth, I'm stopped.

'You can't go any further,' Gus announces. 'Suspected fire on the threes.'

Of course it's level three.

'I need to tell you something,' I pant, 'about prisoners on the threes.'

'Tell the hall staff. I need to deal with the fire brigade.'

I duck out the side gate, breathing deeply but unable to smell any smoke.

'Hurry up or you'll fry,' prisoners cackle.

They're herded up on the exercise yard. My heart clatters in my chest when I see her. Molly. In my haste to get to the hall, I never considered she'd be on shift.

Plumes of cigarette smoke rise into the air as the officers try to keep enemies apart, take numbers, check and filter out the moaning.

I walk up to Molly but, just as I'm about to speak, Ray McCredie scurries over to her. Keeping my face passive as to not give anything away, I observe their interaction. My hands clench and I stuff them into my fleece pockets.

I can't believe this is the guy who's plagued my nightmares. It takes me all my resolve not to scream at Molly to run away. Not to challenge him and really prove what a coward he is. But have I misjudged him? Is he more dangerous than the character he plays?

The fact that I've frozen in place answers my question. My lips are clamped shut. My body rooted to the spot.

'The numbers are wrong,' McCredie says.

Molly and the other officers look around in alarm.

'I need to speak to you,' I say, not addressing anyone specific.

'Now's not a good time, love,' McCredie says.

'It isn't,' Molly echoes.

The faces in the exercise yard are a blur. At first, I think they've forgotten that Kai Spencer moved halls, but I count the bodies myself. Someone's missing. But not one. Not two. Three.

'Sneak back into the building and make sure no one's lying in their bed,' McCredie instructs a pale-faced Molly.

'Are you mad? I'll get my balls chewed if I'm caught.'

'And what do you think they'll do when they realize we've lost three prisoners? Hmm?'

'There're serious external issues between Fred Filan and Adrian Maddox,' I blurt.

'On the pulse, you, eh?' McCredie jokes. 'We picked up on that an hour ago.'

I clench my jaw. 'Really? They need to be split up.'

'I'm sure we can manage it in the hall, actually.'

'This isn't a pissing contest, you know. One of them will get hurt. Seriously hurt.'

'Um, guys?' Molly says.

We both look at her.

'Those are two of the three that are missing.'

43. Adrian

One hour before the fire alarm goes off, I'm still watching Filan when there's activity by the centre console. I press my face against the door to get a better view, but it's just out of my line of vision.

I'm unlocked for lunch and have to force myself out the gaff. Hold my hands so no one sees them shake.

There are different cons behind the hotplate. Filan hovers over them. 'I don't think Maddox looks hungry, boys.'

There're no screws around. I hold out my plate, but no one moves to scoop anything on to it.

'Nah, he's not hungry,' says one of the youngers, trying to impress.

'Move,' Filan growls. I throw my plate, but not with much purpose. I head back to my own and close the door. But it isn't locked.

Once the food's served and the serveries tided away, I head over to make some toast. It's important I keep my energy up.

Spence should be doing this deal, the chicken. Filan's coke is concealed in my waistband, along with the tool I've made to take him out.

The place is quiet. Deserted. I grab the Wet Floor sign and stick it above the storage shelf to mask the CCTV camera.

When the toaster pops the bread, I jump. Take a deep breath.

'Oi. Oi,' Filan growls.

I flinch. Look behind his shovel-head to make sure the floor sign's stayed in place.

He takes a step closer and my hand that's buttering my toast clenches around the plastic knife. It won't do much damage, but it's better than fuck all.

'I guess I owe you.'

'Don't forget it,' I smirk. Relax. Let go of the knife. 'How are you paying for the coke?'

'I'll get money paid into your PPC.'

I swallow. Just him and me. My insides writhe, but I try not to show it. Crick my neck instead. The tool in my joggers feels cold against my skin. I don't take my eyes off him. Not for a second.

I hand over the coke, but he doesn't take it.

'I have a question,' he says. 'Have you ever been able to batter someone on your own? You must be such a disappointment to the Shire.'

My eyes widen.

'What? You think I didn't know? You're a fucking Shire Boy? I despise Shire Boys. I like to plunge knives into their necks. Scar their faces. Make them disappear . . .'

He chuckles, and I want to smash his face in. My hand moves towards my concealed weapon. This is it. My chance at redemption. It's me or him, and I fancy my chances.

'What can I say? I wanted to see what all the fuss was about. My uncle Chet used to rage about you all the time when I was growing up.'

'Shame what happened to him. You hear he cried, right? When I plunged my knife into his ribs. A right pussy.'

The smile disappears from my face. Uncle Chet has been missing, presumed dead, for years. I'm desperate to ask the question, get the answer that's eluded the Shire

Boys for years. But at the same time, not wanting to give him the satisfaction of asking. Begging.

'You stay out of my way. And I'll stay out of yours,' he sneers. 'I'm not scared of you, wee man. I've peppered bigger men than you.'

'Just like the shitebag I've always been told you are. You're no one in here, Filan. A loser. I have this place sewn up. I set my boys on you, and you're fucked. There's not one single person in here that'll come and save you.'

He grins. 'Not even your pals, the screws. Ya grassing rat.'

I take a step closer, ready to paste his face over the floor.

'The difference between you and me,' he adds, 'is I don't need to have other folk fight my battles. I know how to use my hands.'

He sticks his hand into the back of his joggers and pulls out a fucker of a weapon. A piece of metal that's been filed down into a sharpened point. Ripped-up towel is wrapped around the handle to give it grip. Holds it up like a trophy. Slips it back into his pocket.

'But you're a dirty wee bastard. And somebody wants to get you even more than I do.'

I frown. 'Who?'

Then a menacing voice says behind me, 'Me.'

I whirl round.

Rampage.

'When did you get out the digger, mate?'

He stands with Filan. Pulls his beefy hands out of his pockets. It takes a second to register that his hands are blue. That he's wearing gloves.

Rampage reaches over. Smashes the fire alarm.

He's on me in a second. His big hand gripping my neck. My fight-or-flight response kicks in and I scratch at his arms.

'You're an all right cunt,' he says through clenched teeth,

'when you're good for something. The rest of the time I can't fucking stand you.' His grip tightens and tears escape from my eyes.

'Ram. Mate,' I croak, but it's no good. My vision blurs. Darkens.

'Did you grass on big Sinclair too? Is that how he got shipped?'

His words are muffled. But the next one is clear.

'Here.' Filan.

My sight is going, but I see the tool he passes to Rampage.

'Teach the grassing wee bastard a lesson.'

44. Kennedy

As soon as the all-clear's given, Molly and Officer Emma Warren begin escorting sixty-six prisoners back inside. For them, the excitement of the day is over.

I brief the first line manager and together we go to Maddox's cell. It's empty.

'Where the fuck is the wee bastard?' he seethes. Molly and the rest of the officers look sheepish. After all, they've lost not one, not two, but three bodies on their watch.

A search commences as soon as the prisoners are locked up.

'In here,' screams a voice.

I follow them into the servery. At first, all we can see is blood. Pooling under his grey body.

'Oh fuck. Not again,' says Officer Warren, putting her hands to her face. Molly takes a step closer, reaches down and places her fingers on his neck.

At the same time, she reaches for her radio. 'All stations, all stations, code red on Hayworth level three. Repeat. Code red. Hayworth three.'

She clicks off the button and takes a step back.

Nurses and other officers run into the hall.

I look down at the body on the floor one final time before returning to the centre console. I've seen enough. I sit before I fall down. A numbness takes over my senses, dulling everything.

What does this mean?

As I trudge along the section, I hear a shrill voice say, 'Is he dead?'

In the hurry to evacuate the hall, none of the empty cells are locked.

While the nursing team works away in the pantry, as the officers look on, helpless, I slip into Maddox's cell. Close the door. It's cleaner than I'd have expected. The bed's made. The bin's empty. The counter has no marks. The magnolia walls lack the expected graffiti. His clothes are folded away in the small cupboard space provided.

I don't have much time. Scout – McCredie – could clear out the cell before it can officially be searched by the security unit. If I don't look now, there will be nothing in it for Security to find.

I run my hand through his clothes. Rustle the contents of his bin. Check his canister of sugar – a popular concealment method. I shake his cereal box, content it only contains Coco Pops. Peer into his shampoo. His shower gel.

There's no TV in his room to search. The only place left is the mattress. It's easier for me to pull it off the frame. Check every corner for a slit. The bed box is similarly empty. Suspiciously empty.

I rub sweat from my hairline. There's nothing in the room. Disappointment floors me. I'm about to head out of the room, worrying at my lashes, when a glint of blue catches my eye line. I squint. There's something there. Outside his window. On the ledge.

I hurry over. Push open the window. There's enough space to put my hand through, but not much else. I pat my fingertips to feel it. The window frame presses hard into my flesh as I extend my fingers. Scrape the skin.

I should be wearing gloves, but there's no time to find any. I feel it. Touch it delicately so I don't knock it over. My pinkie finger gets purchase and I slowly drag it towards the open slit of the window.

I grasp it. Yank it inside. Originally, the blue piece of plastic had been a piece of cutlery. A knife. A spoon. The end's been snapped off, leaving only the handle. But the part's been melted down and now resembles a star screwdriver.

I look around the room with fresh eyes. There's a panel by the wall that connects to the personal alarm system. If something happened to an officer, they'd press their alarm and get assistance. Quicker than using a radio.

The bottom screw in the panel has a scrap of blue material stuck inside.

My heartbeat quickens. There's going to be something inside the panel, but the manufactured screwdriver keeps slipping in my sweaty fingers. I glance out of the observation hatch. No one's looking for me. All attention's still on the pantry.

A few of the lads are kicking off about being locked up. But no one's paying them any attention either.

I wipe my palms down my trousers and try again. The screws aren't tight, as if Maddox didn't have the time to secure them. I don't know what I'm about to find, but the first screw is out. The second. Left top and bottom. I slide the panel to the side.

Press myself up to the wall to peer inside. And there it is. With no thought to the fingerprints, I remove the phone and stuff it into my trouser pocket.

With sweat running into my eyes, I reattach the screws before taking the screwdriver with me.

I slip out of the cell. Out of the hall.

45. Kennedy

The beat-the-boss phone burns against my leg as I hurry back to the IMU.

'An ambulance has just come down the drive,' Jacob announces as I let myself into the unit.

'Yeah, someone's hurt.'

My heart hammers in my chest as I try to maintain an air of nonchalance. My fingers shake as I attempt to log on to my computer. I keep touching my pocket to make sure the phone is still there. If it fell out between the hall and the unit, I'd be fucked.

'Staff, or—'

'Prisoner. Maddox.'

'Oh.'

'Yeah.'

'Victor will be along any minute,' he says. 'He phoned, looking for you.'

'OK.'

I look up at the clock. I can't go home until I check the phone. But I can't check the phone until Jacob goes home.

When Jacob isn't looking, I remove the phone and hide it in my top drawer just as Victor enters.

'What's happening?' I ask.

'The paramedics have stood down. There was nothing that could be done by the time they got there. This is all we need,' he adds, rubbing his scalp.

His words sink in. Another death in custody. A murder, in custody. The papers will have a hard-on for this.

'What about Filan?'

'He was found in another cell. Says he slept through the fire alarm.'

'Bullshit.'

'Exactly.'

In my drawer, the phone buzzes. My heart freezes as Victor frowns at me. I clear my throat.

I try to remember where we were in the conversation. 'Where was he?'

'He'd decided to move into a recently vacated cell. One of the pass ones. I've asked Tim Reilly for a paper from every officer on duty. I'm already considering asking the Governor to split up the staff group on that division. It's not a good mix.'

I nod. Stare at my closed drawer. Praying it doesn't ring. I should've checked it was on silent before I left the hall.

'I'll stay on for the police,' I say, feigning indifference.

'On a Friday?'

I shrug. 'Someone has to. And I'd rather clear my desk than come into it all on Monday.'

'Don't stay too late. I'll tell the Ops FLM to walk you out to your car. Get home safe. And have a nice weekend.'

I only feel like I can breathe again once he leaves and locks the door behind him.

Twenty minutes until home time. 'Why don't you get yourself away, Jacob? Make the most of the weekend.'

'Nah. I'll wait on too. Until the incident overview comes in. HQ will want that recorded on the system as soon as possible.'

I wave him away. 'Don't be daft. There's no point in us both staying. I'll deal with the paperwork when it comes in.'

Jacob peers at the clock. 'Are you sure?'

'Yes. Go home.'

He grabs his stuff and leaves, and I'm finally alone with Maddox's mobile phone.

46. Kennedy

I stand at the window. Watch Jacob as he toddles up the drive to his car. Only when he drives away do I return to my desk. The only people that can access the IMU are gone.

Tim Reilly has reported the incident to the police. Briefed the Governor. There's nothing I need to do but look at the phone.

I double-check the door is locked, even though I know it is. Even though no one else can access the area. Sit at my desk and boot up the phone.

Security Code: ------

Fuck.

I pluck an eyelash as I consider my options. The sting grounds me. His date of birth?

Access Denied
Security Code: ------
Three more options

It takes me all my resolve not to throw the tiny phone across the office. I clench my hands into fists. Count to ten. Suck on my top lip.

I try his date of birth back to front. The error message is immediate.

Access Denied
Security Code: ------
Two more options

Shit.

I take in the room as I try to calm myself down. My eyes

land on the recent copy of *NEDitorial*. Thomas 'Bar' Linney is grinning to me on the front cover. Maddox's uncle Bar. His hero.

I find Linney on the prison record system. Memorize his date of birth. And when that unlocks the phone, I almost don't believe that it's worked.

I'm in.

I can't explain what it is that makes me look at his contacts before I read the messages. I have to use the nib of my pen to navigate the phone; my sausage fingers are too big.

He has a number for his uncle. A couple more associates. A big leap forward to identifying the prick. All I have to do now is get a list of staff mobile numbers from HR – a task that will have to wait until Monday.

But when I see Laura, the HR officer, in the ladies a short while later, the question blurts from my mouth before I can stop myself.

'How are you managing being back at work, Kennedy?' she asks, rinsing soap from her hands.

'Fine. Can you get me a staff number?'

Laura frowns at me in the mirror, all niceness evaporated.

'A staff number?'

'Their mobile number. Victor asked me to ask,' I add, hoping she doesn't notice my face flush at the lie.

'I'm not permitted to do that, and you should know better than to ask.'

'It's life or death,' I persist as she violently grabs paper towels from the dispenser.

'Then I'm afraid you are going to have to find someone more senior to request it. I'm sorry. It's more than my job's worth to give you that information.'

She pushes past and speeds from the ladies before I can

pressure her any further. I wash my own hands, my thoughts ticking away. I could tell another white lie. Tell Victor I got intelligence from phone calls. About McCredie. He trusts me too much to ask for proof.

And then. First thing on Monday morning, I'll have my answer. My evidence of McCredie's corruption.

Three days away from proving it's McCredie. From ending this nightmare.

Back in the IMU, my own phone ringing startles me. It's Ellie.

'What's wrong?'

'You need to come home, Kennedy. Right now. We need to talk.'

I slip the beat-the-boss phone into my top drawer and hurry home.

47. Kennedy

'I can't believe you've kept all this to yourself,' Ellie says when I confess everything to her.

Another bang, followed by a whizz. The irony that this has happened on the worst weekend of the year. At least our cat's deaf with old age.

'You've risked your job. What if you're found out?'

'I don't care any more. Bruce, Molly, they're all correct. The job's fucked. Maybe I am better off leaving. Find something else.'

The wine tastes good but, mixed with the antidepressants and lack of food, I feel it go straight to my head. It doesn't stop me from taking another sip.

'If it will finally make you happy. That's all I care about. It's all I've ever cared about.'

'Me too. About you, I mean.' I stroke her hair. 'That's why we had to end it. I see the way you look at babies. You deserve to be a mother. And I'm not the one to give you that. I can't make you happy. Not like that.'

She goes to say something but stops herself. Nods.

'Do you think we're safe now that he's dead? If you can prove McCredie's behind it all?'

'I will be able to prove McCredie's involvement.' I look down at the glass of wine. 'But Maddox could have arranged anything before he died. Deleted incriminating messages. There could be revenge for him being killed . . .'

I don't want to think about it any more. I'm sick of thinking about it.

'I could speak to Nihal, from work. He's a whizz with technology. Might be able to unearth something.'

I shake my head. 'I don't want to drag any more people into this. Not with these gangsters. We could still be at risk. I can't have that on my conscience, along with everything else.'

'What do you want to do? We could go and stay with my parents for a few days until things calm down?'

I'd rather face my chances here. 'You go. Stay safe at theirs.'

'No. I'm not going without you.'

A tear escapes her closed eyes. 'I love you, Kennedy.'

'I love you, too. But I can't keep myself safe while worrying about you too. Please.'

We sit there, holding hands, for ages. Neither of us willing to move.

'If only Laura had given me McCredie's number.'

'She was just doing her job. You have to respect her integrity for that.'

'I suppose.'

My phone beeps.

We need to talk.

'It's her,' I say.

'Ignore it.'

'I bet she has it. McCredie's number. If only she was trustworthy. I could've asked her for it. Save me having to wait all weekend.'

'Don't engage, Kennedy. Please.'

'I won't.'

But the irony of it irritates me more than I care to admit. The fact that it's in such easy reach but I still can't get it.

'I could ask Jacob to ask his uncle.'

'The Governor? Do you think that's wise?'

Of course it's a stupid idea. I can't risk Jacob getting involved either. I think back to our chat the other day. How he looked after me. How he looks for the best in everybody.

'Wait!' I shout, spilling my wine.

'What?'

'The noticeboard.'

'I don't know what you're talking about.'

'At work.' I smile. 'His number. It's on the staff notice-board.' Once I start chuckling, I can't stop. 'That's where I can get it. Right now.'

But the spilled wine in front of me stops me.

'Come on,' says Ellie, sensing the change in mood. 'I'll give you a lift back. If his number's there, will you contact Victor?'

'It is there. I saw it the other day.' I pick up my wine and gulp it down. 'Let's go.'

48. Kennedy

I wrap myself in my hoodie to protect myself from the wet. The night air floodlit by colourful, noisy lights.

Ellie uses my fob to access the car park by the main entrance. A dog walker takes his sweet time walking over the pedestrian crossing with his bulldog, unfazed by the downpour. It makes me glad we have a cat.

'Two minutes,' I say, taking the fob from her.

'Please be quick.'

Keeping my head down, I rush to the staff area, fobbing the pad to gain access. Only then can I calm down.

It's still there, like I knew it would be. Shit, I think. I haven't brought a pen. Or anything to write it down. So I do the only thing that I can – I snatch the business card, ripping it off the board.

'Kennedy.'

Shit. I stuff the business card into my pocket. Don't turn around. Fear flares my body. The staff break is over. There's no one to hear me scream.

She rushes over and places a hand on my shoulder. 'We need to talk, Kennedy.'

'Well. Talk then,' I say, turning round.

Her face is pale and devoid of make-up. Bags hang under her eyes. Her hair is wet from the rain.

'Here?'

'You're not welcome in my house. I don't trust you.'

She forces a laugh. Looks away. 'That's fair, I guess. Can we at least go upstairs and sit in the comfy seats?'

She's wearing a light cotton jumper over her white shirt. No coat.

'Go then,' I order. Sighing, she relents.

'Speak.'

'I don't know where to begin, babe. I know you have questions, and I want to tell you everything. But I can't. It's not safe.'

I shake my head. 'You keep saying that. Why are you here? If you can't tell me anything.'

I pick at my nails until she answers. 'I'm trying to explain some things. Like. No, I'm not Scout. He's so much bigger than this. Than me. Please don't ask me to tell you who he is. It's really not safe.'

She doesn't know I know it's McCredie.

'OK.'

'I work for Scout. He told me where and when to get stuff and who I was to give it to. In return I was paid. That's all it's safe to say.'

'OK.'

'It's not as glamorous as it used to be. Scout's always been greedy. Maddox got greedier. I want out, but it's complicated.'

'Did you start getting to know me to find out information?'

'Yes. I was paid to.'

I thought her words would crack my heart, but I'm too numb. But the pain's on its way.

'You put an email out,' she continues. 'Scout got spooked. He didn't care if you died, just that you were scared into quitting. But other people know about you now. Dangerous people. Just because Maddox is dead, it doesn't minimize the risk to you . . . Or me.'

My teeth chitter. 'I wish you'd let me hold you,' she says.

'Why?' I scoff.

'My intentions might not have been good at the start, I'll admit that. But you have to believe me that I love you. I'm in love with you, Kennedy. I want you to save me. I want out, but I don't know how.'

'Maybe start with the truth?'

'I've known Scout a long time. He's known Thomas Linney longer. You'll maybe know him by his nickname. Bar. They've been friends. Since childhood, really. I'm not too sure on the details.'

'Who is Scout?'

'It's not safe for you to know that yet.'

I laugh sarcastically. 'So, you're choosing a criminal over me.'

'No. I'm choosing my safety over your curiosity.'

Bile rises in my throat. I can't even look at her.

'And my safety means nothing to you?'

'I never said that. Look, there's a few things I need to clarify. Until then, we both have to be careful.'

'How do you expect me to believe you? Everything between us has been based on a lie.'

'I don't expect you to forgive me, babe. But I need help. I'm afraid.'

I punch the leather armchair.

'You don't get it, Molly. I'm actually good at my job. I know who Scout is.'

Her face pales.

'You . . . You can't.'

'It's McCredie. And don't lie to me that it isn't, because I have proof.'

Her eyes widen. She grabs my shoulders, stares fiercely into my eyes.

'It's over, Molly. I have his number. I can prove it. He's been messaging Adrian Maddox on an illicit phone.'

'Listen to me carefully. It's not Ray. He doesn't have anything to do with this.'

We stare at each other, not wanting to break the contact. For the first time, I see her sincerity. The way her eyebrows raise. Her eyes. 'I swear,' she adds. 'It's not Ray.'

'Then who?' I wail. She looks at the ground.

After a second, I pull away. Swat angrily at my eyes.

'We're going in circles here. I have to go.'

'It's me. The number.'

'What are you saying?' I whisper.

'The number on the beat-the-boss? It's mine. Check for yourself.'

All light and sound disappear as I stumble backwards.

'You?'

She nods. A sob escapes from her mouth, but all sympathy, all feeling has vanished from my heart. Five seconds ago, I might have comforted her in a moment of weakness, but I can no longer bring myself to touch her.

Tears tumble down her cheeks. Drip on to her jumper, leaving tiny grey marks. I can't think of anything to say, so there is stunned silence, broken only by her sobbing. 'I told you,' she says at last. 'I always cry over things I saw coming.'

'Get away from me.'

She winces at my growl.

'Kennedy.'

'Get away from me . . . Now.'

Molly reaches out to me but pulls her hand back at the last second. 'Kennedy, I'm afraid.'

I look away. Turn my back. Because my resolve is weakening, even after everything. There's a trepidation in her tone. Her confidence has vanished. It's like I'm meeting the real her for the first time. But it's too late.

'Do you know who else is afraid? Ellie. My best friend. And she isn't even involved in any of this. Fuck off, Molly. I don't want to see you again. You have until Monday morning to hand in your resignation, or I'll expose you.'

'Kennedy, wait. It's not safe . . . Let's get in the car. Drive into the sunset, remember?'

'People have died, Molly. I'm not going anywhere with you. Turn yourself in. It's the only way. And the only way we can – God – I don't know whether to wait for you or to forget about you.'

'I can't go to the police. It's not an option.'

I roll my eyes.

'I have to tell you something else. So you know I'm telling you the truth.' I don't know if she's stalling for time or if she has anything useful to say. 'I'll tell you everything, but you have to believe me – I'm not Scout.'

After a deep breath, she has one more confession for me. 'It was me. In the balaclava.'

I'm stunned.

'I'm sorry, I was just following orders. It was that or . . . hurt you.'

'It was you? The whole time? It was you.' I clutch the armrests so I don't slide off the seat.

'Kennedy, you need to understand the bigger picture. This is so dangerous. Scout is still—'

'You terrified me. You terrified Ellie. And you lied to me about it.'

She reaches out for me again, but I can't bear to be touched by her. 'Get to fuck,' I bark. 'You're dead to me.'

I leave the muster room, stumble down the stairs and out of the building, away from her.

How can I possibly tell Ellie I was wrong? After all this, I feel like I'm back at the start.

'Kennedy, wait!' she screams. But I keep on walking. Back to the car. Back to Ellie. The rain masks my tears.

'It's over!' I shout back.

'Is everything OK?' Ellie asks when I open the passenger door.

'Start the engine.'

Molly appears as I go to close the car door. She grabs hold of the door handle, preventing me from shutting it. Tears roll down her face too, mingled with the rain.

'Take me with you,' she pleads.

'Kennedy?' Ellie says. 'What's going on? Did you make me bring you here so you could see her?'

'No. I got what I came for. Start the car.'

Ellie turns the key in the ignition and the engine roars to life.

'Leave,' I urge. 'Go to the police. The train station. Back to your precious Scout. I officially no longer care.'

She looks over the bonnet. Lets go of the door.

'OK. I'll go. But do you have a jacket or something?'

Her cotton jumper is soaked through. I go to give her my hoodie, but it's equally as damp.

Wiping the tears from my face, I say, 'There's an umbrella on the floor.' Ellie reaches around and grabs my yellow umbrella. Passes it to me, and I hand it out to Molly.

With shaking limbs, she puts it up, cowering under the cover of it, and walks away.

The screaming of a nearby firework conceals my sob. Molly jolts. Ellie screams. A plume of red flowers from the centre of Molly's stomach. Her shoulder.

I look at Ellie. Confused. Why is she screaming?

331

Molly drops to the ground as Ellie emerges from the car. The same red is splashed over my umbrella.

He stands there, smoke wafting from the end of the barrel. His other hand clutching the rope tethered to his menacing bulldog.

'Molly, no!' I scream.

But it's too late.

49. Kennedy

I can't help but think, as the procession makes its slow march down the drive, if the family had already started their Christmas shopping. If they kept the receipts.

I clutch a tissue to my breast. Ellie holds my hand, stroking my thumb. 'Breathe,' she whispers. I nod. Officers flurry past in their best pressed clothes. The shields on their caps shining. They nod their respect at Ellie. They know she's the nurse. That she did all she could.

They line the route awaiting the hearse and immediate family. I could have been in the limo, but politely declined. It didn't feel right. A space was reserved for me in the front row, but I'd already warned Ellie I wanted to stay at the back.

Sixty officers in full dress uniform, faces solemn. Pale. They think about their own funerals. How staff will be lined up for them when their time comes. But this one isn't fair.

As the hearse approaches, the officers salute, holding the pose until the hearse passes.

The lump in my throat makes me choke. 'Do you want to go inside?' Ellie whispers.

'Far too young,' laments Ellie's dad. Grief shadowed on his face.

A young woman, black dress clinging to her heavily pregnant stomach, is the first to emerge from the limo.

'Let's get in,' I say. Ellie puts an arm around my shoulder and ushers me inside the crematorium. We find seats at the back and settle in. She hands me the order of service, but I'm not strong enough to look at the face smiling back at me.

Not Bruce. It's not fair.

A full career and then a heart attack six weeks after you hand in your notice. Is it on the cards for me too? You heard about it happening so much.

The family files in. Wife, his poor pregnant daughter; her face so pale it's translucent. Being held up by her husband, striking in his army uniform.

The coffin follows the grieving family, and I lose it.

'I don't want to speak to the family,' I mutter when the service is over forty-five minutes later.

'That's OK.' Ellie presses the keys of the courtesy car into my hand. 'Go and sit in the car and I'll be there as quick as I can.'

She kisses me on the cheek, and I escape out of the other exit, away from the wave of grief that follows the family outside. Ray McCredie's there, and I stop.

'Hey,' he says, throwing away his cigarette.

'Hey,' I mutter.

'How is she?'

'Who?' I ask, but I know full well who.

'Molly.'

'I don't know. I haven't been to see her,' I lie. I've barely been able to stay away in the days since it happened.

'They're saying your girlfriend saved her life. That true?'

'She's not my girlfriend. And we don't know if – she's been saved. It's still touch and go.'

He sighs. 'Thanks. Anyway. She's a good officer. I liked her a lot.'

I trudge away, not wanting to speak to any wankers.

I switch on the engine and flinch. But nothing happens except a blast of comforting warm air.

I watch in the rear-view mirror and wonder what flowers were left for Maddox. His service was yesterday.

Had someone used Molly to lure me out? Had they got us mixed up because she had my umbrella? Did she know it was going to happen? Did she save my life?

It's not like I could ask her. Not with the coma. The ventilator helping her breathe.

Ellie strolls over to the car. Head down. She waits until I roll down the window.

'Dad wants me to take him to the wake. Do you want to come?'

'No.'

'Is it OK if I go?' I want to tell her no, but I'm not in a position to do so.

'Of course.'

'Head straight home, yeah?'

I nod. Change gears. Start reversing out of the space and rolling up the window. She knows I'm annoyed, but I don't care.

I sit in the queue at the T-junction. Left to home. Right to the hospital. I change the indicator and manoeuvre into the correct lane.

Drive round in circles until a space opens up. Switch off my phone so Ellie can't track me.

I'd never visited the ICU before Molly was admitted, and I was amazed at how big it was. I sanitize my hands. Put on the plastic apron. I walk into the room, not expecting anyone to be there, and watch as Tim Reilly plants a kiss on her forehead.

I take a step back.

'I'm sorry,' I blurt.

'Kennedy. How are you?'

I nod. 'Didn't expect to see you here.'

'It was my turn to visit. I try to limit Clive doing it as much as I can. She looks better today though, don't you think?'

She doesn't. The only skin that isn't covered under gauze and bandages is grey. Her hair is greasy.

'Yeah,' I lie.

'I better get back.'

'The prison's on lockdown. For the funeral. Stay a bit longer if you want.'

'It's OK. I'll leave her in your hands.'

He looks at her again. Fixes the arm of her hospital gown. The gesture is loving. I swallow the lump again. Pour myself a glass of her untouched water the auxiliary must put in on autopilot.

'Is it true they've arrested someone?' Tim asks before he strolls out of the room.

'I don't know. I've . . . had to take some personal time.'

He nods. He understands.

'See you later, pal,' he says, before disappearing.

I take Molly's hand in mine. 'Wake up,' I say. 'I want to help you. Just wake up.' We sit that way for hours as the machines attached to her keep her alive.

'I don't need to know who Scout is. Only if you wake up,' I plead.

But her unconscious state remains, taunting me.

'I'll quit if you wake up. Please,' I whisper.

The room darkens. Nurses carry out checks.

'Come on, let's get you home.' I'm not surprised Ellie's found me. I'm not that unpredictable.

'The police want to speak to you.'

Epilogue

'The police say I'm no longer at risk.'

Victor studies me over his glasses. His fingers steepled. 'That's good.'

I nod.

'Do you want more time off? After Molly and Bruce . . .'

'Did Molly put in a transfer request before . . . You know. Before she was shot?'

'I checked with HR. They never received anything.'

It's what I feared, but maybe she didn't have enough time to write something up? I take a deep breath.

'She wanted out, Victor. She got in too deep and wanted out. We have to protect her. Promise me we can protect her.'

'Kennedy. If Molly survives . . . she might not be capable of returning to her post.'

I squeeze my eyes shut to stop the tears. 'Don't say that. If she comes back – no, *when* she comes back – she might still be involved. With Scout. We need to start an operation. On her. On Scout.'

'And bring them all down?'

I nod.

'She wanted out. She sacrificed herself for me. She knew it was coming. If only I'd invited her into my home . . . When she wanted to talk . . . She might still . . .'

'I can't sit on what you've told me. And I won't pretend you haven't disappointed me by only coming to me now. My hands are tied, Kennedy. I've reported Molly Rana to the police. As soon as she wakes up. When she's ready to be interviewed . . . she'll be questioned under caution.'

But his words go over my head. She did love me. In the end. I can save her.

'Kennedy. See sense. She was involved in a plot to cause you harm. She refused to give you information on who was behind the threat to your life. There's no coming back from that.'

'She knew they were coming, Victor. Coming for me. That's why she asked for something of mine. In the end.' A sob catches in my throat. I cough. 'In the end, she saved me. She chose me. Over Scout. And now . . . Now I have to choose her.'

Acknowledgements

Five by Five is a work of fiction. Prison staff do a fantastic job in complex and tough situations and aspects of the novel have been embellished for dramatic purposes. They don't deserve the negative attention they're often subjected to. I hope this series can shed a light on the difficulties prison staff face.

Forever grateful to the judges of the Penguin Michael Joseph Undiscovered Writers Prize for making my dreams come true: Ayo Onatade, Bea Carvalho, Amy McCulloch and Syima Aslam. My fantastic editor, Joel Richardson. Your patience and attention to detail are astonishing. David Headley for seeing something in my writing. Can't wait to share this journey with you.

The MJ team – Ellie Hughes, Kallie Towsend, Sriya Varadharajan, Ellie Morley. The design team who created the best cover. And to Sarah Day for her excellent copy-editing skills.

Five by Five wouldn't exist if it weren't for so many people. To all the staff, past and present, at Moniack Mhor Creative Writing Centre in the Scottish Highlands. If Moniack didn't exist, this book wouldn't exist. Thanks to Val McDermid, Louise Welsh, Mary Paulson-Ellis, Abir Mukherjee for the continued support. The Crime Class of 2018, 2022 and 2023 – thanks for the laughs, support and shoulders to cry on.

To Francesca Main and Nathan Filer for asking me why I wasn't writing about my job and encouraging me to pick it back up again at Moniack in 2019.

To Neil Lancaster, Vaseem Khan and Lin Anderson for being so kind after Pitch Perfect at Bloody Scotland in 2022 and giving me such good advice. I might have given up writing after that weekend if not for you.

To Lauren North, for your kindness and support.

To Alison, Jane and Kristen and the rest of the Edinburgh Writers Forum gang.

To my beta reader (and Harrogate minder), Mary Picken. I owe you so much. John McLaren, Willie McDonald and Jill Morrison for making sure there's nothing in the book that could get me coded. To all the FLMs and SMT that have supported the book. To Denise, I got this.

To my friends, family and colleagues who have encouraged me to keep going, despite all the setbacks, and everyone else that's supported me on this roller-coaster journey. Let's do it all again!

To No Doubt for making *Return of Saturn* about me even though you don't know I exist. I can't write if I'm not listening to your albums. And for reuniting just as I finished the book.

And finally: Callum. All this is for you and always will be. No one inspires me like you. I'm so lucky to be your mum.

In loving memory of Ruby Wilson 1931–2024.